"Chloe Snow's Diary goes far beyond the expected awesomeness + angst of a freshman in high school, though it has both of those qualities in spades. But Chloe Snow, in all her hilarious brilliance, will also break your heart and make you bawl those 'happy to be alive' tears. Amazing."

—*Lauren Myracle*, *New York Times* bestselling author of *The Infinite Moment of Us*

CHLOE SNOW'S DIARY

EMMA CHASTAIN

Simon Pulse

New York   London   Toronto   Sydney   New Delhi

An imprint of Simon & Schuster Children's Publishing Division
1230 Avenue of the Americas, New York, New York 10020
First Simon Pulse hardcover edition March 2017
Text copyright © 2017 by Emma Chastain
Jacket hand lettering copyright © 2017 by Mary Kate McDevitt

For information about special discounts for bulk purchases, please contact
Simon & Schuster Special Sales at 1-866-506-1949 or business@simonandschuster.com.
The Simon & Schuster Speakers Bureau can bring authors to your live event.
For more information or to book an event contact the Simon & Schuster Speakers Bureau
at 1-866-248-3049 or visit our website at www.simonspeakers.com.
Jacket designed by Jessica Handelman
Interior designed by Mike Rosamilia
The text of this book was set in Electra MT.
Manufactured in the United States of America
2 4 6 8 10 9 7 5 3 1
This book has been cataloged with the Library of Congress.
ISBN 978-1-4814-8875-4 (hc)
ISBN 978-1-4814-8877-8 (eBook)

For my parents,
Patricia Anne Chastain
and
David Chastain

Monday, August 10

Mom's gone. Not forever, obviously. For four months at the most, she said.

She came in here all shaky, with swollen eyes, and pressed her forehead into my forehead. Her breath smelled like pad thai. She was like, "Please know how much I love you." We both cried. She explained everything: She's going to Mexico to work on her novel. She knows it's sudden, but she also knows I'm mature enough to handle a little surprise. We'll be in touch all the time. We can Skype and chat and talk on the phone whenever we want. Maybe I can go visit her.

She gave me her blue-and-white porcelain rabbit,

which I've always loved, and a journal, and said, "If there's one thing I want you to remember, it's the importance of creating memories." I don't really want to remember this, actually. Plus I already write in this diary every day, but it seemed rude to tell her that.

Tuesday, August 11

Dad made me breakfast before he went to work: banana pancakes, bacon, and a strawberry smoothie. He sat there watching me eat. So did Snickers. I never give Snickers food from the table, but he never stops hoping.

"This is really good," I said.

"You don't have to finish it," Dad said, but I did, because he looked so sad.

"Don't worry," I said. "It's not for very long."

He unscrewed the blender from its stand. He wasn't looking at me.

"She has to work on her novel," I said. "It's impossible to get anything done here. She needs a room of her own."

He laughed, but not a real laugh, and said, "Right."

Wednesday, August 12

Things I love about Dad:

1. His dad jeans
2. His crinkly eyes

3. He sends me cat videos
4. He never yells
5. He still wears the fugly brown tie I got him for Father's Day when I was eight
6. He knows all the words to every '80s song
7. His dad smell (peanuts and limes)

Thursday, August 13

I try to forget that I'm starting high school in a few weeks, but sometimes the fact rushes into my mind and I get sweaty with fear.

However bad it is, it can't be worse than junior high. My theory is, they put the two most evil grades in one building to keep them from infecting everyone else with their awfulness. Basically all I did in junior high was text, straighten my hair, add to my Benedict Cumberbatch shrine, and worry about how to be more popular. Thinking about it makes me cringe.

I want to be different in high school. Like a new person.

And I want to make out with someone. It's so humiliating that I'm a kissing virgin at this advanced age. Everyone halfway normal in my grade had their first kiss at, like, age 10. I've never even gotten a peck on the cheek (I'm not counting my parents or Uncle Julian). And the longer I go un-smooched, the more freakish I feel. If I graduate high school without being kissed, I'll be too embarrassed to kiss anyone during college, and then I'll most likely die without ever even getting to second base. Something has to change fast. This I vow: I will kiss a guy before New Year's Eve. Or maybe it'll happen *on* New Year's Eve. OK, this I vow: I will kiss a guy before New Year's Day. Vow *taken*.

Friday, August 14

Before Dad left for work, he said, "Don't just sit online all day, OK, kiddo?" so I invited Hannah over, and we went to the pool. She put on SPF one billion because she's so pale she's basically light blue. She wouldn't shut up about how scary the first day of school will be. Finally, to get her to stop, I told her my mom left for Mexico on Monday. She gasped.

"It's not a big deal," I said, irritated.

"It seems like kind of a big deal."

I put my sunglasses on.

She said, "What's going on with her and your dad?"

"Nothing. She's working on her novel. That's it."

"Chloe, I'm so sorry."

"Ugh! Don't be sorry! She's writing, not dying."

I know I shouldn't be mean to Hannah, but she seriously drives me insane. The more intense and touchy-feely she gets, the more I turn into a block of ice.

Saturday, August 15

I pulled all my boxes of fall and winter stuff out of the closet, and I. Hate. Everything. It all says, *I have no identity of my own, so I'm going to wear the most generic clothing possible in a desperate quest to blend in.* My flowered sneakers from Hannah I love. The rest I would burn if I could.

I need a makeover. No, not a makeover—that sounds like some gross magazine. I need to dress like the person I really am. Which is . . . what? Hipster. Hippie. Stoner. Emo. Preppy. None of those.

Sunday, August 16

The first thing I do in the morning, lying in bed, before I'm all the way awake, is check everything on my phone. I don't even want to; it feels like I have to catch up on what happened while I was asleep, so I don't fall behind. I've tried to do a phone cleanse before, but the longest I've lasted is three hours. I don't understand why it feels so good to click while you're doing it and so disgusting after you're done.

Monday, August 17

I just talked to Mom!!!!! It wasn't for very long, because her phone was dying. She's in a small town with cobblestone streets and a bullring. She rented a one-room apartment that looks out on a courtyard.

"I miss you like crazy," she said.

"I miss you, too!"

"I can't wait to show you my place, babe. There are these Argentinean kids staying downstairs from me, and they have drum circles under my window 24/7. This morning, a stray cat showed up on my doorstep. She's orange, with one white paw. Doesn't that seem lucky?"

I asked if she wanted to talk to Dad, but she said she had to go find cat food before the stores closed, and she'd call him later.

At dinner, I told Dad everything Mom said. He nodded and smiled. He looked like he had a migraine, but when I asked him if he wanted an Advil, he said he was fine, just tired.

Tuesday, August 18

Things I love about Mom:

1. Artistic
2. Did yoga before it was cool
3. Genius writer
4. Lets me skip school all the time to hang out with her
5. Lets me watch and read whatever I want, because you can't shield your children from the world; you have to introduce them to it

6. Beautiful

7. Compliments me a lot

Wednesday, August 19

Hannah's mom drove us to the mall. She was wearing a pink short-sleeved cardigan and cork wedges with pink straps. On the way there, we talked about Hannah's older brother, Brian, who just left for his first semester at Dartmouth, which according to Mrs. Egan is the best school in the world.

"I'm telling you, Chloe, it's all about the family dinner. Eating together as a family is scientifically proven to raise your SAT score, did you know that?"

Hannah hissed, "Mom, stop."

"Oh, honey," Mrs. Egan said, looking at me in the rearview mirror. "Hannah told me about your mother."

I gave Hannah a look of death.

"She'll be back in December," I said.

"Of course she will!"

I refused to talk to Hannah in the mall until she bought me a soft pretzel and a Diet Coke. Even then I was being a total B. I went to all the stores with her, but I wouldn't try anything on. I sat in the armchairs they put there for boyfriends and husbands and pretended to fall asleep.

Even when Mom was here, we didn't have family

dinner. Usually Dad would make something for him and me, and we'd eat while Mom worked upstairs. Then she would eat carrots and hummus standing up at the kitchen counter. She can't be on a regular schedule, because she's an artist.

I'll do way better on the SAT than Brian. He's the kind of guy who says "She's driving with Mike and I" because he thinks "I" sounds fancier.

Thursday, August 20

There's nothing better than going to the pool. Here's what to bring:

* Sunglasses
* Beach towel decorated with a picture of a
  New York City taxi, to help you dream up ways
  to escape the suburbs
* Pencil case with house keys and money for the
  concession stand
* Book

Then lie in the sun for hours, and do some breast-stroke when you get too hot. Don't feel like you're being lazy, because you're reading *and* working on your tan. I know it gives you wrinkles, but what if you die in a terror-ist attack when you're 20? Then you'll regret wasting your time worrying about sun damage when you could have been living it up and looking cute.

Friday, August 21

Hannah came over seriously crying about our so-called fight. I felt like saying, "I have bigger fish to fry," but I didn't say it, first of all because that would be mean, and second of all because it would be a lie.

I said, "It's not a big deal. Sorry I wouldn't try on pants with you." She almost fainted with relief. It was raining out, so we ate a bag of cinnamon-flavored pita chips and I told her about my kissing vow. She doesn't understand how much I'm suffering, because she kissed Matt Welch last summer at Kayla Price's birthday party, and so now she is a normal human teenager rather than an unkissed freak. No matter how much I ask, she can only describe kissing Matt as "too wet," "kind of strange," and "not what I thought it would be like," which is so frustrating, because I'm dying to know every detail about nose placement and tongue texture and post-kiss facial expressions.

"Don't overthink it," she said, breaking off a corner of a pita chip. "When it's meant to happen, it'll happen."

"No, I need a plan, Hannah. I need to take matters into my own hands. Now help me come up with a list of prospects."

After hours of internet research, we had a list of three guys who are single, reasonably cute but not out of my league, popular enough but not *Popular*, not too druggy, not too mean, not too cocky, and not too player-y:

Zach Chen. Sophomore. Has a man bun (sexy, IMO), sings in an a cappella group (kind of dorky), and plays guitar in a rock band called Deposed Monarchs (again, sexy).

Luke Powers. Junior. Hockey goalie. Has a beautiful flowing hockey mullet like it's the 1970s. At least 6'2" and ripped. Hannah thinks I'm punching above my weight class on this one, but not everyone appreciates his hair, plus his Twitter reveals he's suuuuuper into Settlers of Catan, which, again, is not everyone's cup of tea.

Griffin Gonzalez. Fellow freshman. Has the best name in our class by a mile. Reads a ton, like me. Does a lot of eye rolling and sighing in English class when nonreaders talk. Gives off a vibe like he's counting the days until his PhD program starts. I'm scared of him and think he's a snob but desperately want him to like me.

Little do these guys know that one of them will make out with me before the year is over.

Saturday, August 22

I went to the pool alone. I like doing stuff by myself. It's easier to observe the world when you're not trying to keep a conversation going.

When I went to the concession stand to get a rocket pop, I had to pass this big bunch of older boys. They got quiet as I walked by, but I didn't look at them, so I'm not sure if it was a natural pause in the conversation or if one of them was, like, making a hand job gesture in my direction while everyone died of silent laughter.

After I got my Popsicle, I turned around to head back, and there was one of the guys, in line behind two shivering kids wrapped in striped towels. When he looked at me and I looked at him, I felt like a key sliding into a lock.

"You didn't get me anything?" he said.

"What? Oh, no, I didn't, um . . . Sorry. I don't—"

"Calm down," he said. "I'm messing with you. Wait for me, we can eat together."

While he ordered a SpongeBob ice cream, I studied him. I don't think Hannah would consider him cute. He has a face like bread dough, with raisins for eyes. Plenty of zits on his chin. His hair goes down to his shoulders, and I'm pretty sure it's in dreads. He's extremely tall and about the size of a riding mower, and he has big muscles in his arms and legs. I'm not talking about gym muscles either. Baling-hay muscles, not that there's any hay to bale around here.

I waited for him to pay, and then we went and sat on the bench by the sign-in sheet. It seemed weird that a few seconds earlier, I had never seen this person, and now we were sitting side by side and acting like it was normal. Maybe it *was* normal. I don't know, because I never meet any new guys. I've known everyone in my class since kindergarten.

"Do you go to MH?" he said.

"I'm starting in the fall."

I must have looked petrified, because he said, "There's nothing to worry about."

"On a scale of one to ten, how horrible is it?"

"Two." He was biting his ice cream instead of licking it, which looked so freaking manly.

"You must be popular," I said. "Otherwise you would never say two."

"Oh God." He waved SpongeBob in the air. "That stuff is so stupid."

"You *are* popular!" I said.

"You're not?" he said.

For a second I considered lying, but I realized he would find out the truth on September 2—that is, if he even deigned to notice me at all.

"Nope," I said. "I'm not, like, a loser, but I'm not famous, either. I'm just kind of there."

"I find that hard to believe," he said. I'm pretty sure he was being gallant.

We walked back to the pool together. All his friends stared at us like we were on fire. One of them yelled, "Ask to see some ID!" and they all laughed.

"Ignore those idiots," he said. He walked me back to my chair and said, "What's your name, by the way?"

"Chloe."

"I'm Mac."

We shook hands while a group of young mothers watched us through their big sunglasses. I hate this town. It's teeming with snoops and gossips.

I pretended to read for about an hour, and then Mac and his friends left, and on his way out, MAC BLEW ME A KISS.

Sunday, August 23

!!!!!!!

I was in the midst of an intensive search for Mac online, which wasn't working, because I didn't know his last name or even his real first name.

And then, as I was looking, he added me.

His full name is Macintyre Brody, and I think he has a girlfriend.

He has one of those annoying profiles with no posts of his own, a thousand posts from other people, which he never responded to, and about 10 pictures. There's one of him in someone's basement, wearing a gray T-shirt with the sleeves cut off, holding a red cup. There's one of him in his football uniform, running onto the field and flipping off the camera. And then there's a really beautiful one. His arms are stretched out, and he's laughing. He's just thrown a girl off a dock, and she's hanging in the air like a star, with her long hair flying up behind her. She's wearing cutoffs and a white wifebeater. No bra. She hasn't detagged herself, even though you can see her nipples, so I know her name: Sienna Ross. Underneath the pic, she wrote, *dude i WILL get u back.* If I were Mac's girlfriend, I'd probably call him something boring, like "sweetie." But Sienna calls him "dude." So confident!

I couldn't stalk her profile, because she has superstrict privacy settings, but from the one picture, she looks very athletic and outdoorsy. The kind of person who would survive a zombie apocalypse and who doesn't even need eyeliner to look halfway normal.

Well, that's that.

Monday, August 24

Texted Hannah, *Met a guy named mac at pool. Hot but has gf. Meh.*

She called me immediately and made me tell her every detail. When I sent her the link to his profile, she was like, "He's very handsome," and even though I could tell by her voice that she didn't mean it, I could also tell she was trying her hardest to sound convincing. She really is a good friend.

Tuesday, August 25

I do miss Mom like crazy, but it's kind of nice, being here with just Dad.

They've always fought a lot. Mom throws stuff, not at Dad, but not NOT at him. The week before she left, she winged a wineglass at the backsplash and it broke into a thousand pieces.

Maybe everyone's parents are like that. I don't know. It's not really the kind of thing I talk about with Hannah. I saw her parents get cranky with each other once because they were about to go to the movies and when Mrs. Egan asked how she looked, Mr. Egan said her pants were "not my all-time favorite." She sighed and rolled her eyes, and he said, "What?" in a rude voice. She said, "Being kind is more important than being honest," which I think is true. He said, "Honey, if you don't want to know, don't ask," and it went from there. When they left, Hannah said, "I hate it when they fight," and I said, "Yeah," even though I was thinking, *That was nothing.*

My parents fight about:

1. Whether Dad respects Mom's need to be an artist (Dad says yes, otherwise he wouldn't work to support her while she writes; Mom says no, because he's always throwing his job in her face, like being a lawyer is harder than being a mother and a writer)
2. The state of the house (Dad says it's a pigsty; Mom says he should get evaluated for obsessive-compulsive disorder)
3. Mom's online shopping (Dad says she's spending my tuition money; Mom says he's being melodramatic and controlling)
4. Mom's friends (Dad says they're a bunch of losers; Mom says he's intimidated by anyone who cares more about art than money)

They think I can't hear them because I'm in my bedroom with the door shut, but our house was built in about 1700, and the walls are thin. I could listen to loud music, I guess, but I feel like I have to eavesdrop, to know the worst.

Other times they do disgusting stuff like slow dance in the kitchen with their hands on each other's butts, or sing songs from musicals. That almost drives me crazier than the fighting.

Wednesday, August 26

Dad took me to CVS to buy school supplies. I got high-lighters, fine-point pens, notebooks, and a bunch of folders with unicorns on them. I meant the unicorn folders as a joke, but now I'm worried that everyone will see them and think I seriously love unicorns. Ughhhh.

When I got home, I took my school stuff to my room and spread it out on my bed. There's something so satisfying about new, juicy highlighters and notebooks with crisp edges. They make me feel hopeful, like maybe the school year will go great and I'll suddenly understand math.

Thursday, August 27

After dinner, Dad and I watched *Midnight in Paris*. The point of the movie is, everyone idealizes the past, not realizing that their own era is pretty great and will be idealized by future generations. After it was over, I said, "I still think I'd be happiest in the Jazz Age," and Dad said, "You wouldn't last five minutes without your phone," which doesn't make sense, because if I were born back then, I wouldn't know about smartphones, so I couldn't miss them, which I said, thereby winning the argument. For dessert, Dad had whiskey, and I had a lemon Italian ice, which I flipped over so I could eat the mushy super-sweet part first.

Friday, August 28
Email from Mom!

Dear babe,

¿Que onda? (What's up?) I'm writing to you
from the public library. This is the only place I can
get an internet connection, thank God; you know
how it enslaves me at home. I had to come all the
way to Mexico to escape the siren call of Twitter.

I discovered that if I open the window next
to my bathroom and clamber along a sloped
portion of roof, I can get to a flat section perfect
for sunbathing. I've been sitting out there for
hours every day, tanning and writing.

I'm getting a tremendous amount of work done
but am missing you horribly. Email soon and tell
me everything.

Love,
Your old mom

I wanted to chat her, but she wasn't online, so I
emailed back instead.

Dear Mom,

I miss you! Dad does too. I met a guy at the
pool, Mac. I'm trying to be confident and calm,
like you say, but it's hard because he's so cute
and I can't tell if he likes me or not. He added
me on Facebook, but I think he has a girlfriend.
Thoughts?

Well, *adios* for now!
xxoo Chloe

Saturday, August 29

I'm at Hannah's. We just sobbed our way through *The
Notebook*. I was mostly faking it; I think she should have
married the reliable guy with bright-blue eyes and a jaw
like a box—what's so bad about him? Now Hannah's
online and I'm writing. I feel lonely at her house today. I'm
dreading this sleepover. What's the point of sleepovers,
anyway? There's all this pressure to stay up until 5 a.m.,
and you eat too much candy, and the next day you feel
disgusting and you usually cry about something dumb
because you're so tired. Even when you go to bed at a normal hour, you can't sleep, because Hannah's house smells
wrong, and there's a ticking clock in her bedroom. Then
in the morning you have to eat with the Egans, who have

eggs for breakfast, a thing with which I cannot deal.

I'm going to kick Hannah off her phone and make her talk to me about my kissing campaign. Should I go for Griffin Gonzalez first, since he's in our class and the most similar to me? Or should I aim higher? And if the latter, does "aiming higher" mean starting with Luke Powers or Zach Chen? These are the important questions Hannah has to pretend to care about, because she's my best friend and that's how it goes.

Sunday, August 30

The landline rang this afternoon. I let Dad get it, like I always do. I hate answering the phone if I don't know who's calling. A few minutes later, I heard him raising his voice, so I snuck upstairs to eavesdrop. The door was closed, and I couldn't hear much. ". . . If you think I'm going to . . . ," "mind-bendingly irresponsible . . . ," ". . . *Eat, Pray, Love*, it's your real life . . . ," and ". . . of course she's upset; she's just hiding it." That's the one that made me feel guilty for listening, so I snuck downstairs again. Snickers was hanging out by the sliding doors, keeping an eye on the backyard. I sat next to him and scratched his neck, which he wasn't in the mood for, since it was distracting him from his important squirrel-watching duties.

Eventually I went back upstairs. The door to Mom

and Dad's room was open. Dad was taking Mom's clothes out of the closet and throwing them on the bed.

"I wanted to talk to Mom," I said.

"She had to go." He yanked her long green dress off its hanger and tossed it onto the pile.

"What are you doing?"

"Organizing."

"Are you throwing out those clothes?"

"Mom asked me to donate some things."

I couldn't see his face, but his voice sounded funny.

"Can I have them, then?" I said. "If she doesn't want them anymore?"

He turned around to look at me. "Well, I guess," he said. I could tell he didn't want to let me, but he couldn't think of a reason to say no. Too bad! That's what he gets for lying.

I had to make six trips to my room to move all Mom's clothes in there.

If I had to describe her style in two words, I'd say SCARVES GALORE. Picture a gypsy yoga teacher, and then add more bangles than you thought, and that's Mom.

Monday, August 31
Thank God for Snickers. I was lying in bed crying last night and he jumped up and stared at me with a worried

look on his face. Then he burrowed into the sheets, headfirst, and fell asleep. If only he didn't fart on me all night long, he'd be the perfect dog.

Tuesday, September 1

School starts tomorrow. I'm wearing Dad's old Fun Run T-shirt and trying to snuggle with Snickers, but it's 85 degrees outside, so he's just not that into me. I'm ready for cold weather and sweaters and apple cider. School! Let's do it!

Wednesday, September 2

In a word: blah.

It was hot today, but I still wore tights and a sweater-dress to get into the spirit of autumn. This girl with tons of hair looked me up and down and said, "Aren't you *hot?*" and I said, "*No,*" (so clever!) even though I was sweating like a pig. Then the girl opened the locker right next to mine. Great.

Hannah and I have one measly class together: English, with Miss Murphy, who looks like an explorer. She's tan and her hair is a mix of blond and gray. She was wearing tight jeans, a black blazer, and no makeup. After school, I saw her driving away in a red Jeep with the top off. We're reading *The Crucible* first.

Griffin Gonzalez is in our English class too. I "accidentally" bumped into him as we were leaving, and he said, "Oh, sorry." My campaign is officially under way!

I have lunch at 11:12 a.m., all by myself. What kind of fascists make people eat lunch in the morning? When I'm grown-up, I'm going to sleep till 11 every day and then eat brunch with my artist friends.

I was reduced to sitting with Gloria Lingley, who has never had a haircut in her entire life (her mom won't let her). She went on and on about this piano player called Keith Jarrett, never noticing that I don't even know who that is. I don't think I said anything but "erk" and "unhh" all lunch.

Sienna Ross is in my Spanish class and so are all her stupid popular friends. I guess they left their language requirement until the last minute. Sienna was wearing a waterproof sports watch and no makeup. Her legs are probably longer than my entire body. I think she could feel me staring at her, because she turned around a few times.

The school is basically a bigger version of the junior high: windows so narrow you could barely shoot an arrow out of them, tile the color of barf, and fluorescent lights that make everyone look undead. I got lost four times, but no one pushed me or called me freshmeat or anything. I give the day a C.

Dad's making mac and cheese for dinner, and then probably Mom will call. She's big on debriefing after the first day of school.

Thursday, September 3

The thing is, she's really busy. She can't drop everything and call me. She's probably in the middle of an amazing chapter.

Friday, September 4

Hannah said she thinks she'd make a great nun. What century is she living in? *Are* there even nuns anymore?

Saturday, September 5

Hannah's away this weekend with her parents, so I'm completely and utterly alone. All my homework is done, and I've walked Snickers twice. Neither Zach nor Luke nor Griffin has posted anything new all day. Life is bleak.

Sunday, September 6

Dad forced me to watch *Gentlemen Prefer Blondes*. We ate ice cream from the carton, which Mom never lets us do. Maybe I'll be a gold digger when I grow up, like Lorelei. She doesn't give a single care what anyone thinks of her.

Monday, September 7

Last week, high school seemed like an interesting experiment. Now it's dawning on me that this is my life for the next four years. The bus picks me up at 6:55 a.m., so I have to get up at 6 (6:10 if I don't wash my hair). It's so early

I feel queasy, literally queasy. I can hardly choke down my Pop-Tarts and Diet Coke. I'm half-asleep until about noon. I finally feel awake after dinner, and then it's time to go to bed, but I'm not sleepy, because I'm a teenager, and teenagers are naturally supposed to go to bed late and get up late—that's a true fact from nytimes.com. Our internal clocks are set so we get sleepy around 1 a.m. and want to sleep till noon, so it's basically torture for us to wake up so early. This one school experimented with starting later in the morning, and SAT scores increased by 200 points. Why does our principal hate science and facts?

Tuesday, September 8

Eavesdropped on the girl who made fun of my sweater-dress, which isn't hard, since her locker is right next to mine, and she's always lecturing her minion, Ambreen.

"No one cares about Zach, Ambreen. He doesn't even play a sport. Mac Brody is way more popular."

Ambreen nodded and looked embarrassed.

Why were they talking about Zach? Was Ambreen planning to make a move?

Later in the day, I saw Zach sitting by himself on the front steps, looking for something in his backpack. Without letting myself think about it, I walked over, stood in front of him, and said, "Hi, I'm Chloe." I've never done anything that brave before, but fear that

Ambreen would beat me to the punch gave me courage.

"Hey," said Zach. He sounded surprised.

"Sorry to, like, accost you." ("Like, accost you"? Could I be any faker and weirder?) "I just wanted to tell you, someone sent me a video of your band playing at the Speech and Debate Festival, and I thought you guys were amazing." (Lies. No one had sent me anything. I'd scoured the internet for every video of Deposed Monarchs in existence and watched each one until I had them memorized.)

"Hey, thanks so much," he said. His voice sounded a lot warmer. "That's cool of you to say. We're playing a big show in December at the Sidecar. All ages. You should come. I mean, you could check us out before that, but our other gigs are kinda lame in comparison."

"Yeah, totally. I mean, I'm sure they're not lame. I meant I'll totally come to the December show."

"Rad. Yeah, follow us on Twitter. We'll post all the details."

"I definitely will," I said, not mentioning that I've been following Deposed Monarchs and all its members on Twitter since August 21.

Wednesday, September 9

Best day ever! Hannah's not eating carbs, so she gave me her brownie, and it turned out to have mint chocolate chips in it! Mrs. Egan is a genius! And when we were walking to English, Mac passed us in a huge pack of boys and yelled, "Chloe SNOW!" and pointed at me, and about a hundred people saw. I'm famous. And *then*, after school, I saw Luke Powers walking down the hall alone, and I was so confident after my Mac encounter that I looked him up and down really obviously and then made serious eye contact with him and smiled, *and he smiled back!!!*

Thursday, September 10

Hannah wants me to try out for the a cappella group, the Love Notes (GET IT??). This senior named Bernadette Sanz is in charge of it, and there are only like 15 members, which means they'll accept roughly zero freshmen. Plus, everyone's seen *Pitch Perfect* a billion times and fancies themselves the next Anna Kendrick, so the auditions will probably be crammed with amazing singers. Zach Chen will be there. Maybe I'll have the best audition in Love Notes history, he'll fall in love with me on the spot, and we'll have an adorable story to tell our kids. Or maybe I'll humiliate myself and he'll have to struggle not to laugh. Yeah, the latter sounds a lot more likely. No way am I going to try out.

Friday, September 11

I think I have some memories of 9/11, but that's impossible, because I was a baby. To enjoy being sad, I listened to Nico sing about her failures and her lonely walks in her beautiful, strange seagull voice.

Saturday, September 12

Did a Songs of Summer medley in the bathroom. "Cheerleader" wasn't my strong suit, but "Call Me Maybe" sounded basically like the real thing. Maybe I *will* audition for the Love Notes!

Sunday, September 13

Email from Mommmmmmmmm!

Dear Precious Pony,

I'm *beaucoup* missing you! Last night it stormed—a glorious, terrifying uproar that crashed around my ears and scared the cat half to death. You've never heard thunder until you've heard it resounding through the mountains of Mexico. Today, the sky is the most breathtaking azure.

Progress on my novel continues apace. I simply sit down each day and wait for the muse to visit me, and more often than not, she does.

Re: this boy you've met, how wonderful! He can't fail to fall in love with you. Just remember, a touch of coolness can work wonders. Don't trip all over yourself trying to impress him. You're a goddess, not a puppy.

With fondest love,
Your mama

I'm going to wait until tomorrow to write back. Maybe the touch-of-coolness trick works on mothers, too.

Monday, September 14

The Crucible is so good I read it in two hours. It's about this girl named Abigail who's going out with a married guy, John Proctor. She's popular: everyone's scared of her, but everyone loves her too and wants to make her happy. John Proctor dumps her, and she flips out and starts pretending that all these people are witches, including John's wife (!!!). And her friends go along with it. Actually, it seems like they believe their own lies. They're so in love with Abigail, and so excited to be in a big gang of girls, that they actually hallucinate. Grown-ups take them seriously, including judges and lawyers, and a lot of the so-called witches are killed. And this part blew my mind: it's based on history. All this witch-burning stuff happened, like, a few miles away from here. School! Sometimes it teaches you stuff!

Tuesday, September 15
Eavesdropped on my locker neighbor and Ambreen.

"It's like, mind your own business, you know?"

"Totally," said Ambreen.

"I don't march up to you and say, 'Excuse me, those fries aren't improving your double-chin situation.' So why do people feel free to criticize what I'm eating?"

"Totally."

"It's like, I can't help being naturally skinny. You're body snarking me for something I can't even *control*. And excuse me if I actually like eating cottage cheese and being healthy. How is that your concern?"

"Totally."

Locker neighbor would accuse someone of being a witch in a hot second.

Wednesday, September 16
Dad caught me talking to Snickers, and then he wanted to have a big discussion about am I lonely, do I miss Mom, etc., etc. I said, "I'm fine, but Daddy, listen. There's this singing thing at school. Do you think I should audition?"

"Absolutely," he said right away.

"You didn't even think about it for two seconds."

"You need some extracurriculars."

"I have extracurriculars!"

"Texting doesn't count."

"Hardy-har," I said, but the thing is, he's right. I've taken a bunch of after-school stuff—ballet, soccer, etc., etc.—but nothing sticks, because nothing's as fun as singing along to YouTube in front of the mirror. But if I'm ever going to get out of this no-account town, I have to make myself irresistible to colleges, and that means showing them I'm more than just an excellent English student and a shockingly horrible math student.

Thursday, September 17

Mom called, but I could hardly hear her. Her phone kept cutting out, and finally we both gave up. It doesn't matter, though. We're connected anyway. I can feel what she's thinking. I bet she's sitting on the roof right now, in her big black sunglasses, writing on a notepad.

Friday, September 18

Hannah told me all about Bernadette Sanz, Love Notes president. Apparently she was named after Bernadette Peters and is destined for musical-theater greatness. Somehow she's friends with the popular seniors, including Mac and Sienna, despite her theater geekery.

She had a big part in last year's musical, and everyone thinks she'll get into Juilliard. How smashing for her.

Saturday, September 19

I think Abigail is mean and crazy, but I also think she's cool. She's a teenager who gets an entire town under her control using just words. When John dumps her, she doesn't lie in bed sobbing, like I would. She's like, "No one dumps me and gets away with it. I'm Abigail Williams!" She doesn't feel even a little bit bad about having sex with a married man. All she cares about is herself and what she wants. She gets people *put to death* to punish John! If she were alive today, she'd get into Harvard by lying on her application, then work in an investment bank, pulling off insider trades (whatever they are).

Sunday, September 20

Hannah slept over. When we woke up, we practiced our audition songs. She's been taking voice lessons twice a week after school, but to be 100% honest, I think I sound pretty good, and she sounds medium good.

Breakfast was awkward. She said she wasn't hungry, so I ate a huge bowl of Froot Loops by myself. We weren't talking, so all you could hear was me chewing.

Monday, September 21

Miss Murphy says *The Crucible* is about, among other things, hysteria over Communism in America in the 1950s. Who knew?? Well, Griffin Gonzalez, for one. He was practically falling out of his chair with excitement, and when Miss Murphy called on him, he said, "Arthur Miller was a Communist himself, of course. The real villains of the play are the witch hunters, who are stand-ins for anti-Communists. Liberals are too quick to hold him up as a paragon, when in fact he would have little in common with a contemporary Democrat or progressive."

"That's an excellent point, Griffin," said Miss Murphy, and the two of them proceeded to discuss it for 20 minutes while everyone else stared out the windows.

Going out with Griffin would be like a nonstop book club. I would love it! But I'd have to do a lot of Googling to prepare for our conversations. Plus I wonder if he's the kind of guy who considers gossiping beneath him. I already have a Hannah in my life. I don't need to date another one.

Tuesday, September 22

Sometimes I love walking Snickers after school. He looks so cheerful, trotting along with his collar jingling, smelling everything and looking around for birds. The leaves are starting to change color. Soon it'll be winter, the sky will get dark at 4 p.m., and Snickers and I will freeze our tits off during walks. To everything there is a season. The circle of life, etc.

Wednesday, September 23

It's 1 a.m. and I'm freaking out. Love Notes auditions are tomorrow. It's not too late to change my mind, right? There are plenty of extracurricular options out there. I could join Students Against Drunk Driving! Or run for student council!

Oh God. I don't want to do this.

Thursday, September 24

The auditions were in the auditorium, which is huge and fancy, with about 2,000 red velvet seats. Our school's theater program is really good; that one guy from *Parks and Rec* graduated from here, and so did that lady who does all the impressions. There were about 40 of us, and we all clustered near the stage. Then my locker neighbor stood up and started handing out pieces of paper. "Who is that?" I whispered to Hannah, and she gave me a weird look and said, "That's Bernadette."

We filled in our names, emails, year, other extracurriculars (I wrote "dance," which isn't a complete lie, since I dance in my room in front of my mirror at least four times a week), and vocal part (I had no idea what that meant, so I made a face at Hannah like, *WTF am I supposed to write?* and she showed me her paper. She'd written "soprano," so that's what I put down too). You could tell who the freshmen were: the silent, terrified people. The upperclassmen were making a big production of being totally relaxed. Zach Chen came in late and said, "Chloe, what's up?" to me on his way to sit with the upperclassmen. His man bun looked particularly beautiful today.

A mousy teacher scurried around collecting our papers. Then he got onstage and said, "I'm Mr. Collier, the faculty adviser to this group. Please note that if you gain acceptance to the Love Notes, there will be a small fee charged to cover performance uniforms. Costumes, that is." He glanced offstage. "At this point I'd like to turn things over to Bernadette Sanz, the true leader of this wonderful ensemble." He led us in a round of applause. As Bernadette strode out from the wings, he backed up, still clapping, and practically bowed to her as he made his way offstage. Why are even teachers scared of the popular kids? It's pathetic.

"Thanks, Mr. Collier." Bernadette tossed her hair. Either she'd gotten a blowout in honor of auditions, or she's one of those wizards who know how to make their hair look amazing all by themselves. "OK, listen up, guys. I'm not trying to be mean, but we're a very exclusive group, and we can only accept 15 people max. There are a lot of upperclassmen here who've been in the group before, but no one is guaranteed a spot." A guy in the front row called out, "Yeah, right!" and people laughed. Bernadette glared and said, "Shut up, Roy. *Anyway*, what am I looking for today? Number one, quality. Number two, intonation. Number three, musicianship. Number four, stage presence. You have 32 bars to show me what you've got." While she counted off expectations on her fingers, I stared at her gray nail polish and focused on not throwing up. What the frack was intonation?! How many bars were in my song?? Next to me, Hannah was smiling and nodding. I turned to my left and made eye contact with a cute guy wearing a button-down shirt with small blue checks. We gave each other a look like, *Uh-oh.*

Bernadette held up our information sheets and said, "I'm going to shuffle these and call you up in random order. Let me know if you need me to give you your starting pitch." This made the seniors in the front row boo, for some unknown reason.

Bernadette sat in the front row and worked through the stack of papers. Hannah was called up close to the beginning. She sang an Evanescence song. She sounded good, and she didn't seem nervous at all, just really into the song, which she loves because it's about God. When she got back to her seat, I whispered, "You were great," of course.

Every time Bernadette picked up a new paper, my

heart stopped, and then she'd call a name that wasn't mine. Some people were amazing, some people were painfully bad, some people were painfully quiet. Every time a junior or senior finished singing, people in the audience went "Woo!" and cheered like crazy. No one applauded for the freshmen. Zach sang a slow, sad version of "Where Are Ü Now." A short senior named Josh sang "I've Got the World on a String" and it sounded like a recording of Frank Sinatra. He got many "woos" and a big hand. The cute checked-shirt guy was *so good*. He sang the Subway jingle in a jazzy way, and it was great and funny. When he was done, I clapped for him without planning to, which was awkward, because no one else did.

Finally, *finally* Bernadette called my name, and I lurched out of my seat and crawled over Hannah's knees and walked up the steps to the stage. I could hardly feel my legs.

"Do you need a pitch?" Bernadette said. By this time I'd seen so many auditions that I knew what this question meant, and I shook my head no. I'd practiced my song a million times and knew exactly where the first note was.

I closed my eyes for one second and imagined I was in my bathroom, with Snickers asleep on the bath mat. Then I opened my eyes, took a big breath, and started "Over the Rainbow." Once I was past the first few words, I felt fine. I felt good, actually! I looked over everyone's heads to the back of the auditorium and imagined I was

Dorothy, leaning on a fence and thinking about escaping my boring life. When I got to the end, I glanced down at Bernadette. She looked like she'd just taken a bite of spoiled yogurt.

No one made a peep. I can't remember getting back to my seat; I think I basically blacked out. But I remember checked-shirt guy mouthing *Wow* to me, so I must not have totally sucked. Or maybe he's just nice.

Friday, September 25

Bernadette said that she'll email us the results on Monday, "after consulting with Mr. Collier." I bet Mr. Collier's main consulting duty is to drive to Starbucks when Bernadette needs a fresh green tea.

Saturday, September 26

Mom called today. Apparently there was a bull run in her town, and she watched the whole thing and got close to a huge black bull. Afterward, there was a bullfight, which she hated, because all the spectators were drunk kids from Mexico City.

"The matador had such dignity, though. At one point, someone threw a shoe at him, and he ignored it completely. It was spectacular."

I didn't tell her about the audition. It seemed silly, compared to dying bulls.

Sunday, September 27

Dad makes plenty of money at his boring job. So why does he go jogging in ancient sneakers with actual holes in the toes? Life is mysterious.

Monday, September 28

I didn't get in.

Hannah got in. That guy Josh got in. Zach got in, of course.

I don't know if checked-shirt guy got in, because I don't know his name.

I really think I had a good audition. I feel so sad.

I'm trying to remind myself that a few weeks ago I'd never even heard of the Love Notes, but it doesn't help, for some reason.

Tuesday, September 29

Hannah said, "It's really messed up. You should have made it." She sounded like she meant it.

Wednesday, September 30

Checked-shirt guy stopped me in the hall. His name is Tristan Flynn, he's a freshman, and he just moved here from North Carolina. He didn't get into the Love Notes either!

"Bernadette is awful," he said.

"Her nail polish was so 2013," I said.

"She's probably just threatened by us because we're such amazing singers."

We decided to join the fall chorus, which is open to everyone. And Tristan put his number in my phone!

Thursday, October 1

Well, there's nothing like not realizing you have your period until Chris Fortier hits you in the neck with a dodgeball and then, as you're walking across the gym in defeat, yells, "Hey, Snow, you've got blood on your butt."

Friday, October 2

Was called Blood Butt four times today. Too distraught to say more.

Saturday, October 3

Hannah and I had a Halloween-costume-planning meeting. The key is to start brainstorming early, so you don't panic at the last minute and wind up going as a cat again. (This is an especially pathetic costume when your Puritan father won't let you go as a sexy cat.)

Our ideas so far:

* Mr. Spock and Captain Kirk
* Werewolves

* Ninjas
* Skeletons

Now that I've written down this list, I realize we have the ideas of 11-year-old boys.

Sunday, October 4
Mom isn't too big on holidays—she says our consumer culture has ruined them. One nice thing is, now that she's away for a while, Dad and I can go wild on the decorations without her rolling her eyes or calling us "sheeple."

Today we went to a farm stand and got two giant pumpkins. I'm going to carve mine into a Groucho Marx face.

Monday, October 5
Carving a mustache isn't as easy as it sounds.

Tuesday, October 6
First chorus rehearsal today. It was pretty good! Miss Murphy, the English teacher, is the director, and she winked at me when I walked in, which made me feel like a celebrity. We sang some scales, and it turns out I really am a soprano. We're going to learn a bunch of Christmas songs for the holiday concert. Hooray!

After school, Tristan texted me *fa la la la la la la la la* and I texted him back a Santa emoji. Are we flirting? I think maybe we're flirting.

Wednesday, October 7
Decided not to text or look at my phone at all on the walk home, and noticed that the trees are lit up with red, orange, and yellow leaves, like a beautiful bonfire. This stupid town is kind of pretty.

Thursday, October 8
O

M

G

As I was walking to rehearsal, Mac came around a corner and almost crashed into me. He was wearing mesh shorts and a T-shirt with the sleeves cut off.

"So how's freshman year?" he said.

I shrugged. "It's OK."

"Do you have a boyfriend yet?"

"Not *yet*," I said, trying to make it sound like I was deciding between five different options.

"Good," he said.

". . . ," I said.

He said, "Well, I can't stand here wasting time with you all day. I've gotta go to practice."

"OK," I said, and he said, "Later, skater." And then he winked at me. And then he blew me a kiss!

I couldn't believe my eyes. A KISS! An air kiss, but still.

Friday, October 9

Did Mac technically cheat on Sienna by blowing me a kiss? I feel guilty, even though I didn't do anything besides stare in shock. According to Hannah, I need to stop freaking out about nothing. Ha! Easy for her to say! She has no idea what it's like!

Saturday, October 10

And why did Mac say "good" when I said I don't have a boyfriend yet? He must have meant, "Good, because in my eyes you're 10 years old and too young to have a boyfriend."

Imagine if he meant "Good, because I want to be your boyfriend"?

Sure, and while I'm at it, imagine if I could fly, imagine if I won the lottery, imagine if my parents ever listened to something other than NPR.

Sunday, October 11

Long convo with Mom. She said, "Babe, you'll never guess. Remember the bullfight? Well, I went to a bar afterward—I needed to soothe my nerves. There I was, drinking a paloma, minding my own business, when who should walk in but the matador! We got to talking, and he's really a fascinating person. Masses of black hair, eyes the color of just-cut cucumbers. I'm going to base a character in my novel on him. He's already given me a chapter's worth of material, at least. Isn't that lucky?"

She'd better not fall in love with this bullfighter. Poor Dad would die of sadness.

Monday, October 12

No school today, in honor of Christopher Columbus. I made a whole list of things to do:

1. Bake cookies
2. Read *Lord of the Flies*
3. Paint my nails
4. Come up with amazing Halloween costume idea
5. Walk Snickers
6. Do earth science extra-credit project (something about clouds??)
7. Cook dinner

All I accomplished were numbers two and five. The rest of the day got away from me, by which I mean Tristan and I texted for about eight hours and then I stalked Mac online until dinner, not that there was much to stalk. I wish I could justify adding him to my kissing list, but what's the point of adding "Mac Brody, #1 most popular senior, probable football scholarship recipient, and boyfriend of the unfairly attractive soccer star Sienna Ross"?

Tuesday, October 13

Red alert. Josh, a.k.a. Frank Sinatra, invited Hannah to a party on Saturday night, and Hannah invited me. It's going to be an UPPERCLASSMAN PARTY with BEER and CIGARETTES and maybe even MARIJUANA and perhaps SOMEONE TO KISS, like LUKE POWERS. Thinking about these facts makes me sweaty with fear.

Josh is the short, skinny genius with the voice of Frank Sinatra. By internetting and being creepy, Hannah has figured out that he wasn't popular until last year, when he tutored some kids in his class into not-terrible SAT scores. Now he's the popular seniors' mascot. Someone made a Thank You for Getting Me into College, JOSH! page on FB, and it has 192 likes.

Wednesday, October 14

The thing about health class is, in the handouts, the people offering you drugs are always scary strangers. It's easy to turn down someone you don't know. But what do you say when Luke Powers offers you pot?

Thursday, October 15
Asked Dad if I could sleep over Hannah's house on Saturday. He said, "Of course." I'm a lying monster!!!

Friday, October 16
Gchatted Mom, *what should I wear to a party?*
    She chatted back, *a dazzling smile and a smoky eye.*
    She's so good at advice, even from a million miles away.

Saturday, October 17
Oh God. I'm panicking. Are these jeggings stupid? Do I look like a tragic seventh grader? I *think* my deodorant works, but what proof do I have? Maybe I'm so used to my own smell that I don't realize how stinky I am. Why does my eyeliner always smudge onto my face? I go around looking like a sick raccoon, and Hannah never tells me, and I only realize it when I stumble upon a mirror. What if Mac blows me a kiss again? What if he doesn't?

Sunday, October 18
So that's what a senior party is like.
    It started out like a normal party—people awkwardly

talking and staring at each other—but by, like, 11 p.m. everyone was *drunk*. Hannah and I were the only sober/scared ones. No one tilted our heads back and poured alcohol into us, like I thought they would. Actually, people were hoarding their beer. One guy was carrying a six-pack around in his backpack, so no one would steal it.

Sienna (!!!!!!) offered us some vodka, but I said "Nothankyou" really fast. She squinted at me and said, "You're a freshman?" I nodded. She said, "You know it's my duty as a senior to corrupt you, right?" I must have looked terrified, because she laughed, put her arm around my shoulder, and said, "You're cute. Relax. I'm kidding." I can see why Mac is in love with her. He wasn't there—none of the football players were—but even if he had been, no kisses would have come my way, even the air ones.

Luke Powers was there . . . and all over this girl Danielle de Vincenzo. At one point they started making out, and his friends yelled, "Get a room!" He gave them the finger without opening his eyes. I guess Luke's off the list. Or maybe he should be at the top of it, since he's an enthusiastic maker-outer and appears to be pretty good at it (I was trying not to stare, but I couldn't help myself).

Hannah and I spent most of the time sitting on the couch with Josh, who scares me because he talks in paragraphs. He was like, "Social networks have many of the addictive properties we usually associate with drugs. Do you spend time thinking about social media when you're not on it? Have you ever tried to quit only to find you can't? I'd argue that it's as potent an intoxicant as alcohol. I've been 'clean,' shall we say, for two weeks, and only now are the withdrawal symptoms beginning to subside." Hannah was like, "Oh, yes, fascinating, most interesting." I didn't even try. I just made a HUHWUH? face at him and said, "You're insane! I'm never quitting! How would I spy on everybody?"

The annoying thing is, I don't think Josh is showing off. I think that's just the way he talks.

We technically slept over, because apparently that's what you do at senior parties, but no one went to sleep until 6 a.m. I lay on the floor next to the couch until 8 a.m. Two hours of torture! Hannah was sleeping next to me like a kitten, with a little smile on her annoying face, while my contacts slowly turned into dry, shriveled chips. When it finally felt late enough to leave without making Dad suspicious, I snuck outside and walked the entire way home, which took about an hour.

Dad and Snickers looked so cute and fresh, eating breakfast in the kitchen, that I almost started crying.

Now it's 7 p.m. and I'm going to bed, like a second grader.

Monday, October 19

I have an eye infection from leaving my contacts in all night. Dad had to pick me up from the nurse's office. "Jesus, honey," he said when he saw my eyes, which look like a couple of Atomic Fireballs. I almost confessed everything, but at the last second I held myself back. The doctor gave me some drops and told me that I'm going to incur lasting damage if I continue to be so careless. Jerk!

Tuesday, October 20

Wrote Mom a long, whiny email about my eyes. When I'm sick—well, when I'm sick and she's not in Mexico—she flips out, takes my temperature every hour, and Googles until she's convinced we should go to the ER. In contrast, Dad says stuff like "Buck up, sweetie" and "The more you complain, the worse you'll feel." Which I know is right, but sometimes I want to watch *Phineas and Ferb*, eat tomato soup, and feel sorry for myself, like a baby.

Wednesday, October 21

Miss Murphy was crabby in chorus rehearsal. She said our consonants are awful, and if we'd count, we wouldn't sound so much like a group of snakes. She also said the sopranos sounded "a little shouty." I kind of like it when she's stern with us; it makes me feel like we're a very important group of professional singers getting ready for, like, Carnegie Hall.

Thursday, October 22

Had total nervous breakdown. Sobbed into Snickers's neck. His fur smells so comforting. I don't know what's wrong with me. Hormones, probably. Oh, to be a grown-up and walk around feeling blank and bland all day!

Friday, October 23

Mrs. Egan drove me home after school. (Usually I walk. Dad says even a spoiled brat like me is capable of walking half a mile, but actually he's just too cruel and lazy to pick me up.) Hannah was complaining that she doesn't have time to run anymore, because of the Love Notes. Mrs. Egan said, "When God closes a door, he opens a window," and for some reason, I started sobbing. Mrs. Egan freaked out and pulled over to lunge into the backseat and hug me, which was nice but so annoying, since I wasn't really crying about what she said. I don't know *what* I was crying about.

Saturday, October 24

Hannah and I watched a cat's-eye makeup tutorial and practiced on each other. Somehow we wound up doing hand-clap games from fourth grade.

> *Winstons taste good, just like a cigarette should*
> *Ooh, ahh, wanna piece of pie*

Pie too sweet, wanna piece of meat
etc., etc.

Why were we chanting about cigarettes in fourth grade? What a world.

After she left, I ate an entire box of Hot & Spicy Cheez-Its. I regret nothing!

Sunday, October 25

Hannah sent me 50 texts about the new priest at her church.

I bet Jesus looked like him.

He has golden skin and kind eyes.

His homily was so intellectual.

She's the only person under 60 who puts all the capital letters and punctuation in. Finally I texted, *Hannah you can't bone him he's celibate,* and she texted, *I don't want to 'bone' him! Geez!* which is what she says instead of "God!" or "Jesus!" because she never takes the Lord's name in vain. I texted back, *Who would you bone if you could bone anyone?* I shouldn't tease her, but it's so easy.

No one!

A long pause.

Who would you?

                    Who would I BONE?

Ugh, yes.

                    Mac Brody

                    Easy answer

                    I'd let him do whatever he wanted to me

Chloe!

                    It's not like it's ever going to happen. I'm just telling you the truth

If you feel that way, he should be the only one on your kissing list.

                    I can't wait around for a miracle!

Only Hannah would think I should be loyal to someone who barely knows I'm alive.

Monday, October 26
Mom wrote back!! She said she's been away from email all week because of a research trip. She's sending me get-well thoughts for my eyes.

Tuesday, October 27
Griffin Gonzalez and I walked to our lockers together after English class. He asked if I'm enjoying *The Old Man and the Sea*. I said I don't understand all the fuss about Hemingway. Unspoken emotions, a plain prose style—what's the big whoop? Griffin said he thinks it's hard to appreciate how important he was because everyone who's followed him has ripped him off, so now it seems like he wasn't doing anything special, when in fact he invented a new way of writing. I was half enjoying our conversation, half worrying about whether I sounded smart enough.

Wednesday, October 28
Walked downstairs late at night to get a snack and caught Dad creeping on Mom's FB. He slammed his laptop closed so hard, Snickers jumped. I don't know what this means, and I don't care to think about it. Why do parents have to be so weird?

Thursday, October 29

Tristan texted me:

Just saw miss murphy in the hall

*She has her hair down and
she looks like Mrs. Coach from
friday night lights, amazing!!*

You have to see

I texted back:

Mrs. Coach is my dream mom

And then felt so guilty, because what if Mom knew I'd said that?

Friday, October 30

While all the popular kids in my grade are attending a costume party at Madison Ostler's tonight, I'm going to Hannah's house to play Pictionary with her and her parents.

Saturday, October 31

Another wild Halloween! Hannah and I dressed up in black jeans, black sweaters, and last year's plastic cat noses. Went to five houses before someone said, "Aren't you a little old for trick-or-treating?"

UM, NO!

Sunday, November 1

Forgot to say "Rabbits, rabbits" first thing this morning. That means another month of bad luck.

Monday, November 2

We had a special chorus rehearsal tonight. Dad picked me up, because it was actually hailing, and even he wouldn't force me to walk home through a barrage of ice balls. ("Ice balls," hee hee.) For some reason he came into the music room to find me, instead of waiting in the car like a regular person. It wasn't *that* hideously embarrassing, because rehearsal was over and everyone was talking and packing up their stuff. But then he introduced himself to Miss Murphy. Why? Why???? WHY does he want to be best friends with all my teachers?

"Is she giving you any trouble?" he said.

"Oh, yeah, she's a real handful," Miss Murphy said. They both grinned at me. I felt like they were expecting me to do a trick.

Dad said, "She's really enjoying this. She talks about you all the time."

"DAD," I said, because seriously!! Is he trying to make me sound like a total creeper?

Miss Murphy put her arm around my shoulders and gave me a squeeze. "I'm glad," she said.

Tuesday, November 3

Hannah got her period, probably because I just got my period, which we learned about in health class, and which is so creepy and cool. It makes me feel like nothing but an ape.

Wednesday, November 4

Spent most of chorus rehearsal staring at Tristan. He's so cute and preppy, but preppy almost like he's wearing a costume, which makes it not annoying. Today, for example, he was wearing a navy belt with whales on it, a yellow sweater, boat shoes, and horn-rimmed glasses that I'm pretty sure are fake, because he only wears them a few days a week. If I just saw a picture of him on FB, I'd be intimidated by how good-looking he is, but knowing him in real life, I feel totally relaxed around him. During the break, while we were supposed to be drinking water, we drew a spiral in his notebook and counted off to tell each other's fortunes. I'm going to live in a mansion, have six kids, drive a go-kart, and be a professional gymnast; he's going to live in a shack, have no kids, drive a Porsche, and be a hedge fund manager.

Thursday, November 5

Wasted about five hours after school looking at cat videos and nail art. Decided to quickly check FB before starting my homework and saw that Danielle de Vincenzo is officially in a relationship with Luke Powers. So of course I had to look at every one of her pictures dating back to junior high. I'm disgusted with myself and am never looking at the internet again, ever.

Friday, November 6

Dad made tacos tonight, which I thought was suspicious, because he knows tacos with extra orange cheese are my #1 favorite. I'd eaten five and was wondering whether a sixth would make me feel just full enough or completely gross when he said, "Honey, I need to talk to you about something."

He found out about the party, I thought, but he said, "I talked to Mom last night. I don't think she's going to make it home for Thanksgiving."

"I know," I said. He looked surprised.

"Did you talk to her?"

"No. But she said she'd be away for four months, and it's only November."

He opened his mouth like he was going to say something else, but then closed it and started picking the label off his beer bottle.

Saturday, November 7

Here's what I emailed her.

Dear Mom,

Dad told me about Thanksgiving. You could have mentioned it to me yourself, but whatever. I didn't even expect you to come home, so it's fine. I hope you're having a lot of fun drinking palominos.

Chloe

Sunday, November 8

You know that feeling when you sent a rude email and you're checking your phone every two seconds for the reply? That's one of the worst feelings. It's funny to think that the girls in *The Crucible* never had it. Although I guess they were waiting for real letters, instead, which would be even more nerve-racking.

Monday, November 9

Writing a rude email is bad, but in my opinion, it's also rude to make someone wait two whole days for a response.

Tuesday, November 10

Went to the bathroom during earth science. I didn't really

have to go, but I couldn't handle hearing any more about basalt rock, and when I came out, there was Mac, drinking from the water fountain like a mere mortal. He said, "What's up, kiddo?" I panicked and made a "hrpphmh" sound instead of saying something in English.

God, he's so hot. He makes me feel warm and confused and like I'm about to pass out. Maybe I'll put him on my kissing list in tiny letters: MAC BRODY.

Wednesday, November 11

Mom wrote back! When I saw her name in my inbox, all the hair on my arms stood up.

Dearest Bunny Love,

First, let me apologize for the *obscenely* delayed response. I was away from email for a few days, for reasons too dull to get into.

I sense that you're angry. Please, correct me if I'm wrong—modern technology is wonderful, and I'm oh! so glad I'm living in these times, but one thing computers *aren't* good at is conveying tone of voice, so it's entirely possible I've misread you. But, sweetness, if you are upset, know how profoundly devastated I am to be stuck here under the merciless sun while you and your father celebrate the feast of white oppression. A little joke, sweetheart! I know you love holidays, especially this one (it's #3 on your latest ranking, isn't that right?), and truly I would love nothing more than to see your eyes sparkling above the cranberry sauce and hear your sweet voice. But what kind of example would I be setting for you if I dropped the most important work of my life to indulge my sentimental longing for home? No, I've always wanted you to know—to really *know*, by seeing the example I set—that women can be just as hard-driving and committed to their careers as men. And so while you stuff yourself into a stupor, know that I'm doing what's best for myself *and* for you, even if you can't see it now. You'll thank me one day, I promise.

I love you above all else, and am, as ever,

Your devoted,
Mama

P.S. It's "paloma," honey, not "palomino." Tequila and grapefruit soda—so refreshing, and much more popular here than margaritas, which are considered hopelessly American.

Thursday, November 12
She knows me well, you have to admit that.

Chloe Snow's Holiday Rankings, last updated 8/1
#1 July 4th (the beach, tanning, fireworks, hot dogs, America, my stars and stripes bikini, our annual backyard BBQ)
#2 Christmas (snow, "Santa" [Dad still makes me a stocking every year], waffles for breakfast, steak for dinner)
#3 Thanksgiving (stuffing, cranberry sauce, the official start of Christmas-music-listening season)
#4 Halloween (secretly I love dressing up)
#5 Groundhog Day (Dad and I watch *Groundhog Day* and have a carb blowout)
#6 Easter (cold and gray, plus Hannah always gets her undies in a bunch about my soul and makes me go to church. But on the other hand, Cadbury Creme Eggs)
#7 Valentine's Day (won't be fun until I have a boyfriend, and even then, what if he thinks it's a stupid Hallmark holiday and I have to pretend to agree?)

#8 New Year's Eve (won't be fun until I'm a
grown-up living in New York City)
#9 Arbor Day, Presidents' Day, blah, blah, all the
others are dumb

Friday, November 13

While drying my hair, I realized Hannah hasn't been messaging me much this week, so I held the dryer with my left hand and with my right pointer typed: *r u dead or wut*

I saw the comment bubble with the ellipsis, so I knew she was typing. Then the bubble went away. Then it came back. By the time she got her wording just perfect, my hair was totally dry.

Hi! I need your advice on
something, actually. Can you
sleep over tonight? Mom is
making white lasagna!

That comma kills me! It's like texting with the queen of England. I guarantee I have way better grammar than Hannah, because all I do is read, write in this diary, and get amazing grades in English. But texting isn't about good grammar. It's about speed and creating the illusion of conversation.

Saturday, November 14

HOT GOSSIP: Hannah is in love with Frank Sinatra, a.k.a. Josh Menaker. Apparently they've been texting each other nonfreakingstop, which is why she's neglecting me. But there's a problem. Hannah is not allowed to date until she's in college (I still don't get why God cares if you make out with another teenager, but whatever), which we've already talked about 1,000 times, but which is now actually important, since we're not just discussing what Hannah would do if Channing Tatum asked her out (although that *is* an important hypothetical). Now there's a real skinny but cute guy who messaged her this:

You + me + movies on friday =
unprecedented levels of fun??

Please say yes so i don't curl up
and die like the awkwardest of
awkward turtles

Frank Sinatra isn't my type, but I admit, that's pretty adorable.

After three hours of Hannah panicking about what to text back, and OMG, did she really want a relationship right now? I got fed up and said, "I don't understand— are you guys secretly engaged?"

"Of course not."

"Well, you're acting like it. What's the big deal? Tell your parents you're hanging out with me next Friday and go to the movies. It's a date. You're not ring shopping."

That was my advice in a nutshell, but Hannah's such a quivery stressball that we had to go over everything a thousand times, examining it from every angle and imagining what her parents would say if (a) they stole her phone and read her messages, (b) she broke down and confessed after the date, (c) she and Josh decide they have to go to the same college because long-distance relationships are too hard, and on and on. She also made me practice what I'll say on the phone if her parents call and ask to talk to her. We only slept for two hours, and I have dark-purple bags under my eyes today. I'm seriously the best friend who's ever lived.

Sunday, November 15

Dad found his ancient Nintendo system in the basement and we played Super Mario Bros. for, like, eight hours. Dad is amazing at it! We ordered a pizza for dinner. Mom would have flipped her shiz about all the time we wasted *and* all the toxins in the pepperoni, but it was one of the funnest days I've had probably in my entire life, so I only feel a tiny bit guilty.

Monday, November 16

Whenever I see Sienna and Mac in the hall, she's hanging on his arm and staring up at him with Bambi eyes. She has to hunch over to do the staring up, because they're both six feet tall.

Tuesday, November 17

Hung out with Tristan after school!! What happened was, I was walking along reading *To Kill a Mockingbird* on my phone, and I heard someone say, "Ugh, look at that annoying iPhone zombie," and when I looked up, he was standing in front of me, smiling. Neither of us were doing anything, so we decided to watch football practice, since that's what passes for entertainment in our booming metropolis. The bleachers were freezing, but it was nice to sit outside in the chilly air and smell the grass and the dead leaves, and watch Mac running around.

I felt shy, since this was the first time Tristan and I had hung out for real. Mom always says that questions are the key to conversation, so I said, "Do you play any sports?"

"I played soccer and ran track at home—I mean, in North Carolina—and I made it onto varsity soccer here, but I decided not to play."

"How come?"

"It conflicted with chorus rehearsals."

"WHAT?" I turned on the bleacher to look at him. "You

actually chose chorus over varsity soccer?" Maybe it's different in non-prehistoric towns, but here in the Land That Time Forgot, turning down the chance to play a varsity sport—as a freshman, no less—is like saying, "I don't enjoy being popular or admired. I'd rather be a pariah. Thanks!"

Tristan said, "My dad almost stroked out."

I couldn't think of a follow-up question, so we watched the football players for a few minutes.

"Have you met Mac Brody yet?" I asked.

"I know who he is, obviously."

"It's weird how we automatically know who all the popular seniors are, but they have no idea we exist."

"I hate it," he said. "I can't wait to move to New York, where no one knows my business and no one cares how popular you were in high school."

"I want to move to New York too!" I said, and then we talked for a long time about the New York blogs we read, and whether we could somehow go there together to see a show, and whether we want to live in the West Village or Williamsburg when we're old and rich. When we ran out of New York comments, we were quiet for a minute, and then he said, "You have a crush on Mac, right?" and I said, "Ahh! Is it obvious? Does everyone know?" and he said, "I have no idea, but you've been staring at his butt the entire time we've been here."

Maybe I have a crush on Tristan, too. I feel so

comfortable around him, and we could move to NYC and live in a sunny loft together.

I would put him on my kissing list, but he's too real. Griffin and Zach I could kiss with wild abandon and then never speak to again. I wouldn't want to use Tristan for his lips that way.

Wednesday, November 18

I said to Hannah, "You have to admit Mac's butt is so cute and round," and she was like, "Yeah!" and I was like, "You're the worst liar ever." I don't care what she thinks; her type is elves with curly brown hair, and that's fine for her, but I like guys who could break my ribs from too much love, like Lenny in *Of Mice and Men*, but not mentally challenged, of course.

Thursday, November 19

I can hardly remember the time when Hannah and I were invited to exclusive senior parties. Now the weekend stretches out before me like a vast empty plain.

I saw Zach Chen in the hall today, and he did say, "Chloe! You're still coming to the gig next month, right?" and I said, "I'm counting down the days," which sounded maybe a little intense but not too horrible. Somehow it makes me even lonelier, though, imagining that at this very moment Zach is off doing something interesting, having forgotten our conversation two seconds after it happened, while I'm home alone obsessing over him in my diary.

Friday, November 20

Hannah's on a date right now, Dad's still not home from work, I can't ask Tristan to hang out because then he'd know I have nothing to do on a Friday night, and Snickers looked incredulous when I suggested taking a third walk. I guess I'll just sit here by myself, inching closer to death with the passing of each second.

Saturday, November 21

Hannah came over and told me about the date. Here's what happened:

1. They saw that movie where the girl's eyeball gets cut in half in the cabin, and Hannah stared at her knees through almost the entire thing.
2. Josh held her hand, and neither of them got too sweaty, but she started worrying that her fingers are freakishly fat.
3. They went to the bagel store afterward, because there's nowhere else to go in this godforsaken town.
4. Somehow she and Josh wound up shaking

hands instead of just waving goodbye like
normal people.
5. She thinks she's "probably" falling in love
with him.

Well, that's just great. Hannah's engaged to be
engaged, while I'm the world's youngest spinster.

Sunday, November 22

Today is Mom's birthday! I made her a Happy Birthday
sign covered with glitter and stickers and held it up over
Skype. She loved it, I'm pretty sure. It was hard to tell,
because the picture kept freezing. She looks pretty. Different. She's tan, and she's wearing her hair all piled on top
of her head. When she was home, her long hair annoyed
me, and then I felt guilty for being annoyed, because who
cares? It's just hair. She can wear it however she wants.

Monday, November 23

I clicked through all my summer pics to depress myself.
I remember the days when I was tan and semi-attractive.
Now I'm a short, translucent ghost.

Tuesday, November 24

Everyone's acting cracked out because of the short week.
It takes so little to make high school kids happy.

Wednesday, November 25
HALF DAY TODAY OMG FRIENDS NETFLIX
MARATHON WITH SNICKERS AND HANNAH
PARTAAYYYYY

Thursday, November 26
Well, that was definitely the worst Thanksgiving of my life.
I wanted to stay home with Dad, but he thought it would
be too quiet, so we went to the Egans'. First of all, they
don't make anything from scratch—the cranberry sauce
was from a can and the pumpkin pie crust was premade,
which, not to sound like a snob, but Dad would *never* serve
crap like that on Thanksgiving. Then Mr. Egan said grace
before dinner. A quick prayer would have been fine, but
he went on and on for literally five minutes, which doesn't
sound that long, but it's a NIGHTMARISH ETERNITY
for a prayer. There was a lot about the Heavenly Father, gratitude and humility, etc., etc., and I started to think, *What if
I fart by accident?* and *What if I can't help myself and suddenly yell "GENITAL WARTS!" as loud as I can?* Then
Mr. Egan said, "And we ask you, dear Lord, to watch over
those of us who cannot join us here tonight but who are
in our prayers, especially those who have wandered from
your path, oh God. We ask you to hold them in the palm of
your hand and lead them safely home," and I *knew* he was
talking about Mom. I tried to give Hannah the stink-eye,

but she had her eyes squeezed shut, probably because she knew I'd be furious. After grace finally ended, Mr. Egan aimed a big pitying smile at my face, and because I'm a coward I stared down at my plate instead of giving him the finger. He's one of those sporty dads who dress like a football coach on the weekends and wear a gold chain bracelet. I used to like him.

Dad cleared his throat and said, "Did anyone else go to the last town meeting? I know Mrs. Singh is intense, but she has a point about road salt," and then the grown-ups got engrossed in an incredibly boring adult conversation about who knows what. I thought we were safely off the topic of Mom, but when we were eating the disgusting pumpkin pie, Mrs. Egan gently put her fork down, made eye contact with Dad, and said, "How are you holding up?" in this hushed, holy voice that she probably thought made her sound like the Virgin Mary. Dad said, "Just fine, Julie."

She said, "Well, I think you're the strongest, most patient man alive."

"Really, we're OK."

"And Chloe . . ." She turned to look at me AND HER EYES ACTUALLY FILLED WITH TEARS. I wanted to flip the table upside down. "I just don't know how this sweet lamb does it."

Dad looked at me like, *Don't lose your temper.*

So all I said was, "Does what?"

Mrs. Egan said, "Well, get along without your mother, honey."

I was worried I was going to start crying—not from sadness, but from rage. I said, "It's just a few months," which is so *stupid*. It wasn't snappy, or mean, or articulate—it was nothing. I should have said, "She's a good example to me. She's not sitting around making brownies and obsessing about church because she doesn't have a career, like some mothers I could mention. She has her own life."

I did cry in the car, after Dad and I finally, finally got to leave, and he told me about *l'esprit de l'escalier* (I Googled the spelling), which means "staircase wit," like when you think of the perfect comeback on the stairs after you've left the party. I said, "I hate the Egans," and he said, "They mean well," and I said, "They don't. They want to pretend they're being nice and make us feel terrible at the same time. They're concern trolls," and Dad asked what that meant, and I explained it to him, so we both taught each other something.

Friday, November 27

A selection of texts from Hannah:

I'm so sorry if that was weird.

OK, I guess it was weird.

My parents are insane.

Please, please, please don't be mad.

I finally texted her back to put her out of her misery. I guess I'm not mad at her. It's not her fault her parents enjoy tormenting helpless teenagers.

Saturday, November 28
When I woke up this morning, my favorite sheets, the pink striped ones, were ah-comp-PLETE-ly soaked in period blood. FML.

Sunday, November 29
There's the Sunday Blues, and then there's the Sunday Blues After a Long Weekend. It's a whole other level of despair.

Monday, November 30
BREAKING NEWS. There was a fire drill during fifth period today, and I wound up standing next to Zach Chen. He told me my green nail polish was rad (!!) and picked up my hands to get a better look (!!!!!!). And somehow we wound up playing that game where you hover your fingers over the other person's palms and they try to quickly smack your hands before you can pull away.

When everyone started filing back in, he said, "Thanks for entertaining me," and gave me a high five. Progress!!!!!

Tuesday, December 1

December already! Life goes so fast. It seems like just yesterday I was an innocent fourth grader, totally unaware of the period cramps and inner nostril zits that loomed in my future.

Wednesday, December 2

In chorus today, instead of sitting in sections, we stood in circles of four—one soprano, one alto, one tenor, one bass— and sang like that. It's much harder to remember your part when you can't listen to the sopranos on either side of you. Tristan and I managed to get into the same group, and when we sang "faithful friends who are dear to us gather near to us once more," he grabbed my hands, ironically, I think, but still, we have now technically held hands! And this two days after I touched Zach's hands (well, slapped, really, but still). Maybe I'll be able to keep my kissing vow!

Thursday, December 3

Skyped with Mom. It's strange to see her wearing a tank top and sweating, when I'm walking around in earmuffs because Dad refuses to turn the heat up to a normal level. It makes me feel like she's a time traveler.

I felt strange after hanging up with Mom, so to distract myself, I called Hannah and asked her if she'll go to the Deposed Monarchs show with me. She said she was already planning to go with Josh, but I should come with them, and no, don't be ridiculous, I won't be the third wheel; it'll be more fun with me there. Sometimes I really love her.

Friday, December 4

Tristan and Hannah came over after school. It was starting to get weird that the three of us had never hung out. We watched *White Christmas*, because we are wholesome kids. I think it went well. Everyone was a little too polite, but there weren't many awkward silences. We talked about whether we've ever been stoned (no, none of us) or drunk (me and Hannah not at all, Tristan once when he was 11 and snuck a bunch of leftover wine at one of his parents' parties), which somehow segued into the topic of Josh and what a good kisser he is. Hannah's mom picked her up first. When she was gone, Tristan said, "So have you met Josh? What do you think of him?"

We talked about Hannah and Josh for a while, but not in a horrible gossipy way, in an analytical way. Thank God Tristan has opinions about people too. That's the one thing that annoys me about Hannah: whenever I want to discuss someone, she looks pained and lets me go on for a few minutes without responding much and finally says, "I think ____ is really nice, and we shouldn't talk behind her back."

When we were finished with Hannah and Josh, Tristan said, "So where's your mom? Does she work late?"

"Oh. No. Or, maybe. Actually, she's working in Mexico for a few months."

"That's so cool! What does she do?"

"She's a writer."

He was impressed and asked me a million questions about what she's written, and somehow I couldn't tell him . . . I don't know what I couldn't tell him.

Saturday, December 5
Dad and I drove to the Christmas tree farm, and he sawed down a six-footer. It's the honor system: you take a tree, you leave $50 in a red pail balanced on a tree stump. Basically we live in a real-life version of *Our Town*.

Sunday, December 6
Dad went up to the attic and dragged down all these boxes I'd never seen before, and what do you think they contained?! Christmas lights, stockings, glittery Santa ornaments, plastic holly, snow globes, cookie tins, and more, more, more! We spent the entire day listening to *The Nutcracker* on repeat and decorating. Mom would have popped a blood vessel if she'd seen.

Monday, December 7

In English class, I said *Ethan Frome* is really a novel about feminism. Ethan is so scared and passive he's hardly even a real person, but Mattie and Zeena, even though they're horrible and I hate them, take action the only way they can in a society that forces them to be nothing but wives/servants. Miss Murphy said my comments were "very insightful." I looked back at Griffin Gonzalez and he gave me a nod of respect. I am a genius.

Tuesday, December 8

Have I mentioned that Tristan has icy-blue eyes the color of a frozen lake in a fictional New England town? And light-brown hair, like a beautiful pilgrim?

Wednesday, December 9

Wait. Wait, wait, wait, wait, wait. Tomorrow it'll be exactly four months since Mom left. That means she'll be home in 24 hours or less. But why hasn't she emailed me about it? Should I email her? What if she thinks I've forgotten, and she wants to surprise me, and if I email her I'll ruin it? Maybe she's already on the plane! Wait, what's the time difference?

I. Am. Freaking. Out.

Thursday, December 10

It's almost midnight, and she's not here yet. I asked Dad if I could hang out with Hannah tonight, and he was like, "Sure, just don't be back too late. It's a school night." He sounded totally normal—but maybe he's in on the surprise!

Friday, December 11

Most people travel on the weekends, right? It makes way more sense than coming home randomly in the middle of the week.

Saturday, December 12

Maybe she's going to surprise me at the holiday concert!

Sunday, December 13

I finally cracked and asked Dad if Mom's coming home this week. He was unloading the dishwasher, and he stopped with a coffee cup in his hand. "I'm not sure, honey, but I don't think so."

"She said four months."

"I did email her about your concert."

"It's not normal that she just went to Mexico and left us here. It's not very . . . What's so horrible about us?"

He put the coffee cup on the counter. He looked mad. "*Nothing.*"

We both looked at the cup, which was one of Mom's. It had blue bunnies around the rim.

I know I have flaws. I'm self-centered. I'm lazy. I don't do much besides read, text, and Instagram Snickers. And Dad's Dad. He doesn't understand Mom at all, plus he whistles constantly. And sometimes he gets this look on his face like he can hardly wait to stop talking to you and go off to do some lawyering. But are those things the worst things?

When someone leaves you, you think it must be your fault. You look at your face in the mirror and think, *What a stupid face.* It's hard to make yourself believe you're basically OK. A good egg. Not so annoying and awful that people decide to move to another country to get away from you.

Not "people." Your mother. My mother.

Monday, December 14

It's awkward talking to Hannah about chorus. She pities me because I'm not in the Love Notes, which is annoying, because I would way rather hang out with Tristan than take orders from Bernadette, but Hannah would never believe me if I told her that. Plus she's started to say "aca" instead of "a cappella," which is just—there are no words.

Tuesday, December 15

IT SNOWED!!!!!!! SO FREAKING FESTIVE!!!!!!!!

Wednesday, December 16

Here's what we have to wear for the holiday concert: a white button-down shirt, black pants, black shoes, and a maroon vest. We are going to look like a chorus of blackjack dealers.

Thursday, December 17

The concert went fine. Whatever. Mom didn't come. I mean, I didn't expect her to come, but maybe one tiny corner of me did. Like, an inch of my kidney was hoping she'd make it. I couldn't really pay attention, because I was searching the audience for her face, and by accident I came in too early at the end of the "Hallelujah" chorus, and I longed to vanish into a puff of smoke, leaving nothing but a crumpled maroon vest behind. The Love Notes performed after we did. They did a bunch of pop songs, including "All I Want for Christmas Is You," and the crowd loved it, of course. The girls wore matching tight red dresses, and the guys wore red ties and khakis. Zach Chen sang the lead on "Last Christmas." Bernadette had a million solos. Mac, Sienna, and a bunch of other famous seniors even came to see her (which means they also saw my accidental solo. Great).

Zach came up to me afterward and said, "Someone always comes in too early on the second-to-last 'hallelujah.'

It's basically a tradition. Don't sweat it." He looked so cute in his khakis.

"Ah! I'm so embarrassed. Thank you for saying that. You're nice."

"I'll see you on Saturday, right?"

"I'll be there."

He gave me a hug, and I tried to convey, with silent body language, *I would very much like to kiss you at your gig on Saturday. My lips are yours for the smooching.* He gave my arms a little squeeze after we were done hugging, so maybe it worked.

Dad brought me a bouquet of yellow roses, which was embarrassing but nice. Miss Murphy told him how hard I've been working, and he said he's glad I'm showing an interest in something other than my phone, and then they talked for half an hour about boring grown-up stuff while I texted Tristan, who was trapped across the room with his parents and some other adults.

ur dad is so cute to bring
you flowers

Argh embarrassing

Are Hannah and Bernadette
bffs now?

I looked across the auditorium and saw my best friend chatting and laughing with Josh and Bernie. Hannah did come over to tell me how good I sounded and even pretended she hadn't noticed my solo "hallelujah."

Tristan and I met each other's parents (well, parent, singular, in my case). His mom is so beautiful I almost felt bad for Tristan. People must stare at them wherever they go. She has teeth as white as snow and a nose like an "after" picture. His dad looks like a cowboy from an old movie wearing a suburban-dad costume. They smiled at me a lot and said they'd heard all about me from Tris, and Tris and I both turned bright red.

Friday, December 18

I think I'm in love with Tristan. He's so handsome, and so nice, and I'm so comfortable with him. Your boyfriend is supposed to be your best friend, and he's definitely my best guy friend. Plus, if I married him, his parents would teach me how to be effortlessly attractive while still eating all the Double Stuf Oreos I want.

Maybe I should skip Zach's show tomorrow. Maybe I should save my first kiss for Tristan, my true love. But no, that's crazy. Tris might not even like me. Or what if he likes me, and we kiss, and he rears back and says, "What are you *doing*? Haven't you ever kissed anyone before?" and I break down crying and admit that I haven't, and he says, "Um, I just remembered I have a ton of homework"?

I'm going to that show.

Saturday, December 19

Well, I did it. I kept my vow. I popped my kissing cherry. Yay, I guess.

Hannah, Josh, and I got to the show on time, which apparently isn't the cool thing to do, because hardly anyone else was there. It was at 5 p.m. and we were wearing neon-orange wristbands so the bartenders knew not to serve us alcohol, but it was still exciting to be in a dark bar that smelled like beer. Eventually the place filled up, and by the time Zach and his band were three songs into their first set, it was packed. And loud. Hannah dug an extra pair of bright-blue earplugs out of her bag (she was already wearing a set) and tried to hand them to me. I shook my head and screamed, "NO THANKS!" Actually, I was terrified that I was murdering my ears, but I couldn't risk looking like a doofus—what if Zach happened to see me in the crowd?

He wasn't wearing anything unusual, just his regular jeans and T-shirt, but standing onstage, under lights, playing his guitar and pressing his mouth against a microphone, he was transformed into a sex god. It made me so nervous that I screamed "BE RIGHT BACK!" at Hannah and Josh and headed for the bathroom.

When I came out, the music was so loud it shook my skin, and I decided to take a break. I pushed outside and walked around the corner, and there, leaning up against the wall and looking at his phone, was Griffin Gonzalez.

"Hey!" I said, and then, "Sorry, am I talking really loudly? I can't hear anything."

"It's hellish in there."

"Kind of."

"I hate live music almost as much as I hate traveling. Not that I'd tell anyone that. There are some things you're not allowed to dislike at our age."

"You just told me."

"True."

"What are you doing here, if you hate live music so much?"

"I'm friends with the drummer. What are you doing here?"

"Just hanging out."

"Mmm." He seemed to lose interest, and glanced at his phone.

"Actually, I'm here to kiss someone."

He put his phone away. "Anyone in particular?"

"I was thinking of Zach."

He snorted. "I should have guessed."

"What's that supposed to mean?"

"Soulful guitar-playing singer dude. Catnip to girls like you."

And then I walked right up to Griffin Gonzalez and kissed him. A short kiss, on his mouth. I pulled back to see how he was taking it. He looked surprised but not disgusted, so I put my arms around his neck and kissed him some more, and he kissed me back, dryly at first, but then he kind of pried open my mouth with his lips and we made out!! All the articles I've read online say not to be too aggressive with your tongue, but Griffin hasn't read those articles, I guess. It felt like our tongues were attempting to tie each other into bows.

I didn't feel queasy with excitement. A wave of passion did not pull me under. At all times I was aware of where Griffin's hands were (resting on my hips) and whether or not I was making weird noises (no, not too slurpy).

After, oh, less than 90 seconds, I detached myself.

"That was unexpected," he said.

"Uh, yeah," I said. "I guess I should . . ." I gestured to the bar.

"Sure. I'll probably see you in there."

And that was it!

Zach didn't seem as terrifyingly sexy when I went back inside, but he didn't seem like anyone I want to kiss, either.

Actually, I'm not sure Griffin is someone I want to kiss. Aren't you supposed to feel something when you make out with someone? Kissing Griffin was about as exciting as brushing my teeth. With an electric toothbrush, but still.

He's very handsome, but I don't know how to talk to him. He's so cynical and negative and uninvolved. You can feel him hovering above the rest of us, calmly observing us without descending to our level.

I got what I wanted, and now I want something more.

Sunday, December 20

Griffin's not sitting at home right now dreaming of me, is he? He's not looking at all my feeds and falling deeply and irrevocably in love with me, right?

Tomorrow could be the most awkward day of my life.

Monday, December 21

THANK THE LORD, GRIFFIN DOESN'T LIKE ME! IT'S A CHRISTMAS MIRACLE!

He followed me out of English class. I was power walking away, pretending I didn't see him, but he jogged to catch up.

"Chloe! Do you have a second?"

"Oh, hi, Griffin!"

"Listen, it was fun to, uh, see you on Saturday. I was

wondering if we could talk about—I don't know how you feel or what you have in mind—I mean, I don't want to assume anything." He took a deep breath and started over. "I really like you and respect you as a reader, but I don't know if I'm looking for a relationship right now."

I was only a tiny bit offended. Mostly I was so relieved I could have kissed him again from the joy of it.

"Yes! I mean, I agree. I think we're meant to be really good friends who talk about books."

For a second I thought *he* looked offended, but then he smiled and said, "I'm glad we're on the same page."

"On the same *page*, get it?" I poked him in the ribs. "Book friends? Page?"

"Uh-huh."

Oh, the relief of not having to reject a sad miniature professor! I gave him a big hug and said, "Merry Christmas, Griffin."

Tuesday, December 22

Miss Murphy told us to read some novels over the break instead of rotting our brains playing Call of Duty, and everyone laughed sardonically, so I did too, but after class I pretended to be sending important texts at my desk so I could stay behind, and when everyone had left, I asked her what books she thought I'd like. She got all excited and gave me *I Capture the Castle* and *Prep*.

Wednesday, December 23

HALF DAY!!!! Hannah, Josh, Tristan, and I went to McDonald's after school to celebrate. Josh drove, which meant we had to go to the senior parking lot, which meant I saw Mac. He pointed at me and yelled, "Merry Christmas, Chloe Snow!" Everyone turned to look at me like, *Who is that mysterious girl?* or maybe like, *Who is that very short, incredibly awkward girl?* I blushed and waved at Mac. Hannah said, "I guess you made a big impression on him that day at the pool."

I never talk to her about Mac. I don't see the point, when she can't appreciate the perfection of his butt.

We got in Josh's car, a green Volkswagen Jetta with a pine tree air freshener hanging from the rearview mirror, and drove off with all the windows down, blasting Vampire Weekend (of course Josh loves Vampire Weekend). We passed Griffin, and I lunged halfway out my window to scream, "HI, GRIFFIN!" I'll love him forever for accepting my kiss and then not liking me. Really, it all worked out perfectly.

After McDonald's, Mrs. Egan drove me and Hannah to the mall so we could shop for Christmas presents. I got Mom something at Barnes & Noble, just in case.

Thursday, December 24

Christmas Eve. Dad and I ate shrimp scampi and watched *Meet Me in St. Louis* and even sang songs on the couch, looking at the tree. I insisted on doing "The Twelve Days of Christmas," which Dad hates. After we sang "Silent Night," Dad said, "Your voice really is beautiful." He let me open one present, which is a Christmas Eve tradition in our family, and the present I chose turned out to be huge slippers shaped like Boston terriers, which I didn't even ask for, but which are so *me* that they made me feel like crying. I'm just sad, I'm so sad.

Friday, December 25
It's too late to write the whole thing down, but in a nutshell (in a nutCRACKERshell, hahaha), Mom came home!!!!!!!!!!!!!!!!!!!!

Saturday, December 26
Dad's on a run and Mom's taking a nap, so I finally have time to recap. I woke up at 11 yesterday morning, which was bittersweet, because the innocent days when I rocketed out of bed at 5 a.m. to see if Santa came are gone, gone forever—but nothing feels better than getting 10 hours of sleep. I opened my stocking, which was excellent (nail polish, Cadbury fruit and nut bar, lip stain set in a glittery white box, magnetic Scrabble, sequined iPhone case, and a fancy edition of *Sense and Sensibility*), and all my presents (highlight: a wall calendar illustrated with photos of Snickers), and Dad opened his present from me

(a North Face fleece, which cost a g-d fortune in allowance money). While Dad made waffles, I texted Tristan and Hannah and tried to Instagram Snickers wearing reindeer antlers, which didn't work, because he flung his head around violently every time I tried to put them on him. After breakfast, I lay on the couch eating candy canes and reading S and S, which is so good that I'm going as slowly as I can, to make it last. When it got dark, Dad put on some Christmas jazz and started marinating the steaks.

I was half wondering whether I should finally take a shower and put on real clothes, and half thinking about how surprisingly not-sad I felt, when I heard the front door open. Dad and I looked at each other with a wild surmise. Before I even heard her voice, I knew. My heart beat fast. She clomped through the hall in her boots, and then there she was in the living room, standing in front of me, still cold from being outside, looking so different from how I remembered her but exactly the same, too.

"Mommy!" I said, which is embarrassing, and she said, "Rabbit!" I ran over to her, wishing I'd brushed my hair and washed my face, and threw my arms around her, and she smelled a little bit like a plane, but mostly like herself, her mother self.

I heard her say "Hi, Charlie" over my head. She disentangled herself and went over to my dad. They hugged quickly and then kissed on the mouth even more quickly. I've given Snickers longer smooches.

After she showered and changed, we had dinner. I felt too shy to talk much, and Dad must have too, so we mostly listened to Mom's stories about Mexico. Although I tried to concentrate, I couldn't stop staring at her. She was wearing leggings and a blue tunic. Her hair was in a high bun on top of her head, and she wore bright-red lipstick and no eye makeup. I'm used to seeing her in tons of eyeliner, and she looked young and wide-awake without it.

". . . Mexico City gets such a bad rap, but it's gorgeous. I mean, sure, you can't let your guard down on the STC, and the traffic is killing, but the architecture— you'd think you were in Europe."

I'd forgotten the way she turns her wineglass by the stem when she talks and keeps her fork in her left hand to take a bite of meat instead of switching it to the right. I'd forgotten the little lines by her eyes and the exact sound of her laugh. It made me feel guilty, how much I'd forgotten.

After dinner, we opened presents. I gave Mom an illustrated edition of *The Elements of Style,* and she gave me a necklace of turquoise rectangles outlined in silver. It's definitely beautiful, but I probably won't wear it until I'm 40 or 50. It looks like something a glamorous mother should wear. Like Mom.

She and Dad didn't get each other anything.

I went to bed early, to give them a chance to talk. I

lay there awake for about an hour, staring at the ceiling and feeling my heart race. Mom! Home! For good!

Sunday, December 27

How weird, coming downstairs and seeing Mom sitting at the island in her striped bathrobe, drinking a cup of tea and reading the Style section, just like the old days.

She came on a walk with me and Snickers. It snowed overnight, and the bare tree branches were lined with white.

She said, "So, what ever happened with that guy you met at the pool?"

"Mac? Oh, yeah, I was right. He has a girlfriend."

"Hmm. Well, as Nora Ephron's mother said, everything is copy. Some advice? Don't waste time whining about your feelings. Take notes on the sensory details and the conversations. That'll be easier to turn into a novel later."

I don't want to be a writer. I want to be a happy person. But I could never tell her that. It would offend her.

Mom asked about school, and chorus, and what I'm reading, but I haven't seen her in so long that once I gave her the major headlines, I was out of material.

I'm sure it'll go right back to normal in a few weeks.

Monday, December 28

We ate dinner together for the fourth night in a row, which must be a Snow family record. It got off on the wrong foot, because as Dad was putting down the plates of pasta, Mom said, "Oh, I had penne for lunch," and Dad said, "You should have said something," and Mom said, "No, no, it looks delicious, Charlie."

They were extremely polite to each other all the way through dinner, and even during Trivial Pursuit (Mom won—she always does). She read a book to me on the couch and played with my hair, and I almost cried, it felt so nice.

Tuesday, December 29

I'm acting a little different around Dad now that Mom's back. It feels like it used to in the old days: Mom and me on the girly-doing-our-nails-and-reading-magazines team, Dad on the going-for-runs-and-working-late team. A team of one.

Wednesday, December 30

Texting with Hannah.

My mom's back!

!!!!! I'm so happy for you!

Her and my dad are making out all over the place so gross

Aw, cute.

I'm a liar.

I could tell Tristan what's really going on, except I kind of lied to him about it too.

Thursday, December 31

I sat on the edge of the bathtub while Mom did her makeup, and told her about Tristan. "I feel totally normal around him, like I can talk about anything. He doesn't make me nervous."

"And what about Mac?"

"So nervous. Like throw-up-on-my-shoes nervous."

Mom paused with her lipstick in midair. "Let me pass along some wisdom gleaned from my own experience, bunny. Never go for the safe, boring choice. Always opt for the man who makes your stomach churn."

I hope that when she said "safe" and "boring," she wasn't talking about Dad.

It's New Year's Eve. Dad's making jambalaya, and at midnight we'll eat 12 grapes, one for each month of the New Year, and make a wish for each grape. It's a Mexican tradition. I have my wishes all ready, but of course I can't write them down or they won't come true.

Friday, January 1

On the plus side, I remembered to say "Rabbits, rabbits" first thing this morning.

On the downside, everything's terrible.

During dinner, Mom told us about these crazy ruins she'd visited. "Rabbit, you would adore Teotihuacán. You clamber to the top of these pyramids, look down, and I swear you can feel the ghosts of sacrificed virgins fluttering around your ears."

Dad cleared his throat.

Mom reached over and pushed a piece of hair behind my ear. "I can't wait to show you."

"Veronica!" Dad sounded pissed.

"I can't wait to see, Mom," I said. *The virgins will probably haunt me extra hard, since I'm one of them.*

"Chloe, you're not going to Mexico," Dad said.

"But Mom just said—"

"I heard her."

Mom rolled her eyes at me like, *Your father is so ridiculous.*

Dad turned to me and said, "Do you mind hanging out in your room for a few minutes while I talk to Mom?"

I stomped off—*what am I, four years old, being sent to my room?*—and didn't even pretend to go up the stairs; I just lurked in the hallway to eavesdrop, which was easy, because they were both too mad to pay attention to what I was doing.

". . . get her hopes up like that. It's not fair."

"Charlie, don't be ridiculous. She knows I don't mean we're getting on a plane tomorrow."

"No, she doesn't know that. When you breeze in here unannounced, talking about the butterflies and pyramids and saying 'I can't wait to show you,' she starts packing her bags and looking for her passport."

"You underestimate her, Charlie."

"You're not estimating her at all, Veronica. You're not giving her a moment's thought."

Why can't he be nice to her? Why can't he let us go to Mexico, like Mom wants?

Saturday, January 2

Escaped to Hannah's house. Her parents were fighting about when to take the tree down, and she made a face at me like, *They're so annoying*, and I made a face back at her like, *Sorry, it sucks*, but actually I was filled with jealousy.

Sunday, January 3

Family meeting this afternoon. Of course: Why not have a family meeting on the saddest day of the week?

Mom said, "Chloe, I haven't managed your expectations well, and for that I feel absolutely dreadful."

Dad said, "Cut to the chase, Veronica."

Mom glared at him and then turned to me with a pitying expression. "I know it's hard on you, angel. Don't think I don't empathize. But I look back at my mother, trapped in our house like something out of Charlotte Perkins Gilman, and I think, 'What effect did that have on the formation of my character? Wouldn't I have been better off if she'd followed her dreams?'"

Dad said to her, "Enough, Veronica," and then, to me, "Mom's not staying. She's going back to Mexico."

"For a while," Mom said. "It'll be just like last time. I'll go; I'll come back."

"We can come with you," I said.

"Oh, bunny," she said.

"No, I have a plan. I can take classes online, and Dad can teach English as a Second Language."

Mom turned to Dad. He looked back at her like he was waiting, but she didn't say anything, so he turned to me and said, "Mom's going by herself."

"Dad, please say yes. Please. I want to be with Mom."

His face looked crumpled. "I understand, honey. But it's just not possible."

"You don't understand at all," I shouted at him, and stood up so fast my chair tipped over.

Monday, January 4

I never thought I'd be so excited to go back to school. When I walked in at 7:20 and smelled the chicken-fingery air, I wanted to kneel down and kiss the linoleum.

Tuesday, January 5
Mom's gone again. Already, when I try to imagine the smell of her neck, I draw a blank.

Wednesday, January 6
Tonight I asked Dad why we can't move to Mexico.

"My job is here," he said. "And your school is here."

"But people change jobs and schools all the time."

He looked at his plate. "There are plenty of reasons it's not a good idea."

"Are you hinting that Mom doesn't want us to move there?"

He didn't say anything.

"Well, she *does*," I said. "She loves me so much, and she wants me to live with her, and you're keeping us apart."

His face got red. "I know you miss Mom."

"That's not the point!"

"Don't yell at me, Chloe."

"May I be excused?"

I left before he answered and barely got to my room before I started crying.

Thursday, January 7
Mom married the wrong guy. I mean, I know if she'd married someone else, I wouldn't exist. But her husband/ my father should be a sensitive, brilliant, interesting

artist. Maybe an alcoholic painter, or a poet with a terrible temper. Someone who would understand why she can't rot away in the suburbs. Someone who would say, "Move to Mexico? Why not?" Someone with a sense of adventure.

Friday, January 8
Hung out with Tristan after school. I felt kind of shy after not seeing him for the whole break. But it was only awkward for a few minutes. Then we started talking about whether we'd rather be buried or cremated, and it felt normal again.

Saturday, January 9
Big news: Josh touched Hannah's boobs under her shirt over winter break. In other news, I'm still a spinster.

Sunday, January 10
Texted Hannah:

> *Do you think Tristan is boring and safe?*

?? No. I think he's smart and handsome.

Sometimes I love Hannah.

Monday, January 11

I think if Mom knew Tristan, she'd really, really like him. Just because I'm comfortable around him doesn't mean he's boring.

Tuesday, January 12

Tristan walked me home. He bumped my arm once, and I said, "Whoops, sorry," and he said, "My fault." Did he do it on purpose????????

Wednesday, January 13

Tristan texted:

> *Did you see? Musical auditions*
> *start 1/25! Miss murphy directing*

Ugh. The theater geeks are the most annoying people on the planet, always crying and shrieking and slapping each other.

> *Not interested*

> *But its the sound of music!*

That's my dad's favorite musical. We've watched it hundreds of times. We know all the words. Mom says it's a nacho plate in movie form, and I know she's right, but Dad's also right that it's funny and wonderful. Plus it reminds him of his mom, who's dead, so he wins.

Ok, interested.

Tris texted to ask if I want to watch it together this weekend.

He basically asked me out!!!!

Thursday, January 14

Tristan and I will never get divorced, because we want the same life. Sure, it's important to love each other and be attracted to each other, but it's even more important to agree that the suburbs are stifling and New York is the only possible place to live.

Friday, January 15

Hannah came over and helped me pick out an outfit for tomorrow. I tried everything on and decided to wear my green V-neck sweater, since (a) it's preppy and (b) it creates the illusion of boobs.

Saturday, January 16

I have never been more humiliated.

I just got back from Tristan's house, which Mom would

hate and call a McMansion, but whatever, I kind of like a two-story foyer and a chandelier in every room. His parents weren't home, which made me nervous, because what would stop us from getting drunk and having sex if we wanted to, which we did, right?

We watched the movie on the living room couch. The TV was beautiful and about six feet long, but hung over the fireplace, which meant you had to tip your head back to watch it. My neck was killing me. Luckily, I got so distracted by the plot and by Julie Andrews's sick voice that I forgot my neck, and even forgot how nervous I was about sitting next to Tristan on the couch.

You know how when a movie ends, the room seems extra quiet, and you feel sad and strange unless you quickly start watching YouTube videos or checking your phone? That happened, but we didn't watch or check anything. Tristan looked at me, and our faces were kind of close together, and I blurted out, "Do you ever, um, think about what if something happened between us?"

I know. I'm like a 14-year-old female Shakespeare.

Tristan had the strangest look on his face.

"Sorry, that made no sense," I said. "What I'm trying to say is, I think you're amazing" (oh God) "and I can kind of imagine dating you."

He just looked at me. Time passed. The glaciers

melted and the earth turned on its axis. I wondered what would happen if I got up and ran out of the room without saying another word.

He said, "I think you're amazing too, but I don't think we should go out."

I picked up a throw pillow and pressed it over my face.

"Stop," he said.

"I can't look at you," I said.

"You're one of my best friends—" he said, and I took the pillow away and said, "Don't, don't, let's just pretend I never said anything, *please*," and he said OK, and we talked about this and that for a few minutes, and then I said I had to go, and I texted Dad to pick me up, and oh, I've ruined everything and I'm so, so, so embarrassed.

Sunday, January 17
Text from Hannah.

So??? How did it go???

Text from Tristan.

Hey, Chloe! Hope everything's OK and you're having an awesome day!

Since when does he punctuate properly in texts?

I'm going to pretend I dropped my phone in the garbage disposal by mistake.

Monday, January 18

It's MLK Day, which is making me feel guilty about being in the depths of despair. What's not perfect about my life, when you think about it? I'm a white girl with a lawyer dad. I'll almost certainly go to college. When's the last time someone asked to touch my hair, or followed me around a store to see if I was going to steal something? No one's ever going to shoot me because I'm wearing a hoodie and holding a squirt gun. I don't have problems, not really.

Tuesday, January 19

Saw Tristan in the hall, and we *waved* to each other and didn't stop to talk. That's not awkward or anything.

Finally told Hannah what happened. She looked so sad for me, which made me want to pull her hair and yell insults about Josh's height.

Wednesday, January 20

Forget Tristan. I have to throw myself into audition prep. I read the *Sound of Music* entry on Wikipedia. I downloaded the soundtrack and am listening to it constantly. I printed out the audition dialogue from the theater club website. And before I fall asleep, I imagine that it's 1938,

I'm a nun-in-training in Austria, and I'm lying on scratchy sheets, thinking about how to be holier. Basically, I pretend I'm Hannah.

Thursday, January 21

Obviously Bernadette will be Maria, and probably all the freshmen will get cast as background nuns, but I'm going to audition for Liesl. Maybe a miracle will occur and I'll get the part, and Rolf will be hot, and Miss Murphy will force us to make out onstage.

Ughhhh. Every time I think about kissing, or boys, or the musical, or anything at all, I remember the Night of Humiliation and get douche chills.

Friday, January 22

My room looked abnormally bright when I woke up, and when I pulled the blinds up, there was snow! Everywhere! Probably four inches on the ground and more falling—the good kind too. Tiny little flakes. I looked at my phone, and there it was, a beautiful text saying school was closed. I raced downstairs to tell Dad; it was so early in the morning, I forgot I was mad at him. I asked him if I had to shovel, and he sighed and said he guessed not. Before he could change his mind, I ran upstairs and jumped back into bed. I slept till 12:30 and then put boots and a coat on over my pajamas and took Snickers for a walk. There were no cars out, and all I could hear were flakes hitting my hood and the snow squeaking under my feet. When I got home, I sang "Sixteen Going on Seventeen" in the bathroom until it sounded right.

I had just made my signature Snow Day drink (half hot chocolate, half mini marshmallows) when I heard the doorbell ring. Zounds! What if it was an evil snowplow man, planning to abduct me? But on the other hand, what if it was a UPS guy with a present from Mom? I ran to the front door, and when I opened it, there was Tristan. His cheeks and nose were red from the cold.

"Did you walk here?" I said. Our houses are three miles apart.

"I have to talk to you," he said.

He followed me back to the kitchen. I tried to look dignified and sexy, even though I hadn't brushed my hair and was still wearing my pajamas.

"Do you want some hot chocolate?" I said. We were both standing by the counter. His boots were dripping all over the floor.

He said, "Remember the other day? At my house? After we watched *The Sound of—*"

"Yes," I said. Had he come all the way over here to humiliate me again? Hadn't I suffered enough already?

"I'm sorry about what happened," he said.

"It's fine." This was agony!

He pulled his hat off and scrunched it between his hands. "I didn't mean to—I thought maybe you knew."

"Knew what?"

"OK. OK. OK. I have to tell you something."

And then, even before he said it, I *did* know. It was like reverse déjà vu.

"I'm gay," he said. He looked nervous but defiant.

"OK," I said.

"OK what?"

"OK . . . good. I mean, that means you would have turned me down even if I was a supermodel."

Wrong thing to say. Selfish. Irrelevant. I immediately regretted it. But I didn't have time to Google! I couldn't look up "how to respond when your friend comes out and you want him to know it's fine that he's gay and you don't mind."

"It's fine that you're gay. I don't mind," I said.

He glared at me. "That's great, Chloe. I'm so glad you don't mind. That's really all I care about."

"I'm sorry I keep saying the wrong things."

He looked at the door, like he was considering leaving. His face was tired. "Whatever. No one's ever had the right reaction."

"What's the right reaction?"

"Just . . . normal. I don't know. I like guys. Why do I even have to tell anyone and deal with their facial expressions?"

"I'm sorry."

"What are you *sorry* about?"

"Just . . . I'm sorry the world is stupid."

He looked down at his boots and then took them off and sat down at the kitchen table. I sat down next to him.

"How many people have you told?" I asked.

"No one here. Four at my old school. And then everyone found out."

He folded his hat in half. It's green and navy striped, with a pom-pom on top. "One of the girls I told acted sympathetic, like I had cancer. Another one said she knew it all along. Lawrence asked me why I was telling him. This girl Ruby jumped up and down, like I'd gotten into Harvard. I think she was the one who spread it around. The popular girls, like, adopted me. I loved it at the time, but now I look back and it makes me embarrassed for myself. And the popular guys hated me and called me names in the hall."

We looked at our hands.

"Was Lawrence one of the popular guys?" I said.

He laughed. "No! He was this kid I liked."

"Straight?"

"Super gay."

"But he didn't like you back?"

"I guess not. No, that's not true. I think he did like me. But he was closeted, so . . ."

"But why?"

"Chloe, I just told you the popular guys would call me a faggot in the hallways. This girl in high school came out, a lacrosse player, and her coach kicked her off the team. She didn't even make up an excuse. She said the situation was distracting in the locker room. It's not like on TV."

I thought about our school. Maybe 50% of the kids think you're born the way you're born and there's nothing else to discuss. 20% are like those popular girls at Tris's old school and would die of excitement if they got to have a gay best friend. (Am I in that 20%?! Ugh, maybe. In my defense, I was in love with Tris before he came out to me.) 15% still say "that's so gay" and use the F word. And 15% post online about hating the sinner, not the sin. Last year this guy with long curly hair named Ian tweeted a long thing about gay people trampling on his religious freedom by getting married, although I'm not sure what two people who love each other have to do with his weirdo strip-mall church.

"Do your parents know?" I asked.

"My mom, I'm not sure. My dad, sometimes I think he does. Like the other day he asked me if I'd seen the news about some law that passed in the Midwest, something about how it's legal to refuse service to gay people, and he was like, 'It's such a hard life. I don't see why anyone would choose that.'"

"What did you say?"

"Nothing. I never talk about anything real with him. When he tries to pick fights, I make an excuse to go to my room. He's scary when he's mad."

"Like, he hits you?"

"No, but he throws stuff. He screams."

"My mom, too."

Snickers was asleep on the rug under the table. We listened to him snoring.

"Didn't you kind of suspect?" Tristan said. "I mean, chorus? Musicals?"

"My dad loves singing and musicals too. And maybe this is a terrible thing to say, but you don't sound gay. I mean, you talk like a jock. And you wear all those polo shirts. . . ."

"Not all gay guys wear infinity scarves and use self-tanner, Chloe."

"I know that!"

"Well, good."

I examined his face. He didn't look mad.

Would it be insensitive to drink my hot chocolate? I decided it would show how relaxed I felt, and took a sip. "Are you going to, like, officially come out?"

"No. You can't tell anyone. I'll kill you, Chloe, seriously."

"Fine! I was just asking." I felt excited and smug that he'd confided in me, just me, and then I felt bad for selfishly focusing on myself again, and so I made grilled cheese sandwiches and tomato soup. After we ate,

I walked Tristan home through the snow, which took forever, because it's impossible to walk briskly in winter boots. When we got to Tris's driveway, we hugged good-bye and then put our mittens on the sides of each other's faces and squeezed.

Saturday, January 23

I have so many questions for Tristan, including:

* Have you ever kissed a guy?
* If yes, what's it like?
* Have you ever kissed a girl?
* If yes, is it different from kissing a guy?
* What base have you gotten to?
* What *are* the bases? Because third base
  confuses me, and Yahoo Answers is no help.
* Do you have a crush on anyone at our school?

But I don't want to pester him or offend him.

Am I an idiot for not suspecting anything? I thought it was an offensive cliché that a lot of gay guys like musicals. It turns out I don't know much about anything.

Sunday, January 24

Tristan came over to do audition prep. It's always weird to see someone after you've had a big emotional thing.

I think we were both nervous, because the first half hour was like, "Can you believe it's snowing again?" "I know! I'm so sick of winter." But finally he said, "Remember when I came out to you on Friday?" and grinned, and then we started goofing around. After we ate lunch, we made a list of the most disgusting things we could think of. These were the best ones:

* Smears of tuna and red lipstick on a plastic spork
* A hairless cat eating its own barf
* Dog poop sprayed with Mr. Hicks's cologne

We were laughing so hard I had to run around the room to stop myself from peeing my pants.

Monday, January 25

First day of auditions! There are three days of first-round auditions; callbacks are on February 1.

There were, mmm, about 200 people trying out. It made the Love Notes auditions look like small potatoes. (Where does that come from, "small potatoes"? What's so bad about them? I think I'm the human equivalent of a small potato.) Tristan and Hannah and I sat together. Bernadette sat right in the front row. I kept trying not to look at her and failing. Even the back of her head looks conceited.

Miss Murphy sat on the edge of the stage with her hands tucked under her thighs. She was wearing a white button-down shirt, tight khaki pants, and brown boots. She looked ready for a theatrical safari.

She introduced the music director, the assistant director, and the producer, and then said, "I'm Miss Murphy, and I'm new to the theater program here. I hope you can learn something from me, as I expect to learn from you. I'll rely on the upperclassmen, in particular, to help me navigate." Bernadette sat up straighter in her seat.

"As you all know—at least, I hope you do—the musical this year is *The Sound of Music*. It's not edgy. It's not new. It's not *The Laramie Project* or *Spring Awakening*. But it's classic, and it's earnest, and I think those two qualities are important. It's also pretty funny. And who can resist Captain von Trapp carrying a riding crop? Not me!"

There are all kinds of horrible teachers. One kind is nervous and weak. The bad kids enjoy trampling on this kind, and the good kids hate the teacher for being too powerless to grind down the bad kids and get some teaching done. Another kind is arrogant and unfair. They don't teach you anything during the unit, and then test you on random stuff they never went over and make fun of you for getting a C-. Another kind is good at teaching but rude to the kids because they're trying not to be weak. Another kind is really into popular kids and lets them get away with skipping pop quizzes and doing makeup tests three weeks late. I could go on and on. But Miss Murphy isn't any of these kinds. She looks confident. She has good posture. She has a little smile on her face, like she's about to make you laugh. She talks in a natural, easy way, like *I'm an adult, and you're a kid right now, but someday you'll be an adult, and I'm pretty sure you'll be a smart and funny one.* She can make a joke about Captain von Trapp's sexy riding crop, and you don't feel embarrassed for her or yourself. You feel like you'll probably steal the joke and use it later.

She handed out forms kind of like Bernadette's, but with one million fields to fill out. Under "Interests" I wrote, "Goofing around with Snickers, my Boston terrier. Being tan. Novels. Doritos." "Top 3 Roles": "Liesl, Baroness Schraeder, Maria (ha!)." Under "Previous Experience," I wrote, "Chorus! :D," which could be interpreted as kissing up, but oh well.

I looked at Hannah's paper. Her interests were ballet, church, studying French, and skiing, and she had to use the back of the sheet to list all her previous experience. Tristan's interests were New York City, street-fashion blogs, and music composition.

Miss Murphy had us rearrange ourselves into groups according to which part we wanted to audition for. I sat with the Liesls, Tristan sat with the Rolfs, and Hannah sat with the Marias, which was the hugest group, of course. Miss Murphy handed out packets with the audition dialogue and songs, which I didn't need, because I've memorized them. Then a few groups, including mine, went off with the choreographer, Mrs. Cordoza, to learn a dance routine set to "Do-Re-Mi." The Liesls performed the dance first. I think I did OK. I didn't trip or fall over or anything, and I got at least 75% of the steps.

Miss Murphy paired up the Rolfs and the Liesls to sing and read together, and I got to go with Tristan! We smiled at each other through the whole audition. I have no idea how it went, but it was actually really fun.

Tuesday, January 26

I saw Zach *and* Luke *and* Griffin *and* Mac in the hall today. Zach said, "Hey, Chloe." Luke didn't notice my existence. Griffin and I waved. Mac shot finger guns at me and then blew imaginary smoke off his index fingers.

There's no point in letting myself think about Mac. I have to stop falling asleep while imagining that the school has caught on fire and he's rushed back into the burning auditorium to find and save me, and that as he carries me out in his arms, he says, "You know I'm crazy about you, right, Chloe Snow?"

Wednesday, January 27

Mrs. Egan made chocolate chip cookies for me and Hannah after school. I get it, Mrs. Egan, you're the perfect mother. Shut up.

Hannah was being weird and quiet and said she wanted to do homework, so we took our cookies up to her bedroom. After a few minutes of staring at a paragraph about the Wilmot Proviso, I said, "So what's it like, being felt up?"

"It's . . . oh, I don't know."

"Are Josh's hands sweaty, or cold, or are they nice and dry?"

"Dry, I guess." Hannah was staring off into the distance with a look on her face like she'd just been diagnosed with cancer.

"What's wrong with you?" I said.

"If I tell you something, do you swear you won't tell anyone?"

Another confession! I'm basically Oprah. "Of course. I swear."

She fiddled with the gold cross on her necklace. "I gave Josh a *hand job.*" She whispered the last two words.

"Oh my God!!"

She winced. "Ugh, Chloe. Don't."

"Sorry, it's just exciting! Where were you? What do penises *feel* like? Were you nervous? Did he, like, put your hand right on it? How did you know what to do?"

"Don't make me talk about it," she said.

"Hannah!" She's infuriating. Finally I have a primary source of information, but she refuses to hand over the details.

"Seriously. I feel horrible."

"Why? He didn't pressure you into it, did he?"

"No!"

"What then?"

"My parents would kill me."

"Well, duh."

"I'm supposed to save that stuff for marriage."

I can't believe Hannah's getting all this action when she's not even enjoying it, while I'm sitting here *dying* to give someone a hand job, and no takers.

Thursday, January 28

Skyped with Mom. She said, "I have a surprise," and held up this mangy white dog that looked yellow around the edges. Apparently he was a street dog who followed Mom home and whined outside her door until she let him in, and now she's decided to adopt him. Getting him on an airplane to the States will be a huge pain, but I didn't say anything.

I cried a little when we hung up. I feel so bad for Snickers. He's lying on my bed all cute and innocent. Little does he know he's not Mom's #1 anymore.

Friday, January 29

I GOT CALLED BACK. SO DID TRISTAN. SO DID HANNAH. SO DID JOSH. WE'RE ALL GOING TO BE BROADWAY STARS, AND SOMEDAY THIS VERY DIARY ENTRY WILL GO FOR MILLIONS AT A SOTHEBY'S AUCTION.

Saturday, January 30

Somehow it's still January. There are piles of dirty snow everywhere, and my upper lip is red from constant nose-blowing. You can really see why Ethan Frome tried to sled himself to death.

Sunday, January 31

Watched *The Sound of Music* with Tristan at my house, then practiced scenes for hours. When I went into the kitchen to get more Diet Coke, Dad wiggled his eyebrows up and down at me and winked madly. "You're way off base, Groucho," I said, but he just continued wiggling.

Monday, February 1

I'm not really sure what happened at callbacks.

You could tell Miss Murphy was trying to decide between four people for Maria. Bernadette was one of them. Her voice is amazing, but her acting stinks. She batted her eyelashes and did a baby-doll voice, and when she read with Roy as the captain, she kept poking him in the pecs.

I was in the Liesl callback group (!!!!), and I read with a senior named Liam, but I still felt relaxed, because there's no chance a mere freshman will get an important part. After our scene, we sang "Sixteen Going on Seventeen," which I think is about Liesl being a goofball. She doesn't actually mean it when she says, "I need someone older and wiser telling me what to do"—she's flirting with Rolf. So I pretended Liam was Mac, and we were at the pool, and I was joking around and making him laugh.

The baronesses went, and then it was the Mother Abbesses' turn. Miss Murphy said, "Nadine, will you read for Mother Abbess, and Bernadette, will you read for Margaretta? For Berthe—"

"Excuse me, Miss Murphy?" It was Bernadette. "I don't think I should read for Margaretta. Only because I don't want to waste your time."

"Why would it be a waste of time?"

"Did you talk to Mr. Campana before he left? Our old director? He might have mentioned I was Rizzo in *Grease* last year?"

"If you want to sit out this scene, that's fine, Bernadette."

Miss Murphy didn't sound annoyed, and Bernadette

sat there playing with her necklace in a smug way, like she'd won, so maybe it wasn't as rude and awkward as it seemed to me.

After the nuns went, we took a break, and I ate about a pound of mini Kit Kats to calm my nerves. When we came back, Miss Murphy said, "I'd like to try a few new combinations for act 1, scene 9. Chloe, would you read for Maria, and Josh, would you read for Captain von Trapp?"

It was like someone had snipped the connection between my ears and my brain. "What did she say?" I whispered to Tristan. Most of the other kids had twisted around in their seats to stare at me.

"Get up," Hannah whispered. "You're reading."

Josh was already climbing the stairs to the stage.

"What is it??" I whispered hysterically, which didn't actually mean anything, but Tristan somehow knew what I was asking and whispered, "It's the scene where Maria yells at the captain and he fires her."

I had the walk from my seat to the stage to think about the scene, so I forced myself to stop being surprised and concentrate. I knew the scene backward and forward from watching the movie and reading the script so many times. Maria's frustrated but not angry. She loves the kids and wants the captain to treat them right. By the time I reached the stairs, I'd decided to do mostly me (spunky, short-tempered) with a dash of Hannah (religious, nice).

I was so nervous at first that my voice was shaking a little. But Josh saved me. He was so good that I almost forgot it was him. He stood up ramrod straight and sneered, and it felt like he really was my rude boss. When he criticized the kids' clothes it actually irritated me, and I did a fake-jolly voice when I replied, to irritate him right back.

Miss Murphy had me stay onstage to sing "The Sound of Music," and then I was back in my seat, panting like I'd run a mile. Bernadette stared at me with the sour-yogurt expression until Miss Murphy called her up to read for Baroness Schraeder.

"That was incredible," Tristan whispered, and Hannah squeezed my hand until it hurt.

"It's not a big deal," I whispered to them, but what if it *is* a big deal?

Tuesday, February 2

Happpppyyyyyy Groundhog Day! Dad made vodka sauce with spaghetti, because I like it better than penne, and we watched Bill Murray try to escape Punxsutawney. Well, Dad watched. I stared at the TV without actually seeing anything. All I could think was, *Sound of Music Miss Murphy Bernadette Maria nuns Broadway Josh auditions cast list omg omg omg.*

Wednesday, February 3

We won't find out until Friday. Miss Murphy is going to post the cast list on the website no later than 9 a.m.

Thursday, February 4

Can't eat. Can't sleep. Can't concentrate on anything.

Friday, February 5

Oh my ears and whiskers. I got it. I'm Maria.

Saturday, February 6

Here's what happened!

We're not allowed to have our phones on during class, of course, but I couldn't help it; at 8:58 I snuck mine onto my lap and opened the theater club page. Refresh . . . refresh . . . Mr. Hicks was droning on about an asymptote . . . refresh . . . and then the page changed! It said, *"The Sound of Music* Cast List," and right there, at the top:

Maria Rainer: Chloe Snow
Captain Georg von Trapp: Josh Menaker

I couldn't believe my eyes, and refreshed the page one more time to make sure there hadn't been a mistake, and there it was again! "Maria Rainer: Chloe Snow"!!!!

This time I remembered to scroll down. Bernadette had been cast as Sister Berthe, Mistress of Novices (BURN!), Hannah's name was in a long list under the heading "Nuns"—Ambreen's a nun too—and Tristan is Rolf!!!!!!!!!! A sophomore I don't know named Annabelle Cara is playing Liesl. Olivia Choi is Baroness Schraeder, and Henry Ossler is Max.

I looked around the room wildly, but there were no theater geeks in my class (besides me, I guess. I'm a theater geek now!). Everyone else looked sleepy and/or confused, totally unaware of the earth-shattering news.

Finally the bell rang, and I sprinted into the hall, through the B wing, and up the stairs, only tripping a tiny bit. When I got near Tristan's locker and saw the back of his head, I shrieked and pushed through the crowd, and he turned around and saw me and said, "Ahhhhhhh!" and we grabbed each other's arms and jumped up and down and screamed in each other's faces, and that was probably the best moment of my year so far. We were being the melodramatic squealing theater kids everyone hates, and I didn't care! I'd gotten the lead in the musical, and Tristan was playing the hot bossy guy, and we are only 14 years old!!!!!!!!!!

Hannah found me after lunch and gave me a hug. "I'm so happy for you, Chlo," she said, and I could tell she meant it. And that's why she's going to heaven and

I'm not. If I were cast as an anonymous nun, and she were Maria, I'd be so jealous my eyes would turn green.

"Josh is really excited," she said, and suddenly I realized: I had to pretend to fall in love with Josh! Her boyfriend! Should I acknowledge the awkwardness? Should I ignore it? Should I reassure Hannah that I don't find Josh the tiniest bit attractive, or would that be insulting? Panicked, I just smiled and nodded like a bobblehead.

Between fifth and sixth period, Gloria Lingley came up to me and said, "Hey. I heard you got the lead in the musical." I nodded. She said, "That's cool," and looked me up and down, from my sneakers to my red striped T-shirt. If I'd known everyone in the world was going to talk to me today, I would have chosen a less Calvin and Hobbes-y outfit.

The most amazing part: after school, as I was cramming all my books into my backpack, Mac and Sienna came up to me! Mac said, "What's up, Sound of Music?" and Sienna congratulated me, which was magnanimous of her, considering Bernie's one of her besties. *And then*, when I checked my phone, I saw that she'd followed me.

I wanted to drive fast on the highway, or skip down a busy main street, but I don't have a license and our town has no busy main street, so all I could do was walk home and force Snickers to dance around the kitchen with me. When Dad finally got home from work, I told him what happened, and he said, "Honey! I'm so proud of you!" and poured some

sparkling cider into champagne flutes. I tried to Skype with
Mom, but she wasn't there, so I emailed her the news.

Sunday, February 7
Email from Mom.

> Darling rabbit,
>
> I've decided to name my canine companion
> Hector. It's a rather sophisticated name for such
> a playful, mischievous little thing, but it'll grow
> with him. Nothing sillier than a dignified old dog
> called something cutesy. I can't wait for you to
> meet him; you've never seen such an affectionate
> being. He curls up on my lap as I write and sits
> at my feet when I lounge on the patio. If I dare
> to stop patting him, he puts his paw on my knee
> quite sternly, as if to say, *Ahem—did I give you
> permission to cease your ministrations?*
>
> What wonderful news about the musical!
>
> Your Mommy

I'm in a terrible mood now. I don't know why. Everything's great, so what's my problem?

Monday, February 8

Bernadette came up to my locker after lunch and said, "Just so you know, we all signed a petition and gave it to Miss Murphy."

She was wearing a gray blazer, high-heeled boots, a gauzy blue scarf, and a big gold watch. She looked like a 20-year-old.

"A petition about what?"

"I didn't want you to be blindsided. Miss Murphy will probably make an announcement at the rehearsal today. See you later, sweetie." She pouted her lips at me and made a sympathetic expression, like I was a two-year-old who'd just dropped her lollipop in the sandbox.

Frantically group-messaged Tristan and Hannah.

> *Bernadette said something about a petition? Anyone know wtf?*

(Hannah) That doesn't ring a bell, no.

(Tristan) She came up to me too!! And look what I found on her instagram

He linked to a picture she'd taken of a printout. It was hard to read the type, since she'd put a filter on the pic, but here's what it said:

To: Miss Murphy
From: The Juniors and Seniors

We, the undersigned, would like to formally protest the casting of *The Sound of Music*. While we respect your theatrical judgment to the utmost, since you're new, you might not understand the existing structures of seniority. Many of us have had leading roles in previous productions at this school, therefore we have proven we have the responsibility, maturity, and talent that it takes. While there are some great freshmen, they are not seasoned, in addition they have three more years to take starring roles. Whereas the seniors have only this year. We also urge you to consider the affect your casting may have on the college admissions process for seniors, many of whom are applying to top theatre programs. We look forward to seeing a revised cast list at your earliest convenience. Signed:

. . . and then there was a whole list of illegible signatures. I felt barfy. Texted Hannah:

>   *Did you know about*
>   *this?*

> *No! Josh didn't either. We're*
> *both surprised.*

>   *This sucks*

> *Try not to worry. She's just*
> *upset.*

Texted Tristan:

>   *omg bernie hates me*

> *She hates me too. i'm*
> *gonna text her "dont hate,*
> *appreciate"*

>   *How many people signed?*

> *No idea. i'm guessing*
> *Josh von trapp didn't*

I'm scared

*Of what, all her split infinitives
and comma splices?*

"Existing structures of seniority"

Affect

Top theatRE programs

She's an idiot

This conversation made me feel better, but as soon as I put my phone back in my bag, the barfiness came back. Bernadette, theater star, popular girl, senior, and possessor of great hair, had it out for me. And she kind of had a point. The upperclassmen *do* have more experience, and they *are* trying to get into college. The younger kids (me!) have no idea what we're doing.

After school, I headed to the auditorium for our first rehearsal. I felt like I had Icy Hot running through my veins. Bernadette was already there, sitting in the front row, laughing with her friends and looking at her phone. Hannah and Josh were sitting in the middle with their heads together. Tristan and I huddled together in the back row.

At exactly 3 p.m., Miss Murphy strode onto the stage. She smiled down at all of us and said, "Welcome to the first rehearsal for what's sure to be a wonderful production of *The Sound of Music!*" People cheered and WOOed.

"Before we get started, I'd like to say a word about the casting."

Instantly, everyone shut up, and my scalp prickled all over.

Miss Murphy started walking slowly back and forth. "Here's some context I didn't share with you at the auditions. About a hundred years ago, I graduated from this very high school, and then went to the Juilliard Drama Division. After graduation, I found acting work on and off Broadway for years, then changed tack and got an MFA in directing from Yale. It's not easy, trying to make it as a director in New York—I'd say it's even harder than trying to make it as an actor—but I was doing OK. Pretty well, even."

I looked around. Everyone was rapt. Some people's mouths were hanging open.

"I moved home last year, and now here I am with you, teaching English and directing the theater program. And I don't consider it a step down; I'm truly, truly happy to be here." She looked into the wings for a moment and then back at us. "I'm telling you about my history, not to brag, but to convey to you that I know exactly how scary auditions are and exactly how much it stings when you don't get the part you wanted. And maybe I am bragging a little."

Bernadette was sitting perfectly still, her face tipped up to look at Miss Murphy.

"Part of my job is to create memorable theatrical experiences that will enrich your entire lives. My high school production of *South Pacific* is dear to me in a way that no Broadway show ever could be. I also have a responsibility to put together the strongest cast I can, for a hundred reasons. It makes for a better show. It will burnish the reputation of our program, which will help you as you go out into the world. It's simply the right thing to do. And maybe most importantly, it will give you a taste of the life you're in for if you decide to pursue a career in theater. Yes, connections are important, and work leads to more work. But believe me, no one cared that Nina Arianda had zero professional credits when she auditioned for *Venus in Fur*. If you can blow the doors off, you'll get the part, and that's a lesson you can't learn too early.

"Here's the flip side of that lesson. Even when you're connected, even when you have a résumé as long as your leg, even when you nailed the audition and you're just what they're looking for—most of the time, you *still* won't get the part. And here's what doesn't help: writing a petition."

Everyone looked at Bernadette. Bernadette looked straight ahead.

Miss Murphy smiled, not in a mean way. "Everyone admires moxie, but no director will respond to a demand like that. If you want to be an actor, you have to get comfortable with rejection. And when it happens, you have to smile politely and think to yourself, 'I don't care; that director doesn't know what she's missing out on. I know I've got what it takes, and I'm going to keep chugging along.' I respect the hard work the upperclassmen have put in, and many of them have been cast in leading roles in this production—but because of their auditions, not because of their age."

She clapped her hands together once. "OK, I've gone on long enough. There's no pressure to accept the role you've been offered. If you don't want to participate, shoot me an email by the end of the day, and there'll be no hard feelings. But I sincerely hope everyone signs on, because I think we'll have a lot of fun together. Now, Mrs. Thibault, if you wouldn't mind handing out the rehearsal schedule, we'll go over who has to be where, when, and then we'll start the read-through."

Tuesday, February 9

I need to take a break from texting and analyzing and reanalyzing with Hannah and Tristan. My thumbs are cramping, plus I have rehearsal in five minutes (and every single school day from now till the show goes on in May).

Bernadette tweeted, *haters can't block my shine.* She

(Bernie) won't talk to me or look at me. Neither will her friends. I'm trying not to care. Anyway, Mac smiled at me in the hall today, so at least there's one senior who doesn't despise me.

Wednesday, February 10
I'm learning so much theater lingo, I'm basically Uta Hagen.

read-through = Sitting in the auditorium with the entire cast, reading through the whole script out loud while Bernadette glares at me and everyone wonders why Miss Murphy gave me the lead.

blocking = Miss Murphy telling us where to go during a scene.

stage right = The part of the stage to the audience's left (what sense does that make??).

stage left = The part of the stage to the audience's right (see parenthetical above).

upstage = The part of the stage closest to the scenery.

downstage = The part of the stage closest to the audience.

wings = Offstage—well, actually, the wings are part of the stage, but they're hidden from the audience by curtains. We stand in the wings just before we come on.

diaphragm = Something below my lungs that I'm apparently supposed to use to sing.
off book = The state in which all of my lines are memorized.
Hell Week = The lead-up to opening night, when we will all live in the auditorium and subsist on snacks and energy drinks.

The schedule is, first we analyze all the scenes, then we block them. For the first month, we have separate dance rehearsals with Mrs. Cordoza, and music rehearsals with Miss Kijek, who has purplish-red hair and a sparkly stud in her nose. Today she whipped her hands off the piano and said, "Chloe, do you realize you're breathing entirely from your chest?" then ran over and poked me in the gut. "Your diaphragm is *here*. That's where you get your air." Well, excuse me!

We have to be off book by March. In May, we have a cue-to-cue rehearsal, a tech rehearsal, and a dress rehearsal in full makeup and costumes. That's Hell Week. Then we have two weekends of shows, and the last one falls on my birthday!

Thursday, February 11
I'm sorry to report that Nadine Wallach was cast as Gretl

simply because she's tiny and adorable. She can't sing a single note.

Friday, February 12
Carnation Day. Red means love; pink means friendship; white means secret admirer (according to our school, but can you really trust a word it says?). Someone told me Mac sent a hundred reds to Sienna. I got six pink ones: three from Hannah and three from Tristan. Hannah got a dozen red ones from Josh *and* they're secretly going out to dinner at the one nice restaurant in our town tomorrow night. "Secretly" because Hannah still hasn't told her parents that she now has a life partner.

Saturday, February 13
I wish I could know for sure that someday I'll have a boyfriend. If only I could see into the future, I could relax and enjoy being a bachelorette.

Sunday, February 14
When I came down to breakfast, I found a big heart-shaped box of chocolates at my place. Dad was smiling at me. "Will you be my valentine?" he said.

"Dad, gross!" I said, but not in a mean way.

Tristan texted me a long string of beating hearts and flowers. Hannah texted me, *Happy Valentine's Day! FYI, today is named after a Christian saint.* Snickers, my real valentine, would have texted me something if he had opposable thumbs, a smartphone, and a brain larger than a clementine.

Monday, February 15

Five more days of school, and then it's finally, finally winter break. The rich kids are going skiing, or someplace warm. For example, according to Twitter, Sienna is going to Florida with Bernadette and a bunch of other girls. The poor kids are staying home, and so are the kids with cheap parents (ahem, Dad).

Tuesday, February 16

We ran through "The Sound of Music" a thousand times at rehearsal. Miss Murphy pulled me aside and said, "I'm going to be blunt. It's coming across as fake."

This irritated me, especially because I knew she was right. "I've never seen an alp! I hate nature!"

"Luckily, you're playing Maria Rainer, not Chloe Snow, and Maria loves nature."

I groaned.

"Slow down and think about the words," said Miss Murphy. "The hills have been around for thousands of years—in comparison, Maria is a blip. But that's not a scary thought. By singing with the hills, by communing with nature, she can achieve immortality, at least for a few minutes. While she's on this earth, she wants to soak in all the beauty and life she can. Does that resonate with you at all?"

I nodded. It really did.

"Over the break, I want you to go through the script and find every single spot where you're saying the line or singing the words without really understanding them. And I want you to write those parts out by hand and figure out what they mean."

Great! That sounds almost as fun as lying on a beach in Florida.

Actually, it does sound kind of fun.

Wednesday, February 17

Sometimes I wake up at 3 a.m. and imagine Mom drunk in some bar, probably with the matador, pretending she's fluent in Spanish and laughing at jokes she doesn't understand, and my heart pounds so fast I can't fall back to sleep, and I feel sick with exhaustion the entire next day.

Thursday, February 18

Dance rehearsal is so hard that it hurts to get out of bed and walk up the stairs. I hobble around like an old lady with rickets. On the plus side, I think I have all the choreography down.

Friday, February 19

Rehearsal was a shambles. Half the cast was out, and the other half was too hysterical about break to concentrate. Miss Murphy told us that if we didn't come back from vacation off book, she would murder each and every one of us. "Probably with a knife. And I'll enjoy it," she said. Most people tried to give her a hug at the end of rehearsal. It is a little sad, realizing that we won't see her for an entire week.

Saturday, February 20

First day of winter breeeeeaaaaaak!!!! I'm going to eat whatever I want and ignore all my homework and hang out with my friends and sleep for 12 hours every single night and look at my phone with wild abandon! Yeah!

Sunday, February 21

Dad made me clean the bathroom and take out the trash. Tris is with his parents and Hannah's sneaking around with Josh. Sienna posted a picture of Mac grinning at her from the window of his pickup truck. She captioned it #airportdropoff #missyourfacealready. It's booger-freezingly cold outside. I tried to dance with Snickers, but he went limp. Life is pain.

Monday, February 22

I need to stop stalking Sienna. Why do I know that she drank piña coladas yesterday, ate a salmon burger for lunch today, and got a sunburn this afternoon? Technology is so weird and terrible.

Tuesday, February 23

Went through the script, which took all day. I've been faking three-quarters of my performance. The more I think about it, the worse I feel for Maria. She's on her own in the world. She thought she found a good place—the abbey—but she got kicked out. She's taking care of seven kids, and their dad/her boss doesn't appreciate what an amazing job she's doing. Then she falls in love with him, but she can't even enjoy it, because she feels so guilty about being un-nun-like, plus Georg already has a girlfriend. But whatever happens, she tries so hard to be cheerful and happy. I think that's the best way to be.

Wednesday, February 24

Josh and Hannah stopped by. It was freezing in my house, as usual, and I answered the door wearing my fleece Santa hat and one of Dad's old sweatshirts. I wasn't embarrassed, though, because Hannah's seen me in much worse, and although at first I thought of Josh as Hannah's Boyfriend Who Is a Senior, now I think of him as My Dorky and Smart Theater Husband Who Is Fun to Tease.

I found some chips and salsa and we sat in the living room with blankets on our laps. After some chitchat about how hideously boring winter break is, Josh said, "Chloe, I'm hosting a get-together on Friday evening, and you are most welcome to attend."

"What, like a party?"

"It's a terrible idea," said Hannah.

Josh said, "Hannah is concerned that my guests won't be respectful of my parents' property. I must admit, I think her fear is well founded. Still, I've enjoyed many parties at my friends' houses, and I'd like to return the favor before graduation."

"Who's coming?"

"Oh, I've invited members of several different social groups."

"Can I invite Tristan?"

"Certainly."

"Do you think Mac will be there? Or any football players, I mean?"

"It's quite possible."

I quizzed Hannah about what she was going to wear, but she said she hadn't thought about it yet. Great! Very helpful.

Thursday, February 25

Tris came over and I tried to make him help me pick out an outfit, but he refused to stop looking at his phone and concentrate on my important problems. Finally I said, "Pay attention to meeeeeee," and he said, "Chloe, I'm not your gay pet. I don't know anything about girls' clothes," and I said, "You and Hannah should really hang out more, you would get along perfectly."

Friday, February 26

The real problem is that I can't make myself care about fashion until I find out I'm going to a party, and by that time it's too late.

Told Dad I'm sleeping over at Hannah's tonight, and he told me to have fun and run away if Mrs. Egan tries to concern-troll me. I'm a terrible daughter.

Saturday, February 27

I feel like someone replaced my brain with a clump of wet cotton balls. I'm dizzy and queasy. I told Dad I got the flu from Hannah. I'm a liar, a cheater, and probably an alcoholic.

Texting with Hannah:

I'm so sorry about last night.

I don't know what happened.

Are you mad?

It's fine

No period and a 20-minute response time. She's furious. I don't care!!! She'll forgive me eventually, and I'll never tell her what happened at the party, and everything will be OK.

Too happy to write.

Sunday, February 28

OK. The party. Josh and Hannah picked me up at six on Friday, and we went to his house. I could see why Hannah was nervous. Bookshelves everywhere, an upright piano, a real fireplace, dark-red rugs . . . It wasn't fancy, exactly, but everything looked like it could have been passed down from a great-great-great-grandfather. We spent an hour gathering all the vases and candles and breakable lamps and bringing them upstairs so that no one would smash them.

It's always strange, seeing someone's parents' bedroom. Sometimes if it's your good friend's house and you're poking around in drawers together, you find embarrassing stuff—sexy books, condoms, dingy underpants. But even if you're just dropping off a bunch of fragile knick-knacks and not snooping, it feels too personal. It smells like grown-ups, and there's their bed, right there, the one they sleep in every night, possibly naked, and you can't help but remember that they had sex in order to make your friend, who came out of his mother's vagina.

"What are you doing?" Hannah said. I jumped a mile.

"Finding a place for this picture," I said. We looked at it together. It was a heavy silver frame with a black-and-white photo of the Menakers on their wedding day. Mrs. Menaker was laughing with her head thrown back, and Mr. Menaker was staring at her adoringly. God, it made me sad.

"Come help me hide the wine," Hannah said as she left.

People started arriving at nine. Tristan was one of the first, then a bunch of stagehands, then some soccer people, then that guy Roy from the Love Notes, who's playing Admiral von Schreiber in the musical. He said getting cast as a Nazi freaked him out at first, but now he enjoys thinking about how furious actual Nazis would be if they could see a mixed-race kid playing one of them as a villain.

It was a weird atmosphere, I think because there were jocks and geeks in one place, united by their love for Josh. Also a problem: the Menakers don't have a TV (!!!), so there was nothing to pretend to watch. For a while the jocks were in the living room drinking beer and the theater geeks were in the kitchen drinking beer. Everyone was talking quietly or checking their phones. But then Mac and the football team arrived with big plastic bottles of vodka and rum, plus Coke, orange juice, and Sprite. Suddenly the lights were off, and someone put on nice, gross hip-hop from a few years ago, and it got loud and dancey.

Hannah had no time for me—she was too busy scurrying around putting coasters under people's cups. It was OK, though, because Tristan and I were glued to each other in terror. We tried to talk, but we were too nervous to have an actual conversation. I would say something like, "Is your sister coming home to visit soon?" and he'd say, "I know, totally." It was like we were performing a conversation for whoever might be listening to us (which was no one). When we ran out of material, we resorted to our phones. I looked at every social network in existence, madly liking and hearting and favoriting things just to have something to do with my thumb.

Then Tristan grabbed me hard above the elbow. "Don't look, but I think Roy is checking me out. I said *don't* look—Chloe!"

Roy looked away fast, like I'd caught him. "He's definitely staring at you," I said.

"I can't believe you turned around like that."

"You should go talk to him!"

"Yeah, right."

"Don't be a baby."

"Thanks for being so understanding."

I picked a thread off his collar. "Just go over there and say, 'What's up?'"

"I can't. If I—oh my God. Don't move. He's coming over here. Does my breath smell like quesadillas?"

I leaned in and took a big sniff. "It smells like flowers."

He looked at me like, *Don't tease me; I'm freaking out,* and I said, "Seriously, it does," and then Roy was next to us, smiling and saying, "Shouldn't you two be home studying your lines?"

"Ha! Ha! Yes!" I said, and then I did a little curtsy for some reason, backed up, nearly crashing into a side table, and fled into the kitchen to give the guys some privacy, but the kitchen was infested with a huge group of football players, and in the middle of them was Mac, handing out red cups.

"CHLOE SNOW!" he said, and pointed at me. "Get over here. We're doing shots."

I went like a zombie into the forest of big shoulders and body spray, and took the cup someone handed me.

"To us!" someone said.

"To sloppy blow jobs!" someone else said.

"Happy winter break, ladies," said Mac, and everyone cheered and gulped down their shot. Except for me. I was planning to do it, but when it got to my mouth, I couldn't. I just let the liquid slosh against my lips.

I didn't think anyone had noticed, but Mac looked

at my cup and said, "What seems to be the problem?"

The other football guys were drifting back to the living room. I decided to level with him. "I've never had a drink before. Well, once I had champagne at my cousin's wedding, and my dad lets me have a sip of his beer sometimes, but that's it."

He put his hands on my shoulders and said, "You're adorable, kid. Here." He took the cup and sloshed the contents into the sink. "That ain't the place to start. Let me make you a rum and Coke." He made me one very confidently and fast. He even found a lime and quartered it for a garnish.

"Cheers," he said, and we bumped the plastic lips of our cups.

It tasted good. It tasted like a special variation on Coke—vanilla or cherry. Or rum and lime, I guess.

"I like it!" I said.

He laughed. I'm always making him laugh, and I'm not even trying.

"Don't drink too fast," he said. I nodded and took three big sips in a row. My fingertips and forehead got warm. I felt great. Why had I been hiding in a corner with Tristan? Parties were wonderful! A chance for disparate groups to mingle! A classic rite of high school! I should savor each moment.

Mac jerked his head toward the kitchen door. "Want

to keep me company while I smoke a cigarette?"

It was dark and chilly out. Without asking if I was cold, Mac took off his hoodie, helped me into it like a gentleman, turned me to face him, and zipped me in. I was dying to Google "guy gives you his hoodie flirting?"

He held out his box of Camel Blues, but I shook my head no. I felt wild enough drinking my rum and Coke, which was almost gone. He tilted his head to meet his orange plastic lighter and exhaled a cloud of smoke away from my face.

"So on a scale of one to ten," he said, "how scary is high school?"

He remembered our pool conversation!

I thought about it. Bernadette and her petition . . . English class . . . auditions . . . Tristan . . . Hannah . . . getting my locker open . . . trying to read the printed map to find my classes . . . "Five, I guess."

"Five. That's not so bad."

He sat down on the steps and patted the place next to him, so I sat down too.

A few seconds passed in silence while I tried desperately to think of an effortlessly witty thing to say. This is what my brain came up with:

"You're going out with Sienna, right?"

"Chloe Snow, you know I'm going out with Sienna. Don't be fake. That's what I like about you—you're honest. Ask me a real question."

"Do you love her?"

"Ha! OK. Well. Yeah, sure, I love her. We're a good match. She's acts tough, but really she's the little wife type. She makes me lunch on the weekends. She respects me. You know, she clears it with me before she goes on vacation with her friends or whatever. She shows me her new clothes and if I don't like them, she returns them."

I thought. "What kind of lunch?"

He laughed. "Turkey sandwiches, usually. I like them with American cheese and mayo, FYI. File that away."

"I don't even like making sandwiches for myself."

"Oh yeah?"

I thought more. "And I don't think I would return clothes you didn't like."

"Really! Good thing you're not my girlfriend, then."

We looked at each other. Our faces were close. It was dark in the backyard. The crickets were chirping. He tipped his head toward mine until our foreheads were touching.

"Don't get me in trouble, Chloe Snow," he whispered.

Then he stood up and went inside.

I was too happy to stay still, so I ran into the dark backyard with my arms open and did my choreography for "The Sound of Music" and even sang a little under my breath. That's what people who don't like musicals don't understand: the songs and dancing are for the times when words can't describe your emotions.

I went around and back in through the front door, and who should be standing in the foyer but Bernadette. "Bernadette, hi!" I said, and gave her a huge hug. She patted me twice on the back with a limp hand. "Uh, hi," she said. I didn't care. I weaved through the crowd, which had doubled in size while Mac and I were outside, and I said hello to everyone, including people I'd never technically met before. Everyone said hi back, and why wouldn't they? We all go to the same little high school, for God's sake. Why do we bother pretending we don't know exactly who everyone is? Why can't we all be friends? There was Tristan, sitting on the couch, talking to Roy. I waved, but I don't think they noticed. There was Hannah, on her hands and knees trying to clean up dirt from a potted plant that had tipped onto its side. She looked up, saw me, and called, "Chloe, do me a huge favor and get me a broom or something?" and I smiled and called back, "Sure, give me one sec!" I went to the kitchen intending to find a broom, but before I could, I spotted the counter full of bottles and realized that the first priority was making myself another drink, so I did! Half rum, half Coke, half a lime. "Getting a little Captain in you?" said a football player with a goatee and a chin strap, and I said, "Hell, yeah!" which is something I've never said before in my life, because I'm not a snowboarder, but suddenly I felt like, *I can say whatever*

I want! Why am I so worried about being myself? What is myself, anyway? I have no idea! I'm 14! I could turn out to be anyone!

I stayed till the sun came up, and every time Mac saw me across the room, he winked, and Roy and Tris and I danced to "Teenage Dream" and "Party in the USA," and maybe they were being ironic, but I wasn't. Dad was out for a run when I got home, and I collapsed into bed without checking my phone, so I missed Hannah's texts (*Where are you? I can't find you anywhere. I'm very disappointed. Please call me as soon as you get this,* etc.). I guess she's furious that I never brought her that broom. There's no way she knows about me and Mac, right? No. No one saw us. Plus, there is no "me and Mac."

Monday, February 29

I saw Mac in the hall. He shook his head, smiled, and said, "Trouble."

Tuesday, March 1

Rehearsal was exhausting. When I wasn't onstage, I was trying to find Hannah, who isn't technically giving me the silent treatment, but who *is* giving me polite, frozen smiles and disappearing every time I have a break. And when I wasn't searching for Hannah, I was running into the wings to talk to Tristan, who made out with Roy at the party!!!!!! We whispered as fast as we could, to try to cram all the gossip in.

Chloe: Where did it happen?

Tristan: In the bathroom.

Chloe: The one by the kitchen?

Tristan: No, the one off the study.

Chloe: Did anyone see you go in?

Tristan: No, definitely not. I made sure.

Miss Murphy: CHLOE! Would you care to join us?

(15 minutes later)

Tristan: Did his lips touch any part of your face?

Chloe: No. Forehead touching only. Is Roy a good kisser?

Tristan: His tongue is kind of pointy and hard.

(This makes us die laughing, for some reason, and we fall all over each other trying not to make any noise.)

Miss Murphy: I need Liesl and Rolf right this instant.

(20 minutes later)

Tristan: You swear nothing else happened?

Chloe: I swear on my mother's grave.

We even talked on the phone after rehearsal, 1980s-style.

Tristan: Do you feel guilty?

Chloe: No. Nothing happened. We were just talking.

Tristan: Maybe they have an open relationship.

Chloe: I don't think so. But Sienna was probably cheating on him in Florida, right?

Tristan: She was living it up at the beach! She probably has six STDs by now.

Chloe: If you were her and you found out we touched foreheads, you wouldn't care, would you?

Tristan: I'd scratch your face off in the hallway. (Thoughtful silence)

Chloe: Has Roy texted you yet?

Tristan: Just a GIF of a panda winking.

Chloe: That's great!

Tristan: Has Mac texted you?

Chloe: He doesn't have my number.

Tristan: Oh. Well, that doesn't mean anything.

Chloe: He probably doesn't text anyway. He's too manly to waste time with emoji.

Tristan: No one's that manly.

Chloe: Yeah, you're right.

Wednesday, March 2

Finally cornered Hannah in the dressing room and said, "I know you're mad at me. I'm sorry I didn't stay to help you clean up."

"I don't care about that. I mean, I do, but . . ."

She paused, and my heart started beating like a madman. Had she found out about the erotic forehead touching somehow?

"Were you drunk, Chloe?"

Oh, thank God.

"Not *drunk* drunk. Tipsy."

She fiddled with her backpack zipper. "We promised each other we'd never have a sip of alcohol until we turned 21."

"But that was in fourth grade, Han."

"We're only 14 years old."

"Almost 15."

She looked like she might cry. "I don't want you to change."

I sat down on the folding chair next to her. "I'm not changing! I don't think drinking is as evil as they told us in health class."

She shook her head. "See? You're different."

Maybe I am different, but so is she. She has a serious boyfriend and she drives around with him, adjusting the heat like a mom.

Thursday, March 3

I saw Sienna in the hall today, *and she said hi to me.* She was wearing a striped T-shirt and her sporty watch. She's tan, and her teeth glowed white when she smiled at me.

I hate Sienna.

Friday, March 4

Because I'm so popular and cool, I spent the night reading *Romeo and Juliet*. Shakespeare makes my brain hurt for half an hour, and then it feels OK. It's like when you're untangling a necklace and you finally see where the knot is and how to undo it.

Saturday, March 5

MAC HAS SENT A TEXT MESSAGE TO MY TELEPHONE.

Sup cutie

His name didn't come up, because his number wasn't in my phone, so I wrote back instantly.

Who is this?

Big mac baby

Oh! Hi. Who gave you my number?

That's for me to know and you to find out

After 15 minutes of agonizing, I wrote: *Haha!*

Then I spent a few hours waiting for him to text back. Why, why, why did I say "Haha"? What could be lamer?

Eventually I turned the volume off and put my phone facedown on my table, but that didn't help, because I kept picking it up to stare at it. Then I shoved it in one of my boots, threw the boot into the back of the closet, and went downstairs and vacuumed, which made Dad ask if I was having some kind of neurological event. Finally I woke Snickers up from a nap and forced him to take a dark, windy walk through the woods. He was so mad at me he wouldn't even bark at squirrels.

Sunday, March 6

Mac called me. He picked up his mobile device and used his fingers not to text me, but to *call* my mobile device! When I saw his name come up, my mouth popped open because of the shock.

He acted like calling people is a normal thing people do even when it's not 1996. He asked how my day was, and I said OK, although we're up to My Lai in world history and it's making me sad. I asked how his day was and he said great, because he benched 275 pounds for the first time. Then we talked about his workout for a long time and I told him that last year in gym class we had to run a mile and

I threw up afterward, and he said I should be ashamed of myself for being so out of shape. But he said it in a nice way.

I don't know—it was a normal conversation. Not very flirty. Not too awkward. What just happened?

Nothing happened. He was bored, so he called a random freshman girl. Stop being ridiculous, Chloe.

Monday, March 7

It seems strange that Hannah doesn't know what happened with me and Mac. I would tell her, but I know she'd freak out and say I'm flirting with disaster, or heading for a fall, or some other mom-ish thing. Besides, there's nothing to tell. That's the whole point! She thinks Mac and I met at the pool this summer, he says hi to me sometimes in the hall, and I fantasize about marrying him and having six tiny football players with him, and she's exactly right. What's my big update? "I borrowed his hoodie"? "He had nothing better to do than call a freshman"? Making a big thing of it would be melodramatic, actually.

Tuesday, March 8

Dad picked me up from rehearsal. I was the last one there, as usual. It's strange to see him walk into the auditorium—he looks familiar but out of place, like if Snickers wandered into a fancy restaurant.

I pretended to be engrossed in packing up my bag so

I could eavesdrop on Dad and Miss Murphy and hear anything nice they said about me.

"Chloe's been working hard," she told him.

"I'm glad to hear that. Hey, she mentioned this is your hometown." (Oh my God. Could he be any more embarrassing and dadly, please?)

"Yup."

"You moved back from the Big Apple?" (Worse and worse.)

"I did. My mom's sick, and I wanted to take care of her. Well, 'wanted' . . . maybe more like 'felt obligated.'"

"That sounds tough."

Miss Murphy shrugged. "I bitch at her to stop smoking and boozing. It has no effect, but it's something to do."

"It must be boring here, compared to the city."

"I get a lot of pitying remarks from my New York friends, but I actually like it here now that I'm old and exhausted."

"Ha! Don't talk to me about old. I threw my back out brushing my teeth this morning."

This cracked both of them up. Grown-ups.

Wednesday, March 9

Mac called me again! And we talked for two hours! He told me that when he was a sophomore, he had a senior girlfriend, which didn't surprise me. Normally senior girls don't lower themselves to make eye contact with underclass guys, much less date them, but Mac is Mac.

Her name is Bailey. He sees her sometimes when she's home on break from Skidmore. "Sienna hates it. She pretends not to mind, but then she's like, 'So what did you guys do *exactly*?' and 'Did you talk about me at all?' and 'Do you wish I were shorter?'"

"Why would you want her to be shorter? She looks like a model."

"Because Bailey's tiny. She looks kind of like you, actually."

Is that a flirty thing to say? Tris says definitely yes, but he didn't hear Mac's voice, which sounded normal, like we were discussing what we'd had for lunch. But it's definitely not normal to talk on the phone for two hours, right? No one does that anymore, do they? It means something good, doesn't it? I type these questions into the internet, but I can't find answers.

Thursday, March 10

We're up to "An Ordinary Couple," and holy cats, it's awkward to stand with my arms around Josh, singing about keeping him close to me and kissing him every morning and every night. I accidentally ate Doritos before rehearsal today, and when I said "Sorry about my Dorito breath!" during the break, he said, "Don't worry about it," which means he noticed it.

Friday, March 11

You might think Miss Murphy would cut me some slack in English class since I'm so busy starring in the musical and learning lyrics and choreography for *six* songs, not to mention five reprises, plus acres and acres of lines, but you would be incorrect. I couldn't answer a basic question about the plot today, because I, ummm, hadn't finished the reading, and she gave me a frosty look and said she was disappointed. In my defense, we're reading a novel called *Ragged Dick*, and it's (a) a novel called *Ragged Dick* and (b) absolutely terrible.

Saturday, March 12

Mac called me again. I considered not picking up, since I didn't want him to realize I was sitting at home alone on Saturday night, but it was fine—he didn't even ask me what I was doing. Mostly he complained about his mother. Apparently she's keeping him locked in his room like a political prisoner because she found a bottle of whiskey in his sock drawer. I painted my nails while he told me about it. Before we hung up, he said, "You're easy to talk to." I guess he thinks of me as an asexual underage therapist.

Sunday, March 13

Hannah and I played Disney Scene It? Deluxe Second Edition all afternoon. She's always Ariel, and I'm always

Tinker Bell. I don't understand why she'd rather be a mopey, voiceless fish woman than a fireball with the power of flight, but that's Hannah for you.

Monday, March 14
March is the cruelest month, not April. Because in March, you keep hoping for a warm day, and the warm day never comes. Instead, you get chapped hands, a bad cold, piles of sad old snow covered in dog pee and grit, and seasonal affective disorder (Dad refuses to buy me a sun lamp).

Tuesday, March 15
Mostly worked on "Climb Ev'ry Mountain" during rehearsal. Hannah and the nuns ran through the wedding processional. During the break, Josh and Hannah sat on the floor back-to-back, leaning on each other while they each did their homework. *And* they were sharing a pair of earbuds. It would bring a tear to my eye if I weren't so sick with envy.

Wednesday, March 16
Mac called after rehearsal. I told him I was tired and he said, "Me too. Let's watch a movie."

"How?"

"Get your laptop and we'll stream something together."

He wanted to watch the new Fast and Furious and

I wanted to watch *Mean Girls*. We compromised and picked an X-Men sequel. He fell asleep halfway through, and I listened to him breathe until the movie ended. Then I whispered good night.

I love him so much. As a friend!

Thursday, March 17

I've started bringing coffee to school in a travel mug. I need a little boost to get through the day. Dad says coffee is OK, but he draws the line at cigarettes.

Friday, March 18

Mac stopped by my locker today. He rifled through all my stuff and bent over to look in my mirror. "How's my makeup?" he said in a falsetto voice. Bernadette was pulling out some textbooks next to us. She didn't look over, but she did slam her locker door like she was trying to crush someone's head with it.

Saturday, March 19

When I was in seventh grade, I had a huge crush on Shawn Hall. I used to spend entire car rides to Grammy's pretending he was sitting next to me with his arm around my shoulders. When a good song came on the radio, I'd imagine us starring in the music video, grinding together on a yacht. I told Mom how much I loved him, and she said, "How exciting!" and asked me a million questions. How tall was he? What kind of clothes did he wear? Was he smart, artistic, funny? Had we had any in-depth conversations? And when I answered, she didn't interrupt or point out that I probably wasn't actually in love with him, since I'd never spoken to him. It's weird to think she doesn't know about Mac.

Sunday, March 20

Dad turned off NPR on the drive home from the grocery store, which he never does, so I assumed he was about to tell me he has cancer. Instead, he cleared his throat and said, "So, Watson, I've detected that you and Tristan aren't dating."

I groaned. "I've been telling you that for months!"

"Don't you want to know how I deduced the truth?"

"Sure." He thinks he's Sherlock Holmes.

"A fortnight ago, you farted in front of him and then laughed uproariously."

"I was trying to fart *on* him because he'd said something rude about my velour pants, but he ran away in time."

"Watson, a young lady in love rarely lets slip a toot in front of her paramour."

"How right you are, Sherlock."

He stopped at a red light and turned to look at me. "But how do you explain the mysterious gentleman who's been calling you nearly every evening?"

Oh shiz.

He'd lulled me into complacency with his terrible English accent, and now I was too flustered to think up a diversion.

"That's Mac."

"Since you talk to him for two to four hours at a time, I deduce that he is not a telemarketer but a human of or around your age. We balance probabilities and choose the most likely."

"Dad," I said, in a tone of voice that meant, *I don't want to play BBC anymore.*

"Tell me more about Mac," he said in his regular voice.

We were driving past the mini strip mall. Some kids from my school were hanging out in the parking lot in front of 7-Eleven. That's what passes for entertainment in this two-horse town.

"He's a senior. He's nice. He plays football."

"Is he your boyfriend?"

"No! No, no, no."

"Is 'boyfriend' hopelessly passé? What's the right term?"

"No, I mean, he's not—we're not going out or anything."

"Well, I'd like to meet him sometime."

Meet Mac?! How would I pitch that one? *So, Mac, I know you have a girlfriend who's not me, but would you enjoy coming to my house to meet my father, as if we're in an old-timey novel with courting and betrothals?*

Monday, March 21

Horrible rehearsal. During "do-mi-mi, mi-so-so, re-fa-fa, la-ti-ti," we kept forgetting who sings which syllable. During the tenth long, empty pause where a note should have been, Miss Murphy threw her empty Starbucks cup at us and said, "Boooo! I want my money back!" Louisa burst into tears and ran off the stage, and we wasted 15 minutes while Marta and Kurt followed her and calmed her down. Then everything ground to a halt again when Frau Schmidt decided her blocking made no sense and demanded that Miss Murphy explain her character's motivation.

Tuesday, March 22

Mom called after dinner. It was hard to hear her over all the car horns in the background. I asked where she was.

"I'm in DF! I just had the most amazing tacos al pastor from a street vendor, and I thought, 'I have to call Chloe and tell her about this.' Pork like candy, pineapple like butter, all wrapped up in hot tortillas that fit in the palm of your hand."

I pictured her in her red lipstick and white shirt,

standing on a corner lit up by streetlights and head-lights. I looked around the kitchen. Snickers was sleeping in his plaid bed. There were a bunch of bananas turning brown on the counter. The dishes I'd washed were drying in the rack. It all looked fake, like a stage set.

"What's DF?"

"Oh, I'm sorry—I forgot. 'DF' is what the locals call it. I'm in Mexico City, doing some research."

"The tacos sound good."

"They're exquisite. I can't wait for you to try them."

"Maybe I could visit for Easter. There might be some last-minute deals on airfare. I could tell you about Mac!"

"Rabbit, I would adore for you to come! This month is a bit tricky for me, but let's pull out our calendars and find a time that works, all right? I've got to dash—I love you, sweetheart—*hasta pronto!*"

Wednesday, March 23

We ended rehearsal with the scene where I come back from the abbey and all the children run over and hug me, and I cried and cried. "That was amazing," Annabelle whispered when we were done. "Thanks," I whispered back, because what was I supposed to say, "I'm not actually acting"?

Miss Murphy said, "Nice work, everyone. Chloe, can you come see me about a costume question?"

We sat in the front row and she talked about a quick change in act 2, which was odd, because we'd already been over it, but then, when everyone had left and it was just us in the auditorium, she said, "OK, spill the beans."

I looked at her like, *What are you talking about?* and she looked at me like, *Oh, come on.*

"I'm fine," I said.

She studied the side of my face. It was strange and nice, being alone together in the auditorium. I could feel the seats stretching out behind us and could hear every little sound we made.

"My mom's away," I said. Miss Murphy didn't say anything, just nodded and kept looking at me. I wanted to tell her the rest, but I couldn't. After a while, she said, "You were good today."

"Method acting," I said, and nodded wisely.

She laughed and patted my knee. "That's the ticket, Marlon."

Thursday, March 24

No contact with Mac today. He's called me or stopped by my locker every day for weeks now. What happened? Is he mad at me? Did he finally realize I'm an unimportant ninth-grade theater nerd? Ugh ugh ugh. How did I get myself into this fix?

Friday, March 25

Everything's fine! He didn't call because he was out with his football friends, getting drunk and shooting BB guns in the woods. Phew.

Saturday, March 26

I don't even want to be his girlfriend. I don't! Girlfriends come and go. Sienna? *Ha.* She'll be a distant memory by the time he gets to college. I want to be his best friend. I want to be the one he calls when he's upset. I want to be more than some girl who makes him sandwiches.

Sunday, March 27

Easter would be a lot more cheerful if they moved it to May or June. Hannah made me go to church with her family at 9 a.m., which meant I had to get up four and a half hours earlier than I normally do on Sundays. Everyone was wearing flowered dresses and strappy sandals except me: I wore a long-sleeved dress and thick tights because, hello, it was cold outside. But even though my outfit made sense and everyone else's was insane, I still felt like the awkward one. The minister talked about spring and blossoming flowers and the chance to start over even after you really poop the sleeping bag (I'm paraphrasing). "Jesus died for *your* sins," he said. "And if you truly repent, there is no sin so heinous that God cannot forgive it."

I wonder if talking on the phone to someone else's boyfriend counts as a heinous sin.

After church, we had to stand around the parking lot getting pelted with icy rain while Mrs. Egan talked to all her friends. In the car on the way home, she screwed herself around in her seat to make too much eye contact with me. "How *are* you, sweetheart?" she said. "Have you heard from your mother?"

"Yup," I said. "The big news is, she sold her novel. There was a bidding war and she got a huge advance."

Mrs. Egan drew her head back on her neck, like she'd smelled a fart. "How thrilling," she said.

The minister wouldn't approve of my lies, but I bet he wouldn't approve of Mrs. Egan's child-torturing, either.

When I got home, Dad said, "SomeBUNNY visited while you were out," grinning ear to ear and nodding toward a huge pink-and-yellow Easter basket on the kitchen counter, filled with neon-green grass and Peeps and mini Kit Kats and those pastel eggs with crunchy candy on the outside and chocolate on the inside. He'd even put in a little stuffed rabbit.

I gave him a hug and told him I loved him, because I'm sappy like that.

Monday, March 28

We're doing a life skills unit in health class. Today we learned about "when you ____, I feel ____ because ____" statements and then did role-playing to practice. Olivia Choi and I had to pretend to be sisters. She's so mean to me as Baroness Schraeder that I have to remind myself she doesn't actually hate me in real life. She said, "When you try to hang out with me and my friends, I feel annoyed because I want to spend time alone with them." I said, "When you yell at me in front of your friends, I feel embarrassed because it makes me seem like a baby." We got really into it and hugged each other at the end of the conversation.

I bet I would love to have a sister, but I don't spend too much time thinking about it. It's hard to miss something you've never had.

Tuesday, March 29

I'm jealous of Maria's favorite things—raindrops on roses, whiskers on kittens . . . silver white winters that melt into springs . . . etc., etc. They're so cozy and pre-internet age. My favorite things are:

1. Silver white winters that melt into springs
2. My phone

3. Snickers
4. Candy Crush
5. Cheez-Its
6. Reading books while wearing comfy pants
7. Tristan and Hannah
8. Thinking about Mac

See? A few good ones, but mostly disgusting.

Tristan and I went to the vending machine during a rehearsal break, and I sang him a personalized version of "Edelweiss": "Tristan Flynn, Tristan Flynn, every weekday you greet me; nice and sweet, cool and neat, you look happy to meet me. BFF, may you bloom and grow, bloom and grow forever. Tristan Flynn, let's move to New York and stay there foreverrrrrr." He liked it so much, he bought my Skittles for me.

Wednesday, March 30

Mac was at my locker today, looking through my backpack for my cherry ChapStick, when Bernadette slammed her locker shut and stood there staring at us. Mac noticed and said, "What's up, B?" He held his hand up for a high five, but she left him hanging.

"You have a *girlfriend*," she said.

"*What??*" he said, faking shock.

"Sienna is my best friend. I can't overlook this situation anymore." She made a little circle around us in the air.

"There's no situation," I said. She turned and walked off without even glancing at me.

"Have a wonderful day, Bernie," he called after her.

I looked at him like, *Oh no*, but he waved his hand and said, "Whatever. She's never liked me." He looked a little nervous, though.

Why doesn't Bernadette understand that Mac and I are just friends? Two people who love each other platonically and innocently? If a relationship is so weak that neither person in it is allowed to have friends of the opposite gender, maybe that relationship is fatally flawed.

Thursday, March 31

It's almost midnight, and I'm still alive. No one spit on me in the halls or egged my house. Maybe Bernadette was just giving Mac a warning.

Friday, April 1

Hannah pulled me aside in the hall and whispered, "Chloe, I have to talk to you."

"What's going on? You look like a ghost."

"I think I might be . . . you know." She made a gesture like she was pouring maple syrup over pancakes and then shooting an arrow.

"I have no idea what that means, Han."

She looked around like spies might be watching from the water fountain and then mouthed, *Pregnant.*

"WHAT?" I said, and honestly, my first thought was, *I can't believe she had sex before I did,* but at least my second thought was, *Poor Hannah; her parents are going to chop her head off.*

I grabbed her arms and said, "When did you find out? How are you going to—" and then her face turned sunny and she was laughing so hard she could barely say, "April Fools'!"

Hilarious, I'm sure.

Not only did she get me good, Josh promposed to her in the afternoon. He crouched down in a huge cardboard box and had his friends wrap him up like a present and push him into Hannah's math class. When she opened the box, he jumped out holding a bouquet of red roses.

Prom is in one month and one week. Anything could happen in one month and one week!

Saturday, April 2

Sienna called me. I feel sick. Why did I pick up? Well, I know exactly why: because I thought there was a tiny chance it was Mac calling from a landline somewhere, and I didn't want to risk missing him.

"Chloe? It's Sienna." Her voice sounded small, like she was sitting at the bottom of a well.

"Hi."

"Hi."

Neither of us said anything. I could hear the air floating around in her well. Then she said, "Can you do me a favor?"

"OK."

"Can you back off?"

She didn't say it meanly. She was polite and quiet.

"You probably won't believe me," I said, "but I'm not trying to steal Mac from you."

"You could never steal Mac from me." Still quiet. Firm. Then she hung up without saying goodbye.

It's 3 a.m. I just took my phone to the kitchen and buried it in the snack drawer. Maybe now I'll be able to sleep.

Sunday, April 3

Mac called me before I'd even finished my coffee. "I can't believe she did that," he said. I jumped up from the table and made a hand signal to Dad, trying to convey, *Pardon me. This is a very important call from a classmate about a project we're working on for earth science.* He didn't look too interested.

"It's OK," I said, walking upstairs.

"What did she say?"

I told him.

"Dude, are you serious? It's so wrong, picking on you. You're this innocent little freshman. She's so paranoid!"

"It's not a big deal."

"We're in a huge fight about it right now," he said. "Huge."

"Oh. I'm sorry," I said, feeling more thrilled and delighted than a six-year-old on a pony ride.

"It's like, doesn't anyone understand the concept of friendship? We're *friends*. Two people who are *friendly* with each other. Why does everyone think you must be my sidepiece?"

"People think that?" This was getting better and better.

"And Bernadette's in Sienna's ear telling lies, creating drama for no reason."

"We're just friends!" I said.

"Exactly. See, you get it. It's not that complicated."

We went on like that for 63 minutes, according to my call log. If there's anything more fun than complaining about other people with your beloved senior football friend, I'm not aware of it.

Monday, April 4

Tristan had so much Roy news today at rehearsal. They DM'd all day Saturday. Then Roy's parents went antiquing yesterday, so Tristan went over to his house and they "watched" a movie but actually made out the entire time (!!!!!!!!!). Now he loves the way Roy kisses and pretends he never said his tongue was pointy and hard.

To stall, I asked him as many questions as I could possibly think of ("Did you get a crick in your neck at any point?" "Did you stop to have a sip of water?" "What was the movie about?" "Do you think you're falling in love?" "What's his house like?" etc., etc.), but finally he got a serious look on his face and said, "What's going on with Mac?"

"I told you everything over text, and I already know you disapprove. I can tell when you're being fake because you use weird emoji."

"Tell me again. It doesn't count as much on our phones."

He looked more and more concerned as I told him. When I got to the end, I said, "Can you unfurrow your brow, please?"

"Sorry. It's just—where is this going?"

"My story?"

"This thing with Mac."

"Nowhere. Nothing will change. He's my best friend."

As soon as I said it, I felt bad, because #1, Hannah's supposed to be my best friend, and #2, Tristan actually *is* my best friend. We've never said it out loud, but I know it's true.

"I mean, besides you, obviously," I said.

"Don't you think Sienna kind of has a point? If Roy were talking to someone for hours every day and stopping by his locker every other minute, I would be pissed."

"It's not like that! We're friends! Why doesn't anyone understand?"

"OK, OK, you're friends."

We both picked at our cuticles. Then Tris said, "What about Chris Fortier? He's always staring at you in the hall."

"Chris Fortier? Do you realize that gray baseball hat he wears used to be white?"

"All I'm saying is, I don't want you to get your feelings hurt."

"I would rather eat a used tampon than go out with Chris Fortier."

"Forget Chris Fortier! I'm sorry I mentioned him!"

We'd made up by the time his mom came to pick him up, thank God. My whole life would be ruined if I ever got in a serious fight with Tristan.

Tuesday, April 5

I love rehearsal, even when Bernie's glaring up at me from the front row. Some of the sets are done, and I pretend as hard as I can that it's all real, that I'm a nanny, that I'm falling in love with my boss, that my lungs are full of mountain air.

Dad picks me up nearly every night now. I think he likes it that I'm working so hard, since normally he'd make me walk home in the dark and tell me it's good for my character. Or maybe it's because he loves *The Sound of Music*. Either way, he shows up before I'm done and sits in the back of the auditorium to watch, then comes down to get me. For a while he and Miss Murphy would have long discussions while I died of embarrassment, but I guess they ran out of stuff to talk about, thank goodness, because now they only smile and give each other a little wave.

Wednesday, April 6

Sienna and Bernadette don't hiss at me in the halls or anything; they just pretend I'm not there. But Bernadette still has to twirl around me onstage and look at me "with loving exasperation," as Miss Murphy put it today. Ha ha ha, Bernadette.

Thursday, April 7

Sometimes I forget about Mom for whole days at a time. I almost don't remember she exists. Then I'll see something that reminds me of her, like a box of quinoa, and a wave of guilt drowns me. Maybe I should get a tattoo of her name on my inner arm. Dad would kill me and Mom would think I was being free-spirited and daring.

Friday, April 8

I dreamed that Dad, Snickers, and I were on a boat in a stormy ocean. All three of us were wearing yellow rain jackets, and Dad had a sad, scared look on his face. All day, I couldn't shake off the dream. I can still see the look on Dad's face, and the big waves.

Saturday, April 9

It was 74 degrees and sunny today. Tris and I sat in Adirondack chairs in his backyard.

"What were the 16 screaming emoji about?" I asked. He'd texted me that he had to tell me something important, and then refused to answer follow-up questions.

"Roy is pissed at me. He wants to meet my parents and go to prom together and be, like, a real couple."

"He asked you to prom?"

"Yeah."

"Aren't you happy?"

"I'd be happy if we went to a different school and I had different parents."

"If we lived in a richer town, it would be better. Like, everyone would be all liberal and fancy and bending over backward to be accepting."

"I know. I visited my cousin in Berkeley last year and half her class is bi. There are, like, six trans kids. Everyone was holding hands in the hall."

"Is your cousin a lesbian? Maybe she could talk to your parents—"

"She's secretly dating this guy who works at a pizza place and has a kid. And no one's talking to my parents, ever."

"What would they do if they found out?"

He sighed. "I don't know. Lose their minds. Maybe kick me out. Everything I've found online says if you're underage and you're not sure of the response you'll get, you shouldn't come out."

When I'd arrived, Mr. Flynn had been heading out to bring the recycling to the town dump. Mrs. Flynn had fixed us a plate of crackers, cheese, and jalapeño jelly. She'd even given us a tiny spoon for the jelly.

"I can't imagine them losing their minds," I said.

"You should have seen my dad when I said I wanted to stop playing soccer so I could sing in chorus. He said the F word."

"He called you an F word?"

"No, but almost. He said why did I want to hang out with a bunch of F words instead of doing something I'm actually good at."

We both looked out at the trees. "Do Roy's parents know?" I said.

"Yeah, but they're basically hippies. I guarantee you Mrs. Baker dated girls in college. They'd probably be disappointed if Roy *weren't* gay."

"Well, I hope you and Roy have a huge fight and you don't go to prom, because it'll be so sickening if you and Hannah both get to go and I have to sit at home talking to Snickers and refreshing Instagram."

"You are the most selfish person on the planet," he said, but he was laughing.

I don't actually hope they break up, of course. That would be terrible. But I will be lonely on prom night. Maybe I can use that time to catch up on homework, or start researching colleges, or maybe I'll just Google "no boyfriend virgin happy anyway?" for hours.

Sunday, April 10

Mrs. Egan drove me and Hannah to the mall to look for spring clothes.

"Do you think Sienna Ross would wear something like this?" I asked Hannah, holding up a gray shirt with leather patches on the shoulders.

"Definitely not. Why?" she said, giving me an odd look.

"Just wondering."

I had that dizzy, thirsty, overwhelmed feeling I always get at the mall. We bought smoothies and sat on a bench, looking through a glass barrier to the fountain on the first floor. *Would I die if I jumped into the fountain?* I wondered, but not in a sad way. I think everyone imagines leaping off high places. (Right?)

"I feel guilty," Hannah said.

"About what?"

"Do you think it's terrible that I haven't told my parents about Josh?"

"They would murder you, Hannah. You're not supposed to date until you're 35."

"18, but yeah."

I sucked the last bits of smoothie from the bottom of the cup. "Don't worry about it."

She looked down at the fountain, but I could tell she wasn't really seeing it. "It's hard keeping a secret. I mean, it's easy to keep the secret, but it's hard feeling like the people who love you don't know this big thing about you."

Was she talking about me? I studied the side of her face for clues. Her perfect pink ear, her reddish hair that gets wispy at her neck, her blond eyelashes. It was weird, looking at her carefully. She's so familiar to me that I hardly have to glance at her anymore. I've known her since we were five years old.

I almost said it. I could feel the words in my mouth. *I think something's going on with me and Mac. We talk on the phone almost every day, for hours at a time. He complains to me about Sienna. I love him. As a friend. I think.*

But I couldn't. She wouldn't understand.

Monday, April 11

Hannah and Tristan and I are all in secret relationships. Well, Hannah and Tris are. I'm in a relationship so secret, it doesn't exist at all.

Everyone says, "Ugh, so much drama," and "I hate drama," and "I'm not one of those people who goes around creating drama," but they secretly love it, right? I do! I mean, I don't want people gossiping about me, and I don't want Hannah's and Tristan's parents to kill them, but at least something's happening! At least we're not just sitting around in our bedrooms clicking on the internet!

Tuesday, April 12

I have to stop looking at pictures of Sienna. She posts all the time, everywhere. The trees she sees on her morning run. Her and Bernadette wearing each other's hair as mustaches. Her breakfast (usually Greek yogurt and honey, sometimes oatmeal with berries). Her bulldog (who looks like an idiot). Her perfect thigh, bruised and bloody from a soccer injury. She doesn't try to make herself look beautiful; she just *is* beautiful.

I make rules for myself, like no looking at pictures of her when I'm in bed, or no looking unless all my homework's done, or it's after 9 p.m., or I was nice to Dad all day. After I make a rule, I feel pleased with myself for being so disciplined, and then I think, *Great, I've taken care of that. My willpower is that of an Olympian. Now I can look.* My brain has a million ways to tempt me. *Who cares if you take a quick peek? This is how members of your generation interact. You don't want to turn into some clueless weirdo. Check quickly now, and then you can stop thinking about it and focus on other things. You feel worse when you don't check. Isn't it better to have the facts?*

After I stalk her, it takes me hours to feel normal again.

I just looked. There was a new one of her squinting against the sun with her hair blowing into her eyes.

It's not that I think I'm ugly. I like my face. I like my body! I even love it, like I love Snickers. This nice little body gets me where I need to go and lets me sing and run around the stage. But I'm no Sienna.

Wednesday, April 13
EXACTLY ONE MONTH UNTIL OPENING NIGHT. OH DEAR LORD.

Thursday, April 14
Tris and I discussed boys for an hour straight backstage while Miss Murphy yelled at the nuns. Finally he said, "Do you realize all we talk about now is Roy and Mac?"

"I know. It's gross."

"Tomorrow, let's talk about current events."

"And art and music."

We'll never be able to do it.

Friday, April 15

Tris bought a tux! *Bought*, like an aristocrat. It was on super sale on nordstrom.com, probably because there's not much demand for midnight-blue tuxedos that fit teenagers. He put it on his mom's credit card without asking. "I feel kind of bad," he said, "but she did say I could use it to buy clothes whenever I want." Why can't Dad be more like that?

Saturday, April 16

2 a.m. Can't sleep. This was probably the #1 most awkward day of my entire life.

Dad had to work. Hannah and I were having a sleepover, and she came over early so we could make a cake she'd read about on her favorite blog (which is intended for 45-year-old mothers, of course). Mom and I never bake or cook together. She says she didn't get a master's degree to waste precious hours of her life mincing garlic. I kind of wish we did, though, because it's easy to talk to someone when you're making food together. If you feel like being quiet, you can, and it's not weird, because you can focus on cracking eggs or whatever you're doing. And if you want to say something serious, it's easy, because you can avoid eye contact by staring down at the Oreos you're crushing up.

I said, "Do you think Sienna dyes her hair?"

Hannah was looking at the recipe with her eyes unfocused.

"Han?"

"Huh? Oh." I could see her scrolling back to figure out what I'd said. "Maybe."

"It's kind of hypocritical. I mean, her whole look is about being, like, this effortless athlete, but no one could be that blond naturally. She probably spends tons of money faking it. Don't you think? Hannah?"

She was staring down into her mixing bowl. "I think my parents suspect something."

"Suspect something?"

"About me and Josh. Well, not Josh in particular. I mean, I think they suspect that I'm going out with someone. Last night my mom said how glad she is that she didn't waste her high school years chasing boys, and my dad keeps sneaking up behind me when I'm doing homework on my laptop. I think he's trying to read my email."

"Do you think they looked through your phone or something?"

"Maybe. But Josh and I never say anything real on our phones. Plus he's in my contacts as Jen."

"Then how do they know?"

She pressed the palms of her hands to her eyes. "Maybe they don't."

"Maybe you're being paranoid!"

"There's another problem." She dropped her hands. Her eyes looked red and tired. "I asked Josh when I could meet his parents, and he got very weird. He was like, 'Soon. They're just really busy right now.'"

"He didn't say *that*," I said.

"No. It was more like, 'They're overwhelmed with the pressures of work.' Anyway, I made him tell me the truth. Apparently his parents would be very upset if they knew he was dating a 'Jesus freak.'" She made quotation marks with her fingers.

"You're kidding me. They should be overjoyed that you—"

The doorbell rang. We both jumped a little.

"Who is that?" Hannah said, and I said, "I have no idea," even though I did have some idea, and my heart was already pounding. When I went to open the door, Mac was standing there in gray shorts, white sneakers, and a purple hoodie—purple! That right there shows you how popular he is. He could wear Hello Kitty rompers, and everyone would be like, "Hello Kitty rompers are so cool."

"Chloe Snow," he said, smiling. We hugged and he picked me up off my feet. "Let's go inside," he said. "It's colder than a witch's tit out here."

As we walked into the house, I said, "Hannah's here," and as he said, "Who?" I heard my dad coming in through the back door, calling, "Anyone home?"

And then there we all were in the kitchen, me and Hannah and Mac and my dad. We went through this-is-Mac-this-is-my-dad-I'm-Hannah-nice-to-meet-you, and then it got quiet. Hannah was staring at Mac, looking awed and confused.

"So this is the famous Mac!" Dad said.

"Dad!"

"I'm an embarrassment to my daughter," Dad said. "I think I should be pretending I've never heard of you."

I groaned.

"Can I get you something to drink, Mac?"

"I'm good, thanks." Mac looked comfortable. He leaned a hip against the island and crossed one ankle over the other, resting the toe of his sneaker on the floor.

Dad got a beer from the fridge, opened it, and raised it like he was toasting all of us.

"So, Mac, do you live close by?"

"Nah. We're over in Gates Hill."

"How do you like it?"

Mac shrugged. "It is what it is. Lots of divorced people, like my mom. Lots of little condos." He looked around the kitchen and said, "It must be nice to have money."

My mouth dropped open, and I heard Hannah take

a breath. Dad made a noise, a combination laugh-grunt. Then he looked at me. "I'll be upstairs," he said. He walked out, holding his beer.

Hannah and I were vibrating like scared rabbits, but Mac was still grinning, relaxed, a big warm lion in the sun.

"That was rude," Hannah squeaked. You've got to hand it to her: when she thinks she sees a broken Commandment, she speaks up.

"Just being honest." He shrugged.

She looked back and forth between us. "Are you guys . . . friends?"

"Are we friends?!" Mac moved next to me and put his arm around my shoulders, jostling me against him. "We're practically besties. Isn't that what you gals say?"

Hannah frowned.

"No, seriously, we met at the pool this summer. I got a cramp and started swallowing water. The lifeguard was MIA. Probably taking a dump. Chloe saved me. Jumped right in and pulled me to the shallow end. What stroke did you use, Chloe?"

His arm was still around my shoulders. Hannah looked upset. She could tell from Mac's voice that this was all a joke, a way of making fun of her somehow. If I joined in with him, I'd be making fun of her too.

"Sidestroke," I said.

Hannah looked bewildered. I knew I should be worried—she was finding out I hadn't told her the whole truth about Mac, I was being mean to her, and Mac had been awful to my dad—but all I could focus on was the feeling of Mac's big, strong arm around me and his big, strong hand squeezing my shoulder.

"Hazel, do you mind if I talk to Chloe alone for a second?"

"It's Hannah," she said.

"Right," Mac said.

Hannah looked at me. I looked at the floor.

"Whatever," she said. Her voice was cold. She turned and left, and I didn't say anything. I didn't even watch her go.

"You were so mean to her!" I said, and punched his shoulder, but lightly, because somehow I wasn't actually mad at him. I was flirting with him. A voice inside me said, *You should not flirt with this person. You should find Hannah*, but it was a very little voice, like a baby mouse voice, easy to ignore.

"Don't say that. You sound like Sienna. She's so pissed at me right now."

It took him half an hour to tell me about their fight. (She feels like he's not making enough time for her; he thinks she's too demanding. It's 100% her fault; she doesn't understand him at all.) After he left, I went to find Hannah, but she was gone. She left her flip-flops in the kitchen. She must have gotten her mom to come pick her up. She hasn't answered my texts or calls. Dad's all quiet and thoughtful. I listened to a podcast and did my nail stickers, but it was no fun by myself.

Sunday, April 17

Are you still mad?

Hannah,
pleeeeeeaaaaaseeeeeee

Don't you at least want to tell me why I suck?

Maybe your phone's broken

btw, you leaf your shoes here

*left

Maybe I shouldn't correct my typos at a moment like this

I'm sorry I didn't tell you mac and I are friends now

There's nothing really to tell

*I know you probably think I
shouldn't hang out with him at
all because he has a gf but he
really needs someone to talk to.
Plus he understands me more
than any guy has before or
probably ever will again*

*I guess you don't want to talk
to me right now*

OK, good night

Monday, April 18

Couldn't take the silence at breakfast. Halfway through
my Cinnamon Toast Crunch, I let the spoon clatter into
the bowl and said, "I know you hate him, Dad."

He looked up from his laptop.

I said, "Just lecture me about how awful he is and get
it over with."

He shrugged. "He's a jackass."

"Dad!"

"You asked."

"He's not like that when it's the two of us talking. He

gets mean in front of other people." It's true, I realized as I said it.

I stared at my cinnamony milk.

"We're not rich, are we?" I asked.

"Not the last time I checked."

I felt relieved, but then he sighed, and said, "Let me give you a real answer. Compared to nearly everyone in the world, we're rich. Compared to people in Gates Hill, compared to my parents when they were my age, we're rich. We're not living in the nicest town in the state, and I can't afford to fix the damn septic tank, but we're doing fine."

"You were poor when you were little?"

"We had to wear hats inside in the winter."

"I never knew that."

"I don't want to burden you with that garbage. It's not sad. I'm fine."

"It seems a little sad."

He looked at his hands. "It's no excuse."

"What isn't?"

"Money. Lack of money. It's no excuse for being callow and disrespectful."

"He was being weird yesterday. I think he was nervous."

"I'm not going to tell you not to see him anymore, but I will say that in my opinion, he's not the right guy for you."

He squeezed my hand and went upstairs. I sat there hating him and feeling bad for him at the same time.

Tuesday, April 19

It all makes sense. The way Dad reuses tinfoil and plastic spoons, washes out Ziploc bags, won't let me throw out moldy cheese, refuses to turn up the heat when it's two degrees outside, and goes bananas when Mom buys seven pairs of shoes online, even though she says she's going to return six of them, which she usually forgets to do. Poor Daddy.

Wednesday, April 20

Hannah's been avoiding me all week, and she won't make eye contact during rehearsal. Today I was so upset I couldn't eat the Junior Mints Tris brought for me. But while we were running the proposal bit, Josh got to, "It's something I've known—deep inside me—for many weeks," and the way he said "deep inside me" made me think of sex, and I had to struggle not to laugh, and the surprised look on his face as he watched me almost lose it made me actually lose it. We started the scene over, and his voice quavered when he got to "deep inside me," and this time we both got hysterical. The third time around we didn't even get two words in before we were laughing so hard I had to bend over and put my head between my legs. I heard Miss Murphy groan from the first row. And then I felt two holes boring into my skull and looked into the audience to find Hannah setting me and Josh on fire with her eyes. I'm sure she thought I was a coldhearted B, to laugh when I should be upset about our fight. And probably she hated Josh for not hating me.

Laughing onstage doesn't feel like laughing in real life. It feels like a sneeze attack. It takes you over and you can't stop, even though you're making an exhibition of yourself and you would love to pull yourself together.

I saw Josh giving Hannah a shoulder massage after rehearsal, so I guess she forgave him. I'm still in trouble, though.

Thursday, April 21

Was at my locker swapping my deadly dull algebra book for my deadly dull history book when I heard Hannah's voice.

"Did it even occur to you to wonder how I got home from your house the other day?"

I grabbed my copy of *The Catcher in the Rye* so I'd have a little friend in my hand.

"Didn't your mom pick you up?"

She shook her head. "I walked home. Barefoot! I cut my foot on a rock."

Whose fault is that? I thought, but did not say out loud.

"I'm sorry if I made you mad," I said.

"That's not a real apology."

It's not that she was wrong. But I hated her scolding Mother Abbess tone. Who died and made her my mom?

"What did I do that was so awful?" I said kind of loudly. A few kids passing by turned to look at us.

"You *ignored* me and *ditched* me to talk to your *stupid fake boyfriend!*" Now the entire hall was looking at us. Hannah's cheeks were turning pink, and there were tears in the corners of her eyes. "And I was trying to tell you something important about Josh. I needed to talk to you."

"I guess you're right," I said.

"I am right. And you know what else, that . . . guy, he's a *jerk.*"

It was considerate of her to avoid saying Mac's name out loud, even when she was in the midst of her fury. But I hated that she'd called him a jerk. I hated that she didn't like him.

I pressed *Catcher* against my ribs. "I'm sorry, Hannah," I said. You could hear in my voice everything I felt: annoyed, offended, truly sorry.

She studied my face. "OK," she said finally. "Apology accepted."

I don't think either of us was in the mood to hug, but for form's sake, we gave each other a shallow one, the kind where just your shoulders touch and you pat each other weakly on the back.

Friday, April 22

This is the sixteenth day in a row Mac has called me. I've never talked on the phone so much in my life. We discuss everything. Our teachers, whether French or Spanish is a prettier language, what we want to do after high school. Tonight I told him about my mom.

"She's in Mexico for a few months, working on her novel."

"That's cool."

"I miss her a lot, but she's a great artist. She needs to do whatever it takes to write."

"Can't she write in America?"

"No. It's too conventional and materialistic here."

"You're way more mature than me. I hate my father for leaving. But then again, he's not an artist; he's just a lush."

"My mom didn't leave."

I must have sounded mad, because he said, "No, I know. I didn't say that, sweetie."

Sweetie! He called me sweetie. I love him so much. But as a friend! As my best, best friend, the person I adore and trust more than anyone else in the solar system.

Saturday, April 23

Oh, for the love of cats. It's Dad's birthday tomorrow. What the FRACK am I going to do??? OK, it's 11 a.m. now and I'm still in my pajamas. Think. *Think!* Tie no, coffee mug no, sweater no, no, no, and how would I get to the mall anyway? The only two places I can walk are (1) the arboretum and (2) the pizza place. Could I steal some flowers from the arboretum?!? I'M PANICKING.

Sunday, April 24

It worked out OK! Josh and Hannah agreed to drive me to the mall. It felt 83% normal with Hannah. It helped that I'd asked her to do me a favor, since doing favors makes her feel kind and charitable, her two favorite ways to feel. I had no idea what I was looking for, but as I was wandering around eating an Auntie Anne's pretzel, watching Hannah and Josh hold hands, and feeling frantic, I realized I knew exactly what to get him: running shoes to replace his broken ones! Foot Locker had a good pair of Nikes, mostly black with some green parts. I looked through every single dad birthday card at Papyrus, but they all had glittery golf clubs or footballs or Hawaiian shirts on them, and Dad doesn't like any of that stuff. Finally I found a cute one with a painting of a lighthouse decorated with bunting and balloons. It reminded me of the Cape, where we go for vacation every year, and which is the one thing in this world Dad loves ponying up for. On the inside it said, *A special wish for all that makes you happy . . . today and always / Have a wonderful Birthday*," which is a little cheesy, plus ungrammatical, but the lighthouse painting made up for it. When I got home, I crossed out the upper-case *B* and wrote in a lowercase one.

On the way home from the mall, we stopped at the bagel store where Josh and Hannah went after their first movie date, and I picked up Dad's favorite items: cream cheese, a pumpernickel bagel (shudder), and lox (shudder, shudder). I set my alarm for six this morning, so I'd wake up before Dad. When the beeping started, I sat bolt upright in bed. Then I ran downstairs and made scrambled eggs with about half a stick of butter and put the cream cheese on a plate with the disgusting lox and the disgusting bagel. I was still hanging up crepe paper streamers when Dad came down wearing his *Better Call Saul* T-shirt and pajama pants, and the look on his face was so good!

The best part was his present. As he unwrapped it, I could see his expression change from *I'm going to look delighted, whatever this is* to *I love this!*

At night, I told him we could watch whatever movie he wanted, and I wouldn't complain. He picked *Vertigo*, which was 10% interesting and 90% so boring I wanted to jump off a clock tower. It made me think about Mom.

I'm not sure why. It's not like Dad wants to concoct an elaborate plot to bump her off.

Monday, April 25

I wish I could move into the auditorium. I love the red velvet seats and the gold curtain. I love being quiet backstage. I love struggling to learn the choreography onstage, knowing that people are talking and eating candy down in the dressing rooms. I love it that Miss Murphy lost her mind that one time Olivia said "Macbeth" in the theater. I love that we're trapped here this week while everyone else is on spring break. I love it that we're not allowed to look at our phones anywhere in the theater and that people follow this rule. I love it that I don't think about Mom or Mac or the internet when I'm onstage.

Tuesday, April 26

Mac told me something surprising: he's not having sex with Sienna.

"She's Catholic," he said. "I get it. I'm Catholic too. Yeah, technically we're not supposed to do it before we get married. But at this point, we've been together for 10 months. It kind of feels like she doesn't trust me."

"Totally," I said.

"I would never cheat on her. I love her. We're good together. Did you know we got voted Class Couple? Yeah.

That's no joke. But think about it: How is the Class Couple not having sex?"

"Right."

"Prom is in less than two weeks," he said. "We're supposed to go, get wasted, and screw like rabbits at the after-party, right? But instead I'll get another hand job. Whoop-de-doo. She's denying me a classic high school experience."

"What's wrong with . . . hand jobs?" I said. I could hardly get the words out.

"They're great if you're in seventh grade. I'm 18 years old!"

"Yeah," I said. Via my tone of voice, I tried to give the impression that I'm extremely knowledgeable about penises and know everything about hand jobs and sexual intercourse.

"I wish we were going to prom," he said.

My entire blood supply shot to my ears, and I heard the ocean. "Me too," I said.

"What color dress would you wear?"

"Probably, um, probably green. That's my favorite color."

"You'd look hot as hell in a green dress. I could sneak you in in my back pocket, you're so tiny. Are you a good dancer?"

"I'm OK."

"We'd dance every slow dance together. What would you want to drink?"

"Rum and Coke."

"I'd bring you some rum in my flask. And afterward we'd go to Walsh's beach house and sleep on the sand in the same sleeping bag."

"OK. I mean, I want to."

"Me too. In another world, we could."

I wanted to ask him what was stopping us from doing it in this world, but I didn't have the courage.

Did we have phone sex??

Wednesday, April 27

I bumped into Hannah backstage, by the props table.

"Oh, hello! How are you?" I said.

"Fine. How are you?"

"Great!"

Silence fell. What did we used to talk about?

Leo, the stage manager, bustled over with a long roll of paper and a Sharpie. He unfurled the paper, put my hand mirror on it, traced around it with the Sharpie, and wrote "MIRROR" in the middle of the trace. "I'm doing this with every single prop," he announced, as if someone had asked him. "That way I'll know at a glance when something goes missing." He glared at me.

"Leo, it's not like I lost the mirror," I said. "I'd just eaten a poppy-seed bagel and I had to check my teeth. It's my prop!"

"It's the theater club's prop," he said.

I pretended to be annoyed, but in fact I wanted to hug Leo for interrupting my horribly polite conversation with Hannah.

Thursday, April 28
Email from Mom.

> Darling bunny rabbit! Please forgive my prolonged silence. I've been doing a bit of traveling, researching my book. When you visit, we must go to the Cenotes Dos Ojos, otherworldly caves flooded with bright-turquoise water. I'm thinking seriously about getting my scuba license. Sometimes snorkeling simply isn't enough (did you ever think I'd type *that* sentence? Ha! Ha!). A newlywed on my excursion lost her engagement ring in the water. Her sobs resounded through the echoey chamber.
>
> Well, sweetheart, I think of you constantly and wonder how you're progressing with your studies, your admirers, and your musical.
>
> Please do write.
>
> Your mommy

Friday, April 29

Dear Mom,

I miss you! A lot has happened since we last
talked. Mac's my best friend now! Well, tied
for best friendship with Tristan. We talk on the
phone alllllll the time and we really understand
each other. He is a kindred spirit.

The show opens in two weeks (Friday the 13th!),
and guess what? The last show falls on my
birthday! (May 22nd, in case you forgot, haha.)
DON'T wish me luck. Wish me a broken leg! (Miss
Murphy, our director, is big on superstitions.)

Hasta pronto,
Chloe

Ugh. Reread it right after I sent it and noticed all the
exclamation points.

Saturday, April 30

I woke up this morning to find Tris sitting on my bed,
staring at me.

"Are you real?" I said. My voice sounded creaky.

"Why wouldn't I be?"

"It's a ghosty thing to do, staring at someone who's trying to sleep."

"I told your dad it was an emergency, so he said I could come up." He put his head in his hands. "My mom found the Nordstrom charge on her credit card statement."

I sat up. "What? For the tux?"

"She asked me what I bought—not accusing me, just asking—and I panicked and told her the truth, that I bought a tux because I'm going to the prom, and she was like, 'You're going to the senior prom? Who is this girl?' all suspicious, like maybe I'm being statutorily raped. So I was like, 'I'm going with my friend Roy, because . . . he . . . really wanted to go and . . . couldn't find a girl to go with,' and she got quiet and said, 'Oh,' and now I think she knows."

Snickers woke up with a jump. He looked surprised to see Tristan. He'd be a terrible guard dog.

"I don't know what to do," Tris said. "Should I tell her?"

"I guess you could. But what if she tells your dad? What if they go completely insane and take away your college tuition or something because they're so angry that you're gay? I mean, is it possible they could be that crazy?"

"I don't think so. But I don't know! Maybe. OK. I can't tell her. I know that."

He flopped down on the bed. Snickers and I scooched over to make room for him.

"I'm only even considering it because of Roy's parents," he said.

"What do you mean?"

"They keep bugging me to come out. They get hysterical with joy whenever I go over to their house. They make stir-frys and tell me, 'Oh, we spent our twenties in Brooklyn, we had sooooo many gay friends in those days, and oh, Roy's grandfather was almost certainly gay, so there may be a genetic component.' Then they split a bottle of wine and get all hushed and ask me how things are going with my parents and if I've 'made any progress there.'"

"What does Roy do?"

"Rolls his eyes and tells them to stop, but they ignore him."

"What do you say when they ask about your parents?"

"I say, 'Not yet,' and they look disappointed. They're dying for me to say I told them and they beat me up and then locked me in the basement. They would love that. I guarantee they would ask me to move in with them." He sighed. "I shouldn't complain. They're, like, gay advocates or whatever. But when they start getting sympathetic about my parents, I want to run out of the room screaming. Even though I *hate* my stupid bigot parents!"

"Yeah."

"I wish I didn't have to think about who thinks being gay is evil and who thinks it's wonderful and wishes everyone was gay and who's calling me a fag in the hall because he's gay and scared about it."

I have some nerve being upset about my mother and my stupid non-boyfriend.

Sunday, May 1

Maria has it easy. She doesn't have to lift a finger to break up the baroness and the captain. The baroness does all the hard work for her by grossing out the captain with her evil views. Maria gets to marry him with a clear conscience.

Monday, May 2

Miss Murphy sat us down today and said, "Tech Week starts this Sunday."

Half the kids groaned.

"Silence, worms," Miss Murphy said in an English accent. Then she switched back to her regular voice. "For those of you who don't know, this is the time when we make sure everything's working together—the costumes, the lighting, the sound, the props, the scenery, the hair and makeup. We'll start at 11 a.m. on Sunday with a double run-through. Monday is cue to cue. Tuesday is tech rehearsal. Wednesday is dress rehearsal. Thursday is your day off, and Friday is opening night. If you have questions about any of these terms, please ask an upperclassman or Bing it on Google." (That's Miss Murphy's classic joke about being a clueless adult. It always gets a laugh. I happen to know she stole it from a comedy podcast, but I would never tattle on her, because, after all, who among us makes up all her own jokes?)

Then we ran act 1 in its entirety, which took about seven hours, because half the cast isn't off book yet. Hell Week should be wonderful.

Tuesday, May 3

Something happened today. Something serious. I still can't believe it.

It started when I skipped class for the first time in my life. Mac came to my locker after third period and whispered, "Meet me in the parking lot in 10 minutes." So I did! I kind of thought that when I walked out the door, an alarm would sound and child catchers would jump out of the bushes with nets, but nothing happened.

We got in his truck. A few people saw, but no one important.

We didn't go anywhere special, just to the pizza

place. I got a small Hawaiian, which he said is disgusting, and I said, "Don't yuck my yum," which is what my preschool teacher used to say whenever we *ewwww*ed each other.

That's not important. Forget the pizza and the preschool. What's important is what happened after we got back in the truck. He said, "You don't have to go back, right?" and I said I didn't, even though I was petrified about missing an entire afternoon of classes. So we drove around in his truck, all the way to the next town, listening to music and talking. We were on a back road and I was telling him how much I hate horror movies when he reached over and put his hand on my leg. I kept talking for a while, but then I shut up and reached over and touched his neck. *I'm touching his neck!* I thought, but even as I was doing it and thinking about it, it seemed impossible that it was really happening. Time had slowed down, or maybe it had sped up. Mac ran his fingers along my knee and up underneath my skirt, and I think that's when I started panting. I couldn't help myself. No one's ever touched my inner thigh before, and it sent a blue line of electricity shooting around my body. It was better than anything I've ever felt before, that blue line. I would give up food and music and sleep to feel it all the time.

He pulled over and we were staring at each other and running our hands over each other's legs and arms. I was insane with horniness. I'd kissed one guy before, ONE, but all of a sudden I'd crossed the river and landed on the other side a different person, and all I could think about was, *Sex, sex, sex, sex, sex, I want to have sex with this person RIGHT NOW.*

He said, "Shit, what do we do?"

"I don't know," I said. "It's your decision." I could hardly talk, I was so turned on, and excited, and scared. *He's supposed to be your friend*, I told myself. *He has a girl-friend. You can't be with him.* But Sienna seemed far away and abstract compared to the reality of Mac sitting next to me. Then he put his hand on my face and ran his thumb over my lower lip, and the blue line came back. I knew I shouldn't, but I couldn't help it: I took off my seat belt and crawled onto his lap, and we were kissing, really kissing. His whole tongue was in my mouth, and I wanted to bite it off and eat it like a piece of watermelon, and then he licked my ear and I rubbed up against him over his pants.

"Wait, wait, wait," he said.

I touched his chest (firm but springy, like a mattress), his face (sharp with stubble), his eyebrows (a little damp), his collarbone (more pronounced than mine).

"Stop for a sec," he said.

I didn't want to stop. It was like I'd had earplugs in all year, and now they were out and I could learn him like a language.

"I have a girlfriend," he said.

"I *know*."

"We shouldn't do this." He slid me back to my side, then stared at me, then banged his forehead against the steering wheel.

He drove me back in time for rehearsal. Before I got out of the truck, he kissed my hand and bit my knuckles. Not hard.

Now that I'm writing about it, and remembering it, I can't believe I was dry-humping Mac in his truck a few hours ago, but at the time it was like I'd taken a drug that wiped away my anxious, analytical thoughts. I had my five senses and they were flooded with Mac, but my consciousness had turned off, and it felt so good. I disappeared from myself and turned into a pure body, like an animal. Oh, I hope, I hope, I hope I get to do it again.

Wednesday, May 4

Tris and I had almost nothing to do at rehearsal today, since Miss Murphy was putting the nuns through their paces. We sat in the basement eating rainbow Goldfish and talking about boys.

"I would never guess he'd be the one to stop it," Tris said.

"Everyone thinks he's this big horrible jock, but he's nice. He's super Catholic!"

"Only you know the real Macintyre Brody?"

"Yeah! Don't roll your eyes."

"Will you at least admit that you don't just want to be his friend?"

I snipped off a Goldfish tail with my fingernails. "Fine. I want to marry him, OK? I do. I want him to dump Sienna and take me to prom and then date me all through college. Even if he cheats on me a few times at parties, I won't mind. Then he'll get drafted and realize how lucky he is: he never has to worry that his girlfriend is only with him because he's a famous millionaire athlete. I'll be on Broadway, and when we get married, our wedding will get a little blurb in *Us Weekly*. Not the cover or anything—I'm not crazy!"

"You're *crazy*," Tristan said. "He's never going to dump Sienna."

"He might!"

Tris folded a foundation sponge in half. "I don't get the point of this. Don't you want to go out with someone you can actually mess around with?"

I thought about it. I mean, yes! I'm horny all. The. Time. All the time! I get turned on from the motion of walking around, and from, like, how soft Snickers's fur is, and the fact that there are tiny green leaves on the trees now. Anything! And being around Mac makes it so much worse, which feels so good. Just the smell of his breath! And the smell of his skin! Mac is like a cheeseburger with fries, and all the other guys at school are like withered baby carrots. Even if I can't have the cheeseburger, I'm not going to eat the carrots.

"I want to go out with Mac," I said.

Thursday, May 5

He came to my locker after school.

"We should talk," he said. "Do you have rehearsal?"

"Uh, no." I did have rehearsal. I've never missed rehearsal. I texted Tris.

> *Will you tell miss m I have food poisoning?*

What are you doing??

> *Will explain later, will you tell her?*

Oh god ok fine

We went to Mac's house. Or, not his house, his mom's condo. It's not *that* bad. It's small, and some of the cabinets are crooked, but it's sunny. She wasn't there, but on the fridge there was a picture of her standing next to a

Christmas tree, smiling up at a guy with a big gray mustache connected to a gray beard. "Who's that?" I asked Mac, tapping the guy, and he said "That's Steve" in the same tone of voice you'd say "That's Osama bin Laden." I decided not to ask him anything else.

We went into his bedroom. Here are some of the things in it:

1. A poster of a girl kneeling on the beach with one hand in her mouth and the other one on her cooch, wearing bikini bottoms and a wet sweater (a *wet* sweater, could there be anything more uncomfortable?) with her nipples showing through the open weave
2. A thousand empty Mountain Dew bottles
3. Maroon sheets and a black bedspread
4. Some kind of Xbox or other video game thingy I know nothing about
5. A fish tank with piranhas inside (!)
6. A little photo album that I flipped through immediately. It had a bunch of pictures of Mac as a little kid, mostly official football portraits. He had big biceps even at age seven.

When I write out this list, it sounds not-great. But at the time something about it made me want to take off my pants and get pregnant. Maybe I have a hormonal imbalance.

I sat on his bed. He sat at his desk.

"OK," he said. "We made out yesterday."

"Right," I said. I tried to sound businesslike, because he did.

"Nothing *really* happened."

"No," I said, even though to me, everything had happened.

"And we won't mention it to anyone."

"Definitely not."

"It's not that I think we did something bad."

"Right."

"But Sienna's my girlfriend, and I'm going to be faithful to her."

My blood got cold. "OK."

"Don't say it like that! I'm so attracted to you, you have no idea. No idea." He scrubbed his hands over his face. "When I'm with her, I feel so sure that I love her, but when I'm with you, I forget."

I looked at his pillow. Lucky pillow, to feel his face every night. "I understand," I said.

He came and sat next to me on the bed. Right next to me.

"You can't talk in that quiet voice," he said. "It's too cute."

"OK," I said, and then I started to cry a little, because

I felt so sorry for myself, because I was never going to be Mac's girlfriend, and then he leaned down and kissed me on the mouth, and soon we were lying on his bed grinding against each other like only dry-humping would save the world from an apocalypse, and then he was sitting up again and saying, "What are we doing, Chloe?" and walking around the room in a circle clutching his forehead.

He kissed me again when he was dropping me off, and this time he put his hand up my shirt.

Friday, May 6

Mac came up to my locker before homeroom and said, "Take my bracelet off me, OK?"

"Why?" I said, as I undid the clasp.

"Wear it tomorrow while I'm at the prom and think about me."

He squeezed the back of my neck and walked away. I looked down at the bracelet. It's three strands of braided leather held together with a fishhook. I know where it came from, because he told me on the phone one night: his junior high coach gave it to him after they won the championships. I will guard this bracelet with my life.

Saturday, May 7

Prom is happening right now, as I type. Here are the texts I've gotten so far.

Mac

At pre prom at bernadette's.
Good thing you didn't come, one
of the senior girls would have
pushed you into the pool

> *The joke would be on her*
> *because I love swimming*

Tris

Roy's parents took one million
pics of us. So embarrassing

> *I know, they tagged you in*
> *everything on fb, i'm looking*
> *at you right now. You are so*
> *handsome in your tux!*

I have some news about parents,
will tell you tomorrow

> *Ok. A cliffhanger!*

Mac

I'm not getting in that
photobooth

Tell sienna, not me

*Can't you come here and
save me?*

Tris

*We just slow danced
and everyone stared
even though we were
standing at arms length
jr high style*

*Our school = westboro
baptist church*

*No ones said anything
yet but im scared
someone will*

Mac

*If you see tristan flynn, will
you say hi to him?*

Not sure who that is

Urgh

Tris

Ginny benson just won prom
queen

But her hair is cut into a square!

Someone told me the teachers
are the ones who vote

That explains it

Will you keep texting me til roy
gets back from the bathroom?

His friends scare me

Sure. Tell me what Hannah's
doing

She's feeding Josh a piece of
chicken from her fork

What's sienna doing?

Looking stressed out and staring
at mac. He's on his phone.

Mac

I'm dancing with you

What do you mean?

I'm listening to a slow song
and thinking about dancing
with you

<3 <3 <3 <3 <3 <3

Tris

The after-prom party is the best
part so far. I just put on my
comfy pants!

I've been wearing my comfy
pants all night. You mad?

Mac

How's the after-party?

Ok, you're probably busy
getting wasted

Good night xxoo

Sunday, May 8

Tris's parent news is, he came out to his mom! It happened the morning of prom when she was driving him to pick up his boutonniere. She asked him if his friend would be coming to the house, and Tris said no, they were meeting at a pre-prom party, and could he have a ride? And his mom said of course, and would it be OK if she came for a while and took a few pictures? Of Tris and his . . . friend?

"It felt like an action movie, like we both had guns and were like, 'Drop it!' 'You first!' And then she said, 'If you have anything you want to tell me . . . I mean, I hope you know you can confide in me. . . . What I'm trying to say is, I love you so much, and your dad . . .' And then she started crying and I couldn't take it anymore, so I was like, 'Roy's my boyfriend,' and then we both started crying so hard she had to pull over, and we hugged each other in the Subway parking lot."

"So it was perfect!"

"It was mostly perfect. I asked if Dad knew too, and she said no, and we shouldn't tell him yet, because he's going through such a stressful time at work, so I got mad at her and asked why she's always making up excuses for him like I'll believe them, doesn't she know he's a disgusting bigot? And she said she knows he's difficult in some ways, but he's my father and I can't talk about him that way. But then we went inside and got a breakfast sandwich and talked about the prom, and it was nice again."

I wanted to talk about his dad more, but he was too impatient to give me his prom notes, which were as follows:

1. Pre-prom was more fun than prom. Everyone rolled their eyes and pretended to hate all the pictures, but actually, it felt great having paparazzi, even if they were parents. Plus the whole night was still to come and potentially magical, which was exciting.
2. The dinner was mashed potatoes, green beans, and miniature chickens with their tiny cooked legs sticking straight out.
3. Tris couldn't enjoy his food because of the tiny legs and because he gets so stressed out around Roy's friends, worrying that they think he's boring and too young.
4. It was a Roaring Twenties theme, which meant a couple of ropes of plastic beads on the tables and black and gold balloons in the corners of the ballroom.
5. The DJ played only Top 40 music, and everyone knew all the words even though everyone pretends to hate pop.

6. There were two other gay couples there: Craig and Noam, who are seniors and go to Renaissance Faires on the weekends and don't seem to be aware of the existence of anyone else at our high school, and Mikala and Beth, who probably met in one of their 16 AP classes. Tris couldn't relax and have fun because he felt so nervous. Roy was like, "It's fine. No one cares what we do," and Tris was like, "Everyone's staring at us and some people are laughing, plus it's easy for you to be relaxed; you're leaving in a few months." No one said anything openly awful to them, but some people said accidentally awful stuff, like, "You guys are soooooooo cute!"

7. He and Roy stayed up all night at a theater kid's after-party, and Tris had two beers. The most stressful part was worrying that he had morning breath at 5 a.m. The best part was eating four pieces of pizza because he was starving from boycotting the miniature chicken.

He told me all this during our break in the double run-through. Speaking of the double run-through, it was absolute garbage. The first time was bad; the second time was terrible. Ursula tripped and dropped the tray of pastries into the orchestra pit. Liesl messed up her choreography and stood there looking shocked while the music kept going. When Josh slammed a door shut, the entire wall tipped over and landed in the wings. I forgot two lines, and during "The Lonely Goatherd," I panicked and couldn't remember what came next (it should have been "Men in the midst of a table d'hote") and sang "la la di da dum dee da doo da da" instead.

Miss Murphy didn't even give us notes afterward. She said, in a sad voice, "Tomorrow is a new day with no mistakes in it," which I recognized from *Anne of Green Gables*, but somehow it didn't seem like the right moment to show off.

Monday, May 9

I thought cue to cue would be an easy rehearsal, since we only have to say the lines that cue a lighting or sound change. Well . . . hahahahahahahahaha! I didn't get home until midnight. Little did I realize we'd have to do the excerpts of each scene approximately 396,145,882 times due to unexpected blackouts, mic feedback like an ice pick in your ear, Oscar the lighting guy adjusting his spots while yelling, "Bear with me, folks!" and a bunch of tiny fixes I didn't understand that are apparently crucial. All the actors had to do was stand around and occasionally say some lines in a monotone, since our performances were beside the point of the rehearsal. I had plenty of time to think about Mac's huge hands, and his low voice, and his cute earlobes, and the way it felt to grind against him on his bed, which is the way I imagine heroin makes you feel, like the Milky Way is running through your veins and your whole body has turned into a big beating heart.

Tuesday, May 10

Finally talked to Mac tonight after rehearsal.

"I miss you!" I said. "Sorry we haven't talked in so long. It's Tech Week, so everyone's acting like we're on the brink of curing cancer."

"That's OK."

"Tell me about prom!"

"I texted you."

"Tell me again."

"It was OK."

"Did Sienna look beautiful?" (She did. I'd seen hundreds of pictures of her on Instagram. She was wearing a short red dress and Vans, and her legs looked miles long.)

"She looked nice."

"Is everything OK?"

"Yeah, I'm just tired. Too much partying."

He sounded strange. Not like himself.

Wednesday, May 11

Theater kids still gross me out sometimes. I mean, yes, it's hard to get your homework done when you're in rehearsals all afternoon and night, and yes, Miss Murphy yells at us sometimes, but do they have to be so melodramatic? "I've *literally* never been so stressed out." "Is the spotlight floating around, or am I getting a migraine?" "I don't think she realizes how much pressure I'm under. Like, between yearbook and SAT prep and this, I'm beyond overscheduled." "First Leo screamed at me for falling asleep on the garden puff; now the vending machine is out of Twizzlers. I can't work like this!" OK, that last one was me.

Thursday, May 12

I wish we didn't have today off from rehearsal. There's too much time to think. All my teachers told me to break a leg, and a few of them are even coming tomorrow night. It never occurred to me that they would show up! I guess there's nothing else to do in the Town That Time Forgot. It almost makes me cry, thinking of Mr. Hicks sitting in the dark watching his students strutting around in lederhosen when he could be wearing pajamas and streaming a Ken Burns documentary, or whatever it is teachers like to stream. What if I forget the words again? That freaking lonely goatherd!! Or what if my stage fright makes me shy and quiet? What if I drop a prop, or miss an entrance, or start laughing when Josh says "deep inside me," or skip a section, or dance left when everyone else is dancing right? What if everyone tells me how great I was to my face but then gossips about how terrible I was behind my back, and says, "What did Miss Murphy expect, casting a freshman?" What if I embarrass her and my dad? What if Mac thinks I'm ridiculous?

Friday, May 13

This was the happiest day of my life so far.

I wasn't scared! Well, no, I was terrified all day, and right through the vocal warm-ups and the part where we stand in a big circle and squeeze each other's hands in a chain, to pass the energy around. And then, the worst part of all, standing in the wings before the curtain went up. I'm used to rehearsals, when the seats are empty and all the action is on the stage. It was so bizarre to be backstage and hear the audience out there, talking and laughing and rustling their programs.

Waiting in the wings for the first scene to end was torture. I was thinking, *Approximately 3 minutes until I go on, now 2 minutes and 50 seconds, why didn't I pee one more time, I'm so lazy, now 2 minutes and 40 seconds, are these fake eyelashes going to pop right off, whoa, the audience actually laughed in the right place, I'm going on so soon, so soon, any second now,* and then the abbey scene was over and the lights came down, the curtain closed, and I ran out to lie down onstage and pretend I was relaxing on a mountain.

The first line of "The Sound of Music" came out clear and strong, and after that I knew it would be OK, and it was.

I was excited, and (embarrassing to say) happy to be showing off my voice and my acting. I didn't think about specific people watching me—not even Mac. I could hear people in the audience clearing their throats and shifting around in their seats. But they were in pitch-blackness and I was in the light. And that made all the difference, not being able to see anyone's face. It turned the audience into one big thing, like a hive. And under the spotlight, I felt like one big thing too, like I was a match for this organism watching me.

Everyone was hysterical in the dressing room after the show, screaming and laughing. Miss Murphy came in and told us, in a serious voice, how good we were and how proud of us she was. Hannah and I hugged each other and it felt completely normal. Tris picked me up and spun me around until my legs were parallel with the floor. When I went to the auditorium, a little girl, probably 10 years old, asked me to autograph her program!!!!!!!!!! And my dad was there with a big bouquet of pink flowers (I don't know what kind; I'm not a gardener). Mac couldn't come to the dressing room because he'd seen the show with Sienna and a bunch of other seniors, but he texted me, *You were Broadway good kid*. Miss Murphy came up, and my dad pulled out a second bouquet of flowers for her, almost as big as mine, and she said, "Oh, wow," and then to me, "Your dad's a pretty nice guy," and I only died of embarrassment slightly, because there weren't many people around to notice that my father was creeping on Miss Murphy.

We drove home just the two of us, like normal. I didn't want to listen to the radio, because it would have erased the musical music. My face was still covered in globs of makeup, and my hair was full of gel and hair spray. I made Dad tell me, in detail, everything he liked about the show and my performance, because you can be a narcissist with your parents and not feel embarrassed. When we got home, he ordered pizza, which he *never* does (too cheap), and he let me have a tiny glass of champagne.

Saturday, May 14

Second show, survived! I felt exactly like a Broadway star, arriving with my coffee, drained from last night's performance but ready to leave my heart on the stage again, because that's what actors *do*, darling. It's in our *blood*.

I could get into this flopping-around-and-being-melodramatic thing. Especially when I get to be 80 years old and I can wear a turban and put my cigarettes in a holder, like that lady in *Bullets over Broadway.*

Tris and I ate coconut M&M's while we did our makeup and talked about last night's show and who dropped lines and who keeps stealing focus by making simpering cutie-pie faces in the background (GRETL) and how terrifying it is every time Josh/Captain von Trapp slams the door and we wait in fear for the wall to collapse. I could talk to Tristan about the show for probably five hours in a row and never get bored. He always has something interesting to say, and he understands everything *I* say, because we've been in almost every single rehearsal together, so we have all the same references. Sometimes I still wish he could be my boyfriend. But it's probably bigoted even to think that.

The second show went better than the first. Everyone was relaxed, and we got bigger laughs. Maybe the best part is the curtain call. I stand backstage knowing that the show's over and I didn't mess up. Everyone in the cast runs out in reverse order of importance. The nuns and the party guests, Frau Schmidt and Franz, Herr Zeller, etc., etc., then the kids, and when it gets to Mother Abbess and Captain von Trapp, my heart really starts pounding. And then, at the very end, it's ME! I run out, stand in the middle of the cast, and bow. And people yell for me!

Dad came again tonight. Mac didn't. I looked for Mom in the audience, but of course she wasn't there. I mean, duh.

I think she might come to the last show. If she's coming at all! Which she's definitely not. But since the last show falls on my birthday, maybe she'd want to surprise me. But I can't get my hopes up. They're not up. I mean, I don't even CARE! Whatever. Whatever!

Sunday, May 15

Matinees should be called *flat*inees. The first two shows were like star-shaped helium balloons. Today's was like a small hot-dog-shaped balloon you keep blowing up halfway only to have it sputter out of your lips and land on the floor. It feels unnatural, going into the windowless dressing room caves and then the windowless auditorium when it's sunny out and the air smells like blue sky and new grass. Before we went on, I thought, *Who are all these nice weirdos, paying to sit inside and watch us on a perfect May Sunday?* One of those weirdos was my dad. It's so dadly of him to go to every single show and sit in the front row, where I can see him doing a one-man standing ovation during the curtain call.

I texted Mac to see if he could hang out after the show, but he had plans. It's starting to feel weird, that we've gone so long without seeing each other. Maybe he's mad at me for being so busy with the show. I really want to see him. I bet as soon as we're alone together, everything will be OK.

Monday, May 16
Something about math class is conducive to deep thinking. As I listen to the soothing drone of Mr. Hicks, I let my mind relax. It's like a spa for my brain. Today I was thinking about how happy I am. Spring is here. I'm the lead in the school musical. I'm probably going to spend the summer in Mexico. Snickers's night farting seems to have improved recently. Mac wanted to go to prom with me. Everything's perfect.

But then I thought: Is it? Why haven't I seen Mac since the day he gave me the bracelet? Shouldn't we be making out in his room? He took the wrong person to prom and he knows it—his texts prove it. Why isn't he dumping Sienna to be with me, his one true love?

Tuesday, May 17
When I turned the corner into the senior wing today, I saw Sienna at her locker at the end of the hall. She was trying to put her hair in a ponytail, and Mac was saying, "Here, let me help you," and rubbing his hands all over her head while she laughed and tried to swat him away. It was disgusting. I walked past them like a robot, keeping my eyes straight ahead.

After school I worked up my courage and called Mac. "I feel like I haven't seen you in a year," I said.

"I'm sorry, kid," he said. "I've been hanging with my brosefs. It's senior year; I only have a few more months with these guys."

I said, "You only have a few more months with *me*, too." I tried to sound jokey, but it came out sounding serious.

"True," he said.

I asked him if everything was OK and he said yeah, of course.

I keep going over our conversation in my mind. Sometimes I can convince myself that he meant everything he said. Then I replay it, and I think no, he's different. Something's changed. I feel sick.

Should I call him again? No! Of course not. That would be crazy—I'd only make things worse.

But maybe if I called him, we'd laugh about how awkward our last conversation was, and he'd suggest going out for pancakes.

No, he wouldn't. If I called him, he wouldn't pick up, and then I'd accidentally leave a desperate voicemail, and then I'd obsess over the voicemail for three hours, and then I'd text him a funny GIF that he wouldn't respond to, and then I'd never be able to fall asleep.

Wednesday, May 18

When I got to the theater for the one rehearsal we have this week, Olivia said, "So what are you doing?"

"Um . . . walking to the dressing room."

"I mean, do you have anything planned for the run-through?"

She must have been able to tell from the look on my face that I had no idea what she was talking about. "Today's the goofy run-through. Everyone does bits, makes jokes? It's a tradition. You really didn't know?"

I marched off to yell at Josh for not warning me. He was in the guys' dressing room, ironing his uniform.

"Are we supposed to do, like, a comedy routine?"

"Chloe, there's no need to panic."

"Do you have something planned?"

"If I did, I wouldn't tell you. The idea is to cause you to corpse."

"What, like pretend to be dead?"

"To corpse is to laugh uncontrollably onstage. It's a British expression. You remember, we corpsed when . . ."

"Don't even say it."

The nuns twerked during "Dixit Dominus." Kurt delivered all of his lines in a Cockney accent. Tris sang Liesl's parts during "Sixteen Going on Seventeen," and she sang his. Josh got me in act 2, scene 1. He turned to watch the baroness walk away, and when he turned back around, he was wearing black glasses with a fake nose and mustache attached. I don't think I've ever laughed so hard. Why? It was only medium-funny. But the shock and horror of him surprising me during a scene, and the terror of imagining him doing something like that during a live show, made me hysterical.

Act 2 was almost over, and I couldn't think of a good gag. In a panic, at the last minute, I pulled off my jeans right before the wedding procession and entered in my underpants, which might sound very daring, but you have to remember (a) I have the physique of an 11-year-old boy and (b) everyone in the show has seen me in my underpants in the dressing room approximately 4,927,053 times. Still, I was wearing a pair of vintage Hannah Montana undies, and I got a big laugh.

Thursday, May 19

Three more shows and then it's all over. I'm pre-depressed just thinking about it. I don't even want to record this, because it's so embarrassing, but I think maybe I really want to do this with my life. Be a theater geek. I know no one makes it, but even if I wound up in the back row of a few off-off-off-Broadway shows, it would be enough. I could wait tables to make rent money, and audition with Tris, and become hardened and cynical. Or maybe

Mac will be a billionaire NFL player by then, and he can underwrite my lifestyle.

I called Mac today, but he didn't pick up. I texted him *I miss you* and then immediately regretted it and sent him a smiling poop emoji to try to undo the damage, which of course only doubled my regret.

He couldn't fall out of love with me this fast, right? I mean, what could have changed between him texting *Can't you come here and save me* from the prom and today?

I have to stay calm and happy and upbeat. Maybe nothing's wrong at all, and this is all in my head. Maybe we'll be messing around in his truck by tomorrow night, and I'll feel stupid for getting so worked up over nothing.

Oh, I adore him, I love him. I can't stand not knowing what he's thinking. I can't stand sitting here, waiting to find out what's happening. I want to know the worst now, and get it over with. I want to call him and say, "Tell me. Whatever it is, tell me," but what if he pretends not to know what I'm talking about? That would be even worse than this torture.

Friday, May 20

What an idiot I am. What a clueless, naive, unobservant garbage-brain.

I was late coming up after the show because I lost my

phone, and it took me 40 minutes to find it. (Josh had seen it lying on the counter and put it in the lost-and-found box, like a sociopath, but that's not important.) When I finally ran up, Dad was sitting in the auditorium. He was wearing work pants, a blue shirt, and a dark-red tie with white flecks on it.

I was in the middle of apologizing when the double doors thunked open, and Miss Murphy came through. "You guys are still here?" she said.

I patted my pockets and tore through my backpack. "Um. Dad. I think I lost my earbuds, too."

He groaned. "Chlo, come on."

"Sorry! Can I run down really quick and look?" It felt like a matter of life and death to find them before I left.

"Hurry up, then."

I ran up the steps and across the stage. I was deep in the wings, about to pull open the trapdoor, when I thought to look in the front pocket of my backpack, and there were my earbuds, coiled up. Feeling relieved, I walked fast back onto the stage, about to yell, "It's OK!" when I saw them. Dad and Miss Murphy, with their arms around each other. He was laughing and his eyes were closed. He looked so happy.

I must have made a sound, because they both looked up at me like I was the monster in a horror movie. Then they jumped apart. Oh, it made me so angry, how scared and guilty they looked.

I walked across the stage, down the stairs, and past them. I heard them murmuring to each other, which doubled my rage. How dare they confer with each other about how to handle me and what to do?

"Chloe," Dad called. His voice was pretty normal. Low, steady, calm.

I didn't stop and I didn't turn around. Outside, it was chilly. Orion stood in the sky. A car raced by with hip-hop thumping. I could hear kids laughing; they must have had the windows rolled down. Probably they were all products of unbroken homes, carefree and happy, on their way to a party.

I considered walking home, or to Tristan's, but what was the point? It would only delay the inevitable showdown.

I waited by the car for a few minutes before he showed up. He unlocked the doors and we got inside without speaking. He put the key in the ignition but didn't turn it.

"I'm sorry," he said.

"About what?" I thought I was mad, but as soon as I started to talk, I realized I was about to cry.

He rubbed his forehead. "Several things."

"Miss Murphy . . ." I had to stop, because my voice was wobbling when I wanted it to sound like a knife.

"I'm very sorry you found out like that just now. I

haven't told you because I didn't know what to say, and I didn't want to upset you. Maybe that wasn't right." He put his hands on the steering wheel. "You know your mother and I have been having some trouble."

"Oh yeah? I hadn't noticed."

"Don't be sarcastic, Chloe." Even after he'd been caught in a criminal act, he expected me to have good manners. It made me want to put my fist through the window.

"I don't want to talk about this," I said.

A pause. "We can talk about it later. But we do have to talk about it."

When we'd pulled into the garage, I said, "Do you love Miss Murphy or something?"

He turned off the engine and looked out the window at nothing, at the side of the garage. "I care about her."

We sat there in silence for a minute. Then I got out of the car and ran inside.

I have to think about this carefully. I want to know exactly what's been going on, but I don't want to talk to him, and I don't want to ask him any questions about *sex* or *love*. Oh God, even typing those words in conjunction with Dad makes me start sweating. I wish someone would hand me a book and say, "I've written an exhaustive investigative report on your father and Miss Murphy. Read this and you'll understand everything."

I've been looking at my phone, checking for vids and pics and hearts and likes and reblogs and snaps. Usually that distracts me from anything, even the worst pain. But it's not working tonight. Even new notifications aren't giving my brain its dopamine shot.

Saturday, May 21
second alast show nad so sad. and so sad about everything dad mom miss mpuryp. wnat mac to love me i think he loves me so who cares lets tell thew howe world! walking homne i really thought about eveytrhing and figued it out but too tired drunk to write now will rembmer in mornig

Sunday, May 22
Worst day of my life. Hungover. No Mom. Last show. Booed during the curtain call. It's my birthday today. Happy birthday to me.

Monday, May 23
Dad let me stay home from school. "Let me" isn't the right term. When he came to see why I wasn't up, I refused to roll over. I stared at the wall and said, "I'm sick." He hovered for a minute, but then said, "OK. I hope you feel better," and left. Is he going to start letting me get away with murder because he feels so guilty?

Because I don't *want* to get away with murder. I want everything to go back to the way it was.

Here's what happened this weekend. On Saturday morning, I snapped awake at 5 a.m. and couldn't get back to sleep. I hid in my room until 10, but all I could find to eat were some old Pop-Tarts, and finally starvation drove me down to the kitchen.

"Good morning," Dad said.

"I don't want to talk, OK? I have the show tonight, and I don't want to get distracted."

He looked at me. "Fair enough."

He was sitting at the kitchen table reading the paper, like he always does. It was enraging. How could he act like nothing was wrong, like the world hadn't exploded? He should have been, I don't know, lying facedown on the kitchen floor, crying. Not resting his elbows on the table and fiddling with his coffee cup.

The show was good. The show was great. I spent the warm-up smiling and laughing, to show Miss Murphy how completely fine I was. Being onstage felt like sitting in a hot tub while drinking a milkshake. As long as I was up there, I didn't have to think about my irresponsible, cheating parents, or that traitor Miss Murphy. Standing in the wings, all I wanted to do was get back in front of the audience so I could stop thinking.

Miss Murphy gave us notes afterward, like she always

does. It's usually one of my favorite parts of the day. It's fun to hear other people getting in trouble, especially for something you noticed they messed up. It's even fun to get in trouble yourself, because it means Miss Murphy was paying attention to you. She didn't say anything to me on Saturday. Once she made eye contact with me, then looked away fast. I tried to burn holes into her face with the power of my hatred.

As I was shoving Pond's cold cream into my backpack, Tris sat down on the counter in front of me. "What's going on? You've been acting really weird all day."

"Something bad."

"Tell me!"

"I will, but not right this second."

"How bad is it?"

I zipped up my backpack. "Not cancer or anything. It's, like, a seven."

Josh and Hannah walked up, and Josh stopped in front of us. "Do you two need a ride to the pits?"

Tris and I looked at each other. "What is that?" I asked Josh.

"Oh, these gravel pits way out near the pond. The seniors have parties there on occasion. You can play music quite loudly, as there are no residential neighborhoods in close proximity. Mac Brody actually dragged an all-weather couch to the location in the flatbed of his truck!"

"Is Mac going tonight?" I asked. I had to know, even if it meant irritating Hannah or making her suspicious. But she was looking at her phone, scrolling fast, and didn't seem to hear.

"I believe he is, yes. I heard him remonstrating with Sienna on the topic earlier today."

"What do you mean?"

"I hate to gossip, but I couldn't help hearing Sienna reminding him that she has plans to visit her grandmother this evening. She refused to entertain a change in plans, even when Mac said tonight's party is sure to be 'epic.'"

I could feel Tris looking at me sternly.

"We would love a ride," I said to Josh.

Hannah couldn't go because she was hanging out with her grandmother, who'd come to see the show, so it was just me, Tris, and Josh. I didn't talk much on the way over. We passed the arboretum, the church in the town center, one of the less-depressing strip malls (the one with a Starbucks), the rows of trees lined with small green leaves—well, gray leaves, in the dark. I cracked my window so I could smell the spring night air. How many of these places had Dad visited with Miss Murphy? Or had they driven to restaurants in other towns? Does he ever really work late? All those times I was home alone with my homework done, trying to entertain myself watching twerking tutorials, was he DOING IT with her?

The pits were creepy and cool, I guess: huge holes in the ground with gravel stretching out around them for at least half a mile. It would be a good place to shoot an alien-planet scene in your low-budget indie movie. We walked up to where a bunch of juniors and seniors were clustered around the couch and sitting on folding beach chairs. Mac wasn't there. When they saw Josh, everyone whooped and cheered. No one said hi to me and Tris. I could feel him vibrating with tension by my side. Normally I would have been vibrating too, especially because I wasn't wearing what you could call a party outfit; in fact, I was wearing my comfy post-show uni consisting of a Tinker Bell sweatshirt and boot-cut yoga pants. But honestly, I did not give one single care. I didn't feel confident. I felt nothing. A bunch of upperclassmen were ignoring two freshmen? Whoop-de-doo. I'll alert the media. The seniors would be gone in a few months, someday we'd be seniors ourselves, and in the blink of an eye we'd all be dead anyway.

"Wait here," I told Tris, then went up to an older guy who wasn't laughing or talking to anyone and said, "Do you have any extra beer?"

He turned to look at me. "Hey, I know you. *Sound of Music*, right? My sister's in that show. Nadine."

"Right, yeah. Gretl."

That seemed to be all we had to say on that topic.

I could have told him Gretl intentionally pulls focus with distracting stage business, but I couldn't muster the energy.

He said, "No beer, but I've got some jungle juice, if you're interested."

"What is that?"

"Everclear, peach schnapps, and about 50 other ingredients. Secret recipe. Help yourself. It's behind that bush."

It was, in a huge orange cooler. I poured out two full cups and brought one over to Tris. He was still standing by himself, pretending to be conducting important business on his phone.

I handed him his jungle juice and he took a sip. "This tastes like someone mixed Hawaiian Punch with Sprite and then added a bunch of poison."

"What do roofies taste like?" I asked.

"Black licorice, probably."

"They don't teach us anything useful in health class. Well, if I crumple to the gravel in a few minutes, just push me into a pit."

"Is that a joke? Roofies aren't funny, Chloe. Are you OK? What's going on with you today?"

I told him. He didn't say "Oh my God, *then* what happened?" like a vulture, or make a dramatic sympathetic listening face, or say "I can't believe he did that" or even "I'm sorry," any of which would have annoyed me and made me stop talking. He listened, looking sometimes off into the distance, sometimes at the ground, and sometimes at my face. When I was done, he asked me how I felt, and I told him, and then neither of us said anything for a while. I could feel the jungle juice warming up my fingers, like a pair of mittens. A poisonous pair of mittens.

"My dad's the boring one," I said. "My mom's the wild one. They can't *both* be wild."

I hadn't thought of that before. It just came out of me because I was talking to Tristan. It's strange when that happens.

Tris nodded. "My mom's the quiet one, and my dad's the right-wing nutjob."

I sat in the gravel next to the bushes and got wasted. Jungle juice and more jungle juice, until my lips felt numb and Tris looked worried. He was attempting to pull my cup out of my hand when I spotted Mac walking toward the couch.

"He's here!" I scrambled up and brushed off my yoga pants. "Tris, do I look OK?"

"Do not go over there."

"Why *not?*" All I wanted was to feel Mac's strong arms around me, crushing me. I wanted to tell him about my dad and hear him call Miss Murphy some horrible dismissive word football players use. He would help me. He *loved* me! He'd kissed me! TWICE! This beautiful senior with the huge hands and the promising college football career talked to me every day, and texted me, and told me things he'd never told anyone. Me, a short freshman with hair the color of oatmeal. Gratitude filled me, and I started dashing across the gravel toward him. My legs felt so free! I was flying! If I could run drunk, I'd be a track and field star! *Stars.* The stars were burning overhead. You never look at the stars when you're in high school. You're too busy staring at your phone or panicking about your life to pay attention to the world. Why don't we go outside to admire the stars every single night?

When I got close to Mac, I jumped. He looked surprised, but he held out his arms and caught me. "Uh, hi," he said, setting me on my feet.

The smell of him! The perfection of him! I couldn't stand it! "I love you!" I said, and got up on my tiptoes and kissed him on the mouth.

He did not kiss me back.

When I opened my eyes, I saw that everyone was staring at us. Juniors. Seniors. Tristan. Bernadette, whose mouth was open in shock. Mac was the only one not looking at me. He was looking at Bernadette, and he looked panicked.

Without deciding to, I found myself backing up. It

turned out Tristan was holding me by the hand, pulling me away. I tried to make eye contact with Mac, but he was whispering with one of his football bros, Ivan. I knew I should feel awkward or upset, but it was like that moment right after you nick yourself shaving your legs but before you feel the sting. Like that moment, but it went on and on.

"Let's get s'more jungle juice," I said.

"You don't need any more drinks," Tris said.

"I'm fine." I tripped on some gravel, and Tris caught me. We were marching away from the pits, toward the road.

"Where are we going?" I said.

"I don't have a plan. It seemed like we needed to make an exit, and I don't see Josh anywhere."

"Was that really, really bard? Bad, I mean? Was it really bad?"

"It wasn't great."

I laughed. This was amazing! I could make an ass of myself in front of the cool upperclassmen and then laugh about it! Why hadn't I ever gotten drunk before?

Tris was shaking his head with his mouth in a straight line.

"You look like Bert," I said. "Remember Bert and Ernie? My dad and I used to watch *Sesame Street* all the time, like, when I was way too old for it. No one else our age even watched that show. It's from forever ago, like the '70s or '60s or '50s or '40s or something. Hey! There was one part where Grover sang, 'The hills are alive with the sound of music,' and the hills moved! They were really alive, get it? I watched that so long ago and now I'm in *The Sound of Music*! Isn't that amazing? I have to show you Grover singing *right now*."

I stopped to pull my phone out of my backpack.

"Let's keep going, Chlo. It's going to take us an hour to walk home from here."

"Why didn't Josh give us a ride?"

"I didn't see him, remember?"

"Oh yeah! I feel like I'm watching a movie about myself, but I keep falling asleep for a minute during the important parts. Anyway, I wish we had more drinks. Let's go to my house and drink my dad's Bombay Sapphire that he loves so freaking much oh I hate him I hate him. Do you think anyone saw me and Mac, I mean do you think everyone saw?"

"Um, I think so, yeah."

"Well, but it's not so bad, right? Because everyone knows we're really, really, really, really good friends and it's not weird to tell your friends you love them."

Tris didn't say anything.

"Right, Tris?"

"Well . . . let's talk about it tomorrow."

"Don't treat me like a baby! I can talk about it now, right now. That reminds me of the Beyoncé song! 'I know you see me now, right now.' That song is so under-appreciated! Did you know it's about dead moms?"

"No."

"This road is nice at night. Look at the trees! Listen to the crickets! It's so beautiful! Tris, I have to tell you something. I love you. I seriously, seriously love you. You're my best friend now. Way more than Hannah."

"I love you too."

"You *do*?? That's so wonderful exciting! I mean wonderful, so wonderful. So exciting! Tris, I really have to pee."

"Now?"

"It's an emergency. Hold my backpack!"

I ran down the grassy slope next to the road and pulled my pants down.

"Go a little farther, Chloe. There are cars driving by!"

"I don't care!"

It felt so good to pee. I've never been that relieved in my life. Unfortunately, I peed all over my pants, and walking four miles in wet, itchy pants kind of killed my mood.

When I finally got home, there was a note on the table: C, *had to go back to work. Leftover mac and cheese in the fridge. Microwave for two min. Love, Dad.* I'd been dreading trying to seem sober when I saw him, but somehow I didn't feel relieved to find he was out. I changed out of my disgusting pants of shame and ate the mac and cheese cold while I drank a beer and tried to look at my phone, which was hard, because I couldn't get my eyes to focus. Then I wrote in my diary, texted Tris (*than you fo everyihng i love uyo soooooooom uch :* :* :**), and went to bed without brushing my teeth, which I've never done ever before, because I care deeply about dental hygiene. The room spun every time I lay down. I tried putting my foot on the floor, which I read about in *Lucky Jim,* but it didn't help. In the end, I pushed my pillow against my headboard and fell asleep sitting up.

When I first woke up on Sunday, I felt OK. My mouth was dry and my eyes felt swollen, but no big whoop.

Then I remembered, and the shock and fear made me jump out of bed.

By the time I got to the bathroom, it was almost too late, and I had to lunge face-first at the toilet to get my barf in there in time. I felt briefly euphoric after throwing up, the way you always do. I brushed my teeth. Then I barfed again. Then I brushed my teeth again. It felt like a lifetime had passed, and it was only 10 a.m. When I looked in the mirror, I saw a reanimated corpse looking back at me. My lips had no color. The skin around my eyes was purple. *I hope you're happy with yourself,* I thought at my reflection.

I climbed into the empty bathtub to think. My dad was cheating on my mom with my formerly favorite teacher and director. Hannah wasn't my friend anymore.

And the night before I'd gotten wasted and attacked Mac in public. I cringed when I remembered sprinting across the gravel toward him. And oh, God, I'd said "I love you." Said it loudly. Had I almost shouted it? I rested my forehead on my knees.

Everyone knew, right? Everyone in the school and probably everyone on the internet now knew that Mac and I were messing around behind Sienna's back. Unless they thought I was a deranged stalker who kissed Mac out of the blue! Would that be better or worse? Well, no. No one would think that, because everyone sees him palling around with me in the halls.

He was never going to talk to me again. Or maybe he was going to call and say, "Chloe, thank you for your drunken act of bravery! You did what I was too scared to do. Now that our secret's out, I've decided to break up with Sienna."

I banged my forehead vigorously against my knees.

Oh no. *Tristan.*

I leaped out of the tub and ran back to my room.

> *I'm so sorry. Thank you for babysitting me. Please forgive me for being a buffoon.*

He texted back right away.

Phew, you're alive.

HAPPY BIRTHDAY!

My birthday. Right. It was my birthday.

When I went downstairs, Dad was making pancakes. My stomach lurched.

"There's the birthday girl!" he said.

I was so angry that he was pretending everything was fine that I said "How's Miss Murphy?" in a nasty tone of voice.

He slid a plate stacked with pancakes in front of me, sat down, and said, "Let's talk."

"OK," I said, because I was too tired and sick to keep stalling.

"OK," he said, and cleared his throat. "Here's the deal. As you've guessed, I've been seeing Miss Murphy."

"Wait. Stop. I changed my mind. I don't want to hear this."

"Give me a second. I won't talk for long, and then you can ask me any questions you want. As I was saying, I've been seeing Miss Murphy."

"For how long?"

"I don't think the details are important."

"At Christmas—were you already dating her at Christmas?"

"I don't want to get into—"

"Just tell me this one thing. Please, I'm begging you."

I had to know, because I had to go back through all of my memories of the musical and Miss Murphy and see which ones were tainted.

"Since March."

"She was being all sympathetic and trying to get me to tell her about Mom and the whole time she was . . ."

"I know this is hard. Let's both try to stay calm and not get mad."

"Why do *you* have to try not to get mad? What do you have to get mad about?"

He laughed, but not a real laugh.

"*What?*" I was crying and trying not to.

"It's been hard for me, Chloe. It was hard when your mom left."

"She didn't *leave*. She went away for a while to work on her writing."

"OK. But she's not here. She's not picking you up from rehearsal or eating dinner with us. She missed your play."

"She didn't miss my play! There's still one left."

"Honey . . ."

I couldn't stop crying. Snot was dripping down my upper lip. "Are you getting a divorce?"

"Chloe."

"If you do, will you marry Miss Murphy?"

He rubbed his eyes. "I haven't thought about those hypotheticals."

"Liar."

He looked embarrassed, which means I'm right. He has thought about it.

"Do you love Miss Murphy more than Mom?"

He paused, and my heart stopped.

"I don't know her as well as I know your mother. We're relative strangers. But she's . . . We're well suited. She's stable and kind."

"Her boobs aren't as big as Mom's."

"Chloe."

"And her butt is flatter."

"That's enough."

"She's having an affair with a married man. That means she's a bad person. And you're a bad person for cheating on your wife."

He looked sad. "That's probably true."

It's impossible to fight with someone who doesn't defend himself.

"I'm done eating."

"You haven't touched your food."

"I'm not hungry."

I stormed upstairs and ate a day-old half sandwich I found in my backpack, which made me feel much better.

On the way to the theater, I looked out at the beautiful soft spring day and wished for a hurricane.

The show. The last show.

It's gross to brag, and I never would out loud, but it's a big deal that I got the lead as a freshman. I've never heard of anyone doing that before. And it's not like I'm one of those kids who've been doing community theater since they were five years old. I'd never even sung out loud in front of anyone but my parents and Hannah before this year.

Mom and I have always been so connected, like we can read each other's minds. I thought, *It's the last show, and I'm the star, and it's my birthday. She'll come.*

It was a relief to get onstage. My performance was good even though my life is falling apart. Maybe it was a sadder version of Maria than usual. I kept thinking, *This is the last time we'll sit on the bed, yodeling. This is the last time I'll leapfrog over Liesl. This is the last time I'll wear this wedding dress. This is the last time I'll make out with Josh.* Backstage, kids were hugging a lot, in typical melodramatic-theater-kid fashion, but it didn't even annoy me.

During the curtain call, I stood backstage trying to memorize every detail. The feel of the scrim against my finger. My scratchy fleeing-through-the-mountains cape. The heat of the lights. The cast's faces in profile, grinning out at the audience. The sound of whooping and cheering. The butterflies in my stomach as I waited to go on. Josh's smile as he looked toward me and held out his arm, which was my signal to run onstage. The blinding spotlight when

I got to center stage. The dark mass of the people in their seats. Mom out there, maybe, impossible to see behind the bright lights, but there and waiting for me.

I was taking my first bow when I heard it: a boo. *Who's getting booed?* I thought, and then I heard another one, and then more, maybe a dozen. And some hissing. It didn't drown out the applause, but it was loud enough that everyone must have heard. I shaded my eyes against the spotlight so I could look into the audience. That's when a guy yelled, "Chloe Snow, you suck!" Laughter. "Chloe's a ho!" someone else yelled—a girl.

I was considering running offstage when Miss Murphy came out from the wings. Was she going to shout at the hecklers? That would only make things worse. But no, when she got close to me, she turned to the audience and took a deep bow. Leo ran out with a big bouquet of flowers for her. She backed up, took my hand, squeezed it tight, lifted it in the air, then brought it down so we could bow together.

The curtain closed and everyone started hugging. I looked at Miss Murphy. She looked back at me. Had I ever studied her face before? It's narrow, like a horse's face. Her skin is very white. She has eyes the color of green grapes, but she doesn't make a big deal out of them with makeup, which I would if I were her.

"Great job," she said. "Great run."

I thought of saying "I hate you" or "You'll never be my stepmother" or nothing at all, but in the end I said "Thank you" in a flat voice and then turned away.

The dressing room was mayhem, with everyone crying and hugging each other yet again, and saying, "I can't believe it's over." I could feel people looking at me. Bernadette and her minions whispered in a corner, burst into laughter, whispered again, burst into laughter, etc. *They're probably not talking about you*, I told myself. *Don't be so self-centered.*

I tried to focus on this memorable moment in my life and notice how everything smelled and looked and sounded and think about what it would be like to see Mom after I'd changed, but all I could think about was the booing. I was feeling so sorry for myself, and trying so hard not to cry, that my stomach hurt. Tris came over and I said, "Just a sec. Let me find my hairpins," and rummaged randomly around in my makeup bag, because I knew if he said something nice, or even looked sympathetic, I would start sobbing.

Hannah came over and said, "Congratulations! Um, this is for you." From the expression on her face and the tone of her voice, I knew she hadn't heard about what happened at the pits. She handed me a pale-pink envelope with my name written really huge across, which is an inside joke we've been making every year since second grade.

I thanked her.

"Is everything OK?" she said.

I nodded.

"That was so weird. I bet it was drunk seniors. They probably picked your name because they saw in the program that you're the lead. Don't you think?"

For a second, I considered it. Maybe the booing was completely unrelated to Mac, and the pits, and Bernadette! What proof did I have that they were linked? None! But . . . no. No. Of course they were linked. Only a psycho would scream "[Person I don't know] is a ho!" or boo a complete stranger. And what are the chances that there are a dozen psychos in one school?

"Maybe," I said.

"Well, I'm sorry it happened. Don't think about it, OK?"

What if I told her everything right there? *I'm in love with Mac and I've been making out with him. I got drunk last night and kissed his mouth in front of everyone.*

She was looking at me anxiously.

"I won't think about it," I said.

"Are you doing anything for your birthday?"

We both looked at the ground. I couldn't remember ever spending my birthday without her.

"Um . . . I was supposed to go to Wendell's, but I'm not feeling too good. I kind of want to go home and go to sleep."

"Well, happy birthday, Chloe."

She hugged me, and I hugged her back. As she walked away, I wanted to say something. But what kind of something? *Why aren't we friends anymore? Do you think we can be friends again? If you knew what I'm really like, would you hate me? Do you think doing so-called bad things makes you a bad person?*

I changed out of my costume for the last time and went upstairs to find Dad. My heart was pounding. Would Mom be standing next to him? What would she be wearing? Would she run over to meet me, or wait until I reached her? There were lots of parents milling around the auditorium, taking pictures and handing flowers to their kids. It took me a minute to spot Dad. He was standing in the front row, staring at the stage like he was expecting the show to start again. He was alone.

"Mom's not in the bathroom, right?" I said when I got to him.

He shook his head no and tried to put his hand on my shoulder. I ducked away.

"I'm so sorry, honey."

Tris came over then, so I didn't have to respond. "Can we skip Wendell's?" I said. Tris said of course. My dad asked was I sure I didn't want to celebrate? I was sure.

The three of us pretended everything was normal, because although I could have talked to my dad, or to

Tris, I couldn't talk to either of them when all three of us were together. Why is that?

My presents were great. Glitter nail polish and a book called *Love, Nina: A Nanny Writes Home* from Tris, and an iPad from my dad, which made me feel spoiled and excited and irritated, because he can't buy my forgiveness. (But it's an iPad!) (It wouldn't matter if it were a car. He's cheating on Mom and maybe has been for years.) I said thank you so so much, I love it, it's perfect, I'm so lucky! Exactly like I would have if everything were OK, and they acted normal too, and then Dad brought out chocolate cupcakes with peanut butter frosting.

And then finally I got to do what I'd wanted to do all night, which was go upstairs with Tris and talk. He lay on my bed; I lay on the floor.

"My mom didn't show up," I said.

"Yeah. It sucks. Are you mad?"

"I guess it's selfish to expect her to fly here for every little thing. She lives in another country. Temporarily, I mean."

"But it's your birthday."

I waited until my eyes stopped prickling and then changed the subject.

"I'm very sorry I got drunk last night."

"It's OK, but Chloe, what if I hadn't been there? You could have gotten hit by a car or date-raped."

I rolled my eyes.

"You could!" he said.

"OK. You're right." I put the crook of my elbow over my eyes so I wouldn't have to look at him as I asked my question. "Do you think the thing tonight was because of the thing last night?"

Silence. I pulled the crook away so I could see his face. It looked troubled, plus he was biting his thumb cuticle.

"It was, right?"

He looked at me.

"What?" I said. "What's wrong?"

"I heard Bernadette talking to Ambreen," he said.

My heart turned into an icicle. "Tell me exactly what she said."

"I don't think—"

"Please. I'm begging you. I'll imagine something much worse if you don't tell me."

He sighed. "I was behind the guys' dressing room door, and they were by the makeup counter right outside. Bernadette was like, 'I saw the whole thing. They were eating each other's faces.'"

"He didn't even kiss me back!"

"Do you want me to tell you or not? Ambreen asked if Sienna knew, and Bernadette was like, 'Oh, I texted her right away. I debated not saying anything, but everyone saw, so she would have found out eventually, and I thought it would be better coming from her best friend. But she already knew. Mac told her right away and begged for forgiveness. I guess he messed around with Chloe a few times, nothing real. He said it was a mistake, but maybe it wasn't a mistake, because it made him realize he only wants to be with Sienna. Kind of romantic. Sienna told me she cried and screamed at him for an hour, but she could never break up with him. She loves him too much. Anyway, can you believe he was cheating on *Sienna* with that nothing little freshman?'"

Tris had gotten really into it and was doing a perfect imitation of Bernadette's vocal fry. I think he'd kind of lost himself in the performance. After he said the "nothing little freshman" part, he clapped his hands over his mouth.

"What else?" I said. "Tell me all of it."

"Nothing else," he said. And then his mom beeped from her car outside.

After he left and I was alone in my room, I opened up my box of treasures (which is actually a shoe box covered in pictures I cut out of my mom's *Vogues* when I was 11) and got out Mom's porcelain rabbit, the one she gave me when she left. It's sitting on its haunches looking worried, and when you hold it for a while, it warms up in your hands.

He only wants to be with Sienna. I was a mistake. I'm nothing real.

Tuesday, May 24

I keep waiting for someone to lock me in my locker or push my head in the toilet and flush, but so far, nothing. Bernadette gives me terrifying looks in the hall—staring, glaring, flaring her nostrils—and I do think I notice seniors looking at me and whispering about me. But maybe I'm being paranoid.

Wednesday, May 25

My heart is dead.

Mac called me. I've never been so happy to see someone's name pop up on my phone. He said he heard about what happened at the last show. "I want you to know, Sienna had nothing to do with that," he said. "I bet Bernadette set it all up."

"Why are you talking about Sienna like that?" I said.

"Like what?"

"Like . . . nice."

There was a pause.

"Listen, Chloe, I think you're awesome."

I started crying, and lifted my phone away from my mouth so he wouldn't hear.

"You make me laugh," he said. "You know I think you're so cute. But we can't hang out anymore. It's not fair to Sienna. She's my girlfriend."

"When . . . ?" I pinched my leg as hard as I could to

make myself stop crying. "Is this because of what I did at the pits? I'm sorry! I was drunk. I was dumb. I'd found out something about . . . It doesn't matter. I'll never do anything like that again. We can go back to the way we were."

"Don't worry about the pits," he said. "It's not that."

"Then what?"

"I just realized I have to do the right thing."

"But what changed?"

"I probably shouldn't tell you this. It's weird not being able to talk to you about everything."

"You can! You can tell me anything you want."

"Sienna and I had sex on prom night. For the first time, I mean. We've been doing it a ton since then. It's amazing. I feel so close to her. Maybe that makes me sound whipped, but it's true."

"Oh."

"I shouldn't have told you."

"No, no, it's OK."

"I actually have to pick her up right now, so I have to go, OK? But we'll talk—we'll talk at some point. You're the best. Never change."

Thursday, May 26

Mac passed me in the hall and waved. A polite wave like you'd give your elderly neighbor when you saw her out walking her dog. It's his second-to-last day of school. Tomorrow's the Senior Costume Contest, and then they're done forever. My chest hurts. I went to the nurse. She took my temperature and said, "You're not running a fever." She's big and soft, like a human loaf of bread. She was so close I could feel her breath on my cheek. I wondered how weird it would be to hug her, and decided very. She let me rest on a cot. I lay on my back and the tears trickled into my ears.

Friday, May 27
I WANT TO BURN DOWN THE SCHOOL AND EVERY EVIL SMALL-TOWN SENIOR IN IT

Saturday, May 28

Mom,

Can you please, please, please come on Skype? I'm sorry to sound hysterical, but I've left you messages on every single place online and I can't find you anywhere and I really, really need your help, OK?

Chloe

Sunday, May 29

Maybe I deserve everything that happened to me on Friday. Probably I do.

Bernadette dressed up as me. When I saw her in the hall, I thought, *Hey, she has the same flowered sneakers I do,* and then I realized. Her hair was in pigtails, which didn't make sense—I never wear pigtails—but I think was a joke about how young I am. She stood there smirking at me and called out "Do you like my costume?" in a little-girl voice that I think was supposed to be an imitation of me. I stood there with my mouth hanging open, and she turned and walked away with her butt twitching. All day people kept coming up to me to ask if I'd seen Bernadette. People I've never even talked to before! Some of them looked openly delighted and some of them were pretending to be concerned for me.

After lunch one of Sienna's friends said "Hey, slut" to me. I'd never talked to this girl before, but when you're a freshman, you automatically know every senior's life story. Riley Isaacson, ballet dancer, wears a fedora inside, apparently does splits over her boyfriend when they have sex (now that I write that down, I realize it's clearly a ridiculous rumor some guy made up). When she said it, I was alone, and she was safe in the middle of a big group of friends, who *ppppbbbb*ted with laughter, covered their mouths, and grabbed each other's arms. She smiled at me and then looked around, obviously proud of herself. The other kids in the hall, the non-seniors, stopped their conversations to stare at me. I could almost see them drafting tweets in their minds.

During the costume contest, which the entire school was required to attend, I saw Mac and Sienna talking and laughing. He was wearing jeans and a Tom Brady jersey, and she was Finn from *Adventure Time*. And not sexy Finn either. Long jean shorts, blue T-shirt, green backpack, white fur hat, hair hidden. She looked more beautiful dressed as a boy than any of the other girls did in their fake eyelashes with their boobs hanging out. Mac pulled on Sienna's hat and she laughed at him and tried to push him away, but she wasn't trying that hard.

As I was walking home from school, a car full of kids drove by, and someone in the backseat sprayed me with a water gun. The people in the car whooped and cheered. They left too fast for me to make out anyone's face. After they'd sped away, I lifted my T-shirt up to smell it and make sure it was water. It was pee. When I got home, I threw my clothes in the trash and took a shower (and cried and cried in the shower, but that probably goes without saying). Then I got my clothes out of the trash and washed them, because it's just a little pee, and Mom gave me that shirt.

Everyone's talking about me online. Some people are using my name, some people are subtweeting, probably some people are posting about it on their little blogs that I'll never find, thank God. I was on my phone all day Friday, refreshing like mad. Every time I saw a new one, my face went numb.

the lesson here is dont mess with senior guys #stepoffbitch

best senior dress up day in world history lmao ;)!!!!!

bernadette ur costume was hilarious tho

thanks man it was hard work making myself look like a busted baby lolol

if i laugh when frosh cry am I a bad person? cause HAHAHAHAHA

I hate to say it, but cheaters get what they deserve.

not afraid to call out chloe. you're an ugly bitch and everyone knows it.

Millions more like that. Nothing from Sienna, at least nothing about me. And this one, from Josh.

I'm disgusted with the vengefulness, prurience, and hypocrisy of my classmates. Let he who is without sin cast the first stone.

I texted him immediately.

Thanks for saying that

I wish I could do something
to help.

> *Did you hear about*
> *freshmen getting sprayed*
> *with pee? From a water*
> *gun? Is that a thing?*

No. Did that happen to you?

> *Never mind.*

Chloe, that must rise to the level
of assault. I would urge you to
contact the administration and
explain to them what's been
going on.

> *Maybe I will*

But of course I won't. That's all I need, for the vice principal or whoever to call Bernadette into his office and tell her I ratted her out. Snitches get stitches.

It's the worst feeling, knowing that everyone's talking about you, that everyone hates you. I can't sleep. I'm so tired, but when I lie down, my muscles clench and my mind races. *Relax, relax,* I tell myself. *Think about the*

Cape. Imagine you're about to walk down to the beach. Splintery stairs. Gulls sailing through the sky. Sun on your neck. It works for a second and then I catch myself thinking about that girl yelling "Chloe's a ho!" or the look on Mac's face when I jumped on him in the pits. I roll around trying to get comfortable, and the sheets get hot and twisted. Finally I fall asleep, and then I jolt awake in the middle of the night to check my phone. It's right there, next to my bed, and people are whispering about me in it. How can I not look? Then I do look, and it's even worse than I thought, and it takes me hours to fall asleep again.

Dad kept asking what was wrong, and I finally broke down and told him. He was so nice. Why can't he make it easier for me to hate him?

Monday, May 30

No school—Memorial Day. It's the first good thing that's happened to me in weeks.

As soon as I woke up, I checked my feed and saw six new updates, including *chloe snow more like chloe HO*, and then something snapped and I deleted myself from everything. Yik Yak, Snapchat, Instagram, everything, everything. It felt like filling a hot-air balloon with helium and slowly drifting away from the ground. When I finished, the room seemed quiet. Everyone is still talking about me, but at least I can't hear it.

But how will I know what people are saying??? What if #chloeho becomes a trending topic?

No. No! Stay strong. Stay off.

After breakfast I finally Skyped with Mom. She was off in the desert doing research or something and just got back today. I told her the whole Mac thing: the prom invitation, the pits, the last show, the Senior Costume Contest. She was like, "Those *monsters*. How *dare* they?" and "You did nothing wrong. Absolutely nothing wrong. Unless being 15 and lousy with hormones is a crime, in which case, lock up every teenager in the known universe!" and "Wait until you're all in your twenties. They'll be stuck in the suburbs, changing diapers, while you're traveling the world and meeting fascinating men." Yeah!!

School tomorrow. How can I do this? I could stay home, but I can't stay home forever. And if I don't show up, people will decide that Sienna murdered me or that I've gone into hiding.

What will I *wear*? Everything looks so embarrassing now, like it could be part of Bernadette's costume. My T-shirt the color of pink cotton candy. Anything with flowers on it. My two-dinosaurs-kissing sweater. I guess I'm too old to wear that stuff. Maybe everyone's right to make fun of me. I'm weird and babyish and maybe I'm a bad person. I don't feel like a bad person, but those ISIS guys probably feel pretty pleased with themselves, too, so.

Tuesday, May 31

I forgot: the seniors are done with school. None of them were there today—Bernadette, Mac, Sienna, Riley. The juniors were strutting around getting used to their power. Everyone stared at me and whispered as I walked by. Some sophomore I don't even know came up to me and said, "Are you OK? If people were talking about me like that, I'd be cutting myself, seriously," which was nice, unless it was really mean. I could feel people studying the back of my head during class. But at least I wasn't worried that a senior would punch me in the hall or smash my teeth into the water fountain spout as I was leaning over to get a drink (for some reason, when I wake up at 3 a.m., that's what I envision happening).

Tris kept coming to pick me up from classes and walk me to my locker. He looped his arm through mine, told me stories in a loud voice, and threw his head back to laugh and laugh at whatever I said, which wasn't much. Basically, he tried to convince all the people darting glances at me that everything's fine and I haven't been ground into baby powder. I thanked him at the end of the day, but I was too shy to say the right words. The right words are, "Thank you for standing by me in my darkest hour."

Wednesday, June 1
Rabbits, rabbits. Although what's the point?

Thursday, June 2
He'll change his mind. He has to. He doesn't really want to be with her. He's confused because he's in a sex coma. After a week or two, he'll remember all the reasons he loves me. Yeah, she's beautiful, but she's boring. I make him laugh! A good sense of humor is way more important than long legs with no scabs on them. After everyone forgets about these last few weeks, he'll show up outside my house in his pickup truck and tell me how sorry he is and what a big mistake he made.

Friday, June 3
I hate him for doing this to me. He made me fall in love with him, and then he took himself away from me.

Saturday, June 4
This is all my fault. I basically forced him to do this. If only I hadn't molested him in front of his friends! If only

I hadn't been so jealous of Sienna! If only I hadn't always texted him first! I'm pathetic and desperate.

Sunday, June 5

I'll never love anyone else the way I love him. I'm sure I'll meet plenty of dudes who are more appropriate for me, and I'll probably even marry someone smarter and nicer than Mac. But no one will make me feel the way he did.

Monday, June 6

The shower is a good place to cry. Standing under warm water is comforting. Plus, the water washes away your tears.

Tuesday, June 7

I've vowed not to talk to or look at Miss Murphy for the rest of time, but I still have to sit through her English class. We're reading *The Great Gatsby*. Today someone said she doesn't understand why Gatsby loves Daisy so much, when she's not that special, and I was dying to raise my hand and say, "That's the whole point, that you can fall in love with anyone if you don't actually know her, because really you're falling in love with a person you've made up," but I didn't let myself.

I don't think Dad is seeing Miss Murphy anymore,

unless he's sneaking off during work. He never leaves the house at night now.

Wednesday, June 8

I feel sad all the time. It's like wearing a big ugly hat. Sometimes I forget about it for a few minutes, but then I see it in my peripheral vision and think, *Oh yeah, the hat of sadness.* Mac Mom Dad Miss Murphy.

For a few seconds after I wake up in the morning, I don't remember anything. Then I move my head and it all comes back to me. I'm wearing the hat.

Seeing Tris helps. Clicking on my phone helps. But even when I have a good day, I have to lie in bed alone in the dark at the end of it.

Thursday, June 9

Most internet advice columnists say your parents' love life is none of your business. Some of them say if you know your friend Joe is being cheated on, you should ask yourself, "If I were Joe, would I want to be told?" and if the answer is yes, tell.

Maybe Mom already knows! Maybe Dad's told her all about Miss Murphy. Maybe they have an open marriage (barf, die, kill, more barf). Or maybe Dad's been cheating on her their whole marriage. Maybe that's why they were constantly fighting. Maybe that's why she shopped online and got drunk before it was dark out and screamed at him about wearing his shoes inside: because she was so furious about his cheating. And maybe she was like, "This is your last chance. I'm moving to Mexico to show you how awful life will be without me. Come to your senses or it's over forever." Maybe she moved without me because she felt it was her obligation to show him how overwhelmed he'd be as a single parent. It was her way of saving their relationship! She's been pining away for me the whole time.

Friday, June 10

Tonight I pulled my treasure box out of the closet. I put Mom's rabbit on my knee and went through all my Mac memorabilia.

* The precious prom bracelet
* The cherry ChapStick he always used to borrow
* A letter he wrote to me on a piece of notebook paper and crammed into my locker after I'd helped him with his English homework. (*Chloe your awesome. Thanks for saving my ass and being cute. You make me smile kid. Love ya.*)
* A Twix bar he gave me once

* A picture of him about to catch a football,
cut out of the local newspaper after the
Thanksgiving Day game

This box of treasures is the second thing I would grab in a fire, right after Snickers.

Saturday, June 11

Dad was watching a spy movie by himself, and I couldn't take it. Being home on Saturday night is depressing enough without your father shoving his loneliness in your face. I marched into the living room and said, "You don't have to be here all the time, you know."

He looked up. "Huh?"

"You're canceling all your dates so I won't have any reason to hate you or whatever. You're constantly in the house. You don't even go on runs anymore."

He turned off the movie.

"Don't turn it off. I don't want to have some big thing."

"It's OK. It was bad anyway. I guess I have been seeing a little less of—Miss Murphy." He tapped his forehead gently with the remote. "It seemed like a good idea to, uh, dial it back a bit."

"GOD, Dad, that's worse!"

"Worse than what?"

"I don't want to feel like I'm in charge of your disgusting love life! I don't want to feel guilty that I'm keeping you from having your *affair*."

"You're not in charge of anything. I made the decision," he said.

I didn't say anything.

"Do you want to eat some popcorn and watch this silly movie with me?" he asked. "We can start from the beginning."

"No, thanks," I said. I really did want to eat popcorn—he makes it from scratch with about a stick of butter—but I couldn't sit there getting my fingers greasy with him after he cheated on Mom. It doesn't matter that he dumped Miss Murphy, if he even did. He still had an affair.

Sunday, June 12

Mac. I think about him all the time. The way he would clap his hands together and look at the sky when I made him laugh. The way his tongue tasted (probably like the food tastes in heaven). His muscles. His eyelashes. The way he looked at me in his pickup truck. The way he touched me in his pickup truck.

Monday, June 13

We were leaving class today when Miss Murphy said, "Chloe, can you hang back for a second?" I did, because I didn't see how to get out of it. When everyone was gone, she sat down next to me, at one of the kid desks. We both faced forward, like there was an invisible teacher in front of us.

"I wanted to say I'm sorry," she said. "I betrayed your trust. There's no excuse for my behavior."

That's right. There's no excuse. She tried to steal a married man away from his wife. She's an immoral thief, like Abigail Williams in *The Crucible*. Neither of them understand: you can't just take the person you want like you're tearing a leaf off a tree. The leaf belongs to the tree. The tree belongs to the leaf. Abigail and Miss Murphy are a couple of greedy children who only care about themselves and what they want.

I know I tried to steal Mac away from Sienna, but that's different. I'm a kid. And Mac should have been my tree in the first place.

"Chloe? Is there anything you want to say?"

I looked down at my hands, which were clenched so hard my knuckles were white. "Don't worry about it," I said. "It's not a big deal." Then I got up and walked out without looking at her.

Tuesday, June 14

I thought people would be tired of talking about me by now, but they're not. People still whisper and stare at me when I walk by in the hall. A junior girl I don't know called "Yo, it's Chloe Ho!" across the parking lot after school today, so I guess that's still a thing. I haven't reactivated any of my accounts, but I'm sure people are talking about me online. It's very restful, not having profiles. It makes me feel like I'm living in olden times. Pine tree forests, birds singing, teenage girls being horrible to each other in person.

Wednesday, June 15

School continues on and on, stretching toward the horizon, approaching zero but never reaching it. Why was I ever excited about snow days when we have to pay for them when the warm weather finally arrives? What a fool I was.

Thursday, June 16

Skyped with Mom. There she was on the screen, sitting in her apartment, wearing a green scarf over her hair and patting her ugly lapdog, saying something about emulating Faulkner and creating different first-person narrators, and I couldn't listen. I felt so sorry for her.

"Don't you agree, sweetheart?" she said.

"Huh?"

"Don't you think she's a stronger point-of-view character?"

"Maybe. Mom?"

"Yes?"

"I have a question. Say you know something, and it might really hurt someone's feelings, but they might want to know."

She pushed the dog off her lap. "What are you getting at, Chloe?"

"Well . . . I don't want to tell you, because it's about a friend, and it's a secret."

"I don't like hints and secrets."

"So you think I should tell."

She leaned back in her chair. "I think honesty is overrated. I think oftentimes people confess something they shouldn't because they want to soothe their own guilty conscience. And it's certainly not your place to confess someone else's secret."

"Are you mad? You sound mad."

"I'm firm in my opinion."

"Well, OK. Thank you. That helps."

Friday, June 17

Dad and I still have dinner together every night. It's been not-great. He tries to talk to me, and I talk back, but politely, not in my real voice. Sometimes I forget to be cold because he brings up something interesting (New York, which Bennet sister I would be, online bullying) and I'll start talking for real. Then I remember and realize he's tricked me into being normal, and I get furious and leave the table.

The worst is when I have a question, like I did tonight. Asking questions puts you in other people's power. You need a favor from them: the favor of telling you information you want to know. So I try to sneak in questions without actually asking them.

"I guess we're not having a Fourth of July party this year."

"Why wouldn't we?"

"Well, it might be weird to have one without Mom."

"It might be OK."

I glared at him. I know what he's insinuating. Mom and her friends don't wear festive attire to the party, whereas Dad likes to wear his American flag T-shirt and I like to wear my red-and-white-striped shorts and my blue tank top with white stars. Mom talks to her friends like, "Patriotism is the last refuge of the scoundrel. I'm surrounded by provincial dolts even in my own house!" It's a joke. She doesn't actually think Dad and I are provincial dolts. She's proud of us for being normal, and herself for being weird.

I wanted to tell Dad it wouldn't be OK, it would be horrible, but I was a little worried he'd cancel the party if he really believed I wanted him to, and I love it way too much for that.

Then I said, "I guess the Cape would be *really* weird without Mom." I wanted to get all my secret questions out of the way in one shot.

Dad put down his beer. "Chloe, we're going to forge ahead, OK? I promise I won't cancel any of our summer stuff. I arranged the rental right after Christmas. I should have told you that before. I'm sorry. It didn't occur to me that you'd be worried."

I nodded and tried not to look relieved. It's so annoying when you think you're being sneaky and then your parents read your mind.

Saturday, June 18

Dear Mom,

I've been thinking. Dad doesn't want to move to Mexico, and that's fine. But couldn't I come live with you? I found an online school that looks legit, and I could take classes in Spanish at the high school in the town where you live. Think about how much my brain

would grow if I learned a second language!
And if Dad doesn't like the idea, we can tell
him how amazing this will be for my college
applications. The essay practically writes itself!!
I promise I won't hang around the apartment
all day pestering you while you try to work.
You probably remember how I used to do that
when I was little, but I've changed a lot. I can
entertain myself now.

I'll be honest with you. This town is bringing me
down. A lot of people hate me, and they tell me
so at school. I know you'll say I should brush it
off, but I can't. I feel sick most of the day, and at
night when I wake up. Also, I miss you. Please
help me. Please say I can move to Mexico when
school ends.

Chloe

Sunday, June 19

Father's Day. I got Dad a Hallmark card, not even one
of those big juicy glittery ones that cost $7.99, and added
"love, Chloe" after the printed message.

Still no word from Mom. I guess she doesn't want
me to move out there.

Monday, June 20

Chloe Rabbit,

What a beautiful email. There are some complications to sort out on my end, but I promise you I will mull over your request and get back to you as soon as I can. OK, angel? I must dash—I'm overbooked today—but more anon.

Mom

When I first thought about it, I was like, *Overbooked? She doesn't have a job or any responsibilities.* But that's the way Dad thinks, or Miss Murphy. Like, wake up at 6, make a to-do list, drink your coffee, go out and conquer the world. That's great if you're a lawyer, or the director of some piddling high school theater program no one cares about. Mom's trying to make great art. To do that, you have to sleep in, take long walks, and wait for inspiration. You can't waste a bunch of time sorting through your email. She *is* overbooked, but not in the way corporate losers and two-bit directors would understand.

Tuesday, June 21

Maybe she'll never come back. *Probably* she'll never

come back. She doesn't love Dad. She loves me, but not enough. I don't make up for living in a place where everyone knows your business and most of the other mothers care more about Pinterest and scented candles and their long bobs than they do about books.

She can't stay in Mexico forever. I bet she and Dad will get a divorce and she'll move to—New York! Yes! That's exactly what will happen! She'll publish her book and live in Brooklyn like she's always wanted to, and go to parties with famous novelists wearing cool glasses. And I'll live there too, with Tris, and on the weekends she'll take me to author get-togethers and say, "This is my incredible daughter, Chloe; she's in the theater program at NYU, but we'll see how long she lasts before Broadway lures her away." And everyone will say, "Chloe, we've heard so much about you! Can't we persuade you to sing something?" I'll protest, but when they won't relent, I'll sing "I Get Along Without You Very Well" and make everyone cry. And on holidays, I'll go home to see Dad. I'll take the train, resting my head against the glass and looking out at the snow mournfully. His hair will be turning a little gray around the temples, and he'll make steaks and put on the Duke Ellington *Nutcracker Suite,* like always. It won't be sad when I leave because . . . because . . . no. He can't marry Miss Murphy. I don't care how guilty I feel leaving him and Snickers all by themselves. He'll have to die alone.

Wednesday, June 22

The last day of classes. I knew I was looking forward to today, but I didn't realize how much until I got home, let my backpack slip onto the floor, and lay right down on the kitchen floor. I looked up at the recessed lights and felt my bones melting into a puddle of relaxation. Then I fell asleep, and when I woke up, the sun was setting and Snickers was licking my face, probably because I looked dead.

Oh, I'm happy, I'm so happy. A whole summer of no one staring at me or whispering about me or feeling sorry for me or being disgusted with me.

Thursday, June 23

Tris and I spent the day lying in front of a box fan. It was too hot to eat anything but Popsicles. We talked about global warming and what irresponsible jerks our parents are for knowing the world was melting and not doing anything to stop it. Then we made a list of horrible things we won't have to do now that it's summer.

1. Wake up in the middle of our natural sleep cycles
2. Get ready for school in the dark
3. Wear a scarf and hat inside in June because the air-conditioning in our school is so Arctic
4. Attempt to be cheerful underneath drop ceilings and fluorescent lights

5. Struggle not to get caught checking our phones
6. Struggle not to fall asleep in class
7. Suffer the humiliation of being too young to drive
8. Deal with the constant backstabbing, gossiping, judging, terrorizing, and French courtier–style struggling for power that define high school life

Tris said he can come to our Fourth of July party, and so can Roy, which I should be happy about. I like Roy, but we never make each other laugh for real. And I would never give him a hard time, like I used to give Josh a hard time. We're very polite and nice to each other. It's kind of awful.

Friday, June 24
Today is Hannah's birthday. I texted her a bouquet, a winking smiley face blowing a heart kiss, and the two girls dancing, but she didn't text back.

She must have heard about me and Mac, and I'm sure she thinks what I did was really wrong.

I think it was wrong too.

Saturday, June 25
This morning Dad yelled up to me to see if I wanted to go to the hardware store with him, which I would normally never do, but the truth is, I've been a little lonely

without school. It would be OK if I were Tris's only friend, like he's mine, but he's busy with Roy, and I don't want to be pathetic, so I never guilt him about not hanging out with me more. Whenever I feel sad, I remind myself that it could be worse. I could be getting booed or pushed or laughed at in the pits. And that helps a lot. But not all the way.

So when Dad yelled up, I yelled back sure, OK, I would go.

The hardware store is the only place more boring than the fine arts museum. I was standing next to Dad gazing at a stack of electrical tape with my eyes unfocused when I heard Hannah's dad go, "Charlie, how are you, man? Haven't seen you in months!" I looked up and there was Hannah, wearing a pink dress and flip-flops I know she bought at American Eagle last summer, because I was with her when she did. How awkward that she'd ignored my text just yesterday.

Dad and Mr. Egan were laughing with their arms crossed and their legs planted wide apart, like a couple of dads. "How's your summer going?" I asked Hannah.

"It's OK," she said. "I'm going to camp in July."

"I'm jealous," I said, which is true. I'm reading *The Yonahlossee Riding Camp for Girls*, and it's making me want to ride a horse and have an affair with a much older man.

There was an awkward silence.

"How's Josh?" I asked, because it was the only thing I could think of.

"We broke up."

"*What?*"

She closed her eyes and smoothed one of her eyebrows. She looked so sad and grown-up.

"Hannah, what are you saying? You guys were practically married! What happened?"

"I don't know. I don't really want to talk about it here."

It hurt my feelings, even though of course it made sense that she didn't want to talk about it next to a bin full of incandescent lightbulbs while our fathers were bellowing at each other about relief pitching.

"OK. Well, I'm really sorry."

"Thanks."

We both looked at the ground. My dad said, "Anyway, we'll see you on the Fourth, right?"

"What's happening on the Fourth?" said Mr. Egan.

Dad glanced at me. "We're having a few people over for a cookout. No big deal. You guys should swing by if you can make it. 4 to 8."

In the car on the way home, Dad said, "Sorry about that. I assumed you'd invited Hannah."

"It's OK."

"What's going on? Did you have a falling-out?"

I shrugged. "Not really. Maybe junior high was as far as we could go."

He didn't say what a shame or try to talk me out of my opinion. If he weren't such a cheating dirtbag, he'd be a good father.

Sunday, June 26

Hannah came over today. Just showed up on my doorstep at noon without texting me first, like we were on an old-fashioned TV show. She looked as fresh as a cucumber. I'd recently woken up. My eyes were swollen like dumplings and I had morning breath mixed with iced-coffee breath. I invited her in and we stood in the kitchen chatting about nothing for almost 45 minutes— finals, the weather, notable status updates. Then she said, "It was kind of weird, seeing you at the hardware store yesterday."

"Yeah, I guess it was."

"It's been weird for a while now, though."

"Yeah."

She took a deep breath. "Do you want to talk about it?"

"OK," I said.

We sat at the kitchen island. It was hot, and my forearms stuck to the granite. My heart was racing. What was she going to say? Then, to my surprise, she pulled out her phone. It wasn't like her to text at a moment like this. She said, "I wrote you a letter so I wouldn't forget anything I wanted to say. Is it OK if I read it?"

"Sure."

She cleared her throat.

"'Dear Chloe: You are my oldest friend. I still remember meeting you in kindergarten. Mrs. Yglesias teased you for coloring a dinosaur pink on the first day, and you were so angry, you wouldn't do any art activities for the rest of the week. It made everyone respect you, including me. I could talk about memories of our times together all day, but I am here to tell you why I feel so upset.

"'Number 1. You stopped telling me things. Maybe this is my own fault. I know I can be judgmental. However, I would like to know about your relationships and about what's going on with your mother. I'm not stupid. When you hid things from me, it didn't fool me. It made me sad to know that you didn't want to talk to me anymore about things that matter. Number 2. You don't ask about my life. When I needed to talk to you about my parents, you ran off with Mac. You never asked questions about me and Josh, and hand job questions don't count. I'm talking about feelings. Now we broke up, and you don't know anything about it. You could have known everything if you'd been interested. Number 3. You've changed. I know you're not from a Catholic family and that's fine. Maybe it's normal to drink and I'm the one who is out of step with what teenagers do these days. But I admit it makes me very uncomfortable to have a friend who drinks alcohol.'"

I thought, *I could get up and leave,* but actually I couldn't. I was too fascinated.

"'Number 4. According to rumors, you and Mac have kissed many times, and probably done more. Please tell me if the rumors are wrong.'"

She looked up at me and I looked back at her with a face of stone. She looked back down at her phone.

"'You might not want to hear this, but what you and Mac did was wrong. You hurt Sienna and you hurt your own souls. I'm not saying the punishment fit the crime. Bernadette and her friends were even more wrong than you. But adultery is a sin.'"

I had to interrupt. "*Adultery?* We messed around a few times. He's not married, Hannah. He's 18 years old. It's not a big deal."

Her face was flushed. "I do think it's a big deal."

"Of course you do. You're the second coming of the Virgin Mary."

She frowned. "I think you know what you did was wrong."

"You know what, you're right, Hannah. You don't know anything about my life anymore. You want to talk about adultery? My dad's been having an affair with Miss Murphy for months."

She looked shocked, like I'd slapped her.

"*That's* adultery," I said. "That's Abigail Williams stuff."

She looked at the table, then back at me. "What's so different about you and Miss Murphy?" she said.

"Besides the fact that she's stealing someone's husband and I'm an innocent teenager who kissed someone else's boyfriend a few times? And by the way, thanks for that sensitive response to the news that my parents' marriage is over and our director is dating my dad. You're so selfish, Hannah."

"No, *you're* so selfish. You're such an only child."

I reared back.

"You are," she said. "You don't care about anyone but yourself. Have you even noticed that Sienna's lost a ton of weight and has huge dark circles under her eyes? Do you ever wonder how your parents are feeling? Are you aware that other people exist in the world?"

"Yes to all of it!" I said.

She stood up. "I don't believe you. And by the way, I'm not a virgin anymore."

Now she's gone and I'm so mad I want to punch a wall. How dare she lecture me about my behavior? How dare she judge me for drinking and falling in love? And how dare she have sex before me?

Monday, June 27

Oh my God. Hannah's right about everything.

It's the middle of the night. The realization woke me up.

I'm Abigail Williams.

I'm the bad guy.

I'm exactly like Miss Murphy.

I tried to take Mac away from his girlfriend. I can think of a million reasons why I'm different from every other person who's done the same thing, but in my heart I know what I did was wrong. He was wrong too, but that doesn't make me less wrong.

Tuesday, June 28

Called Hannah first thing in the morning.

"You were right," I said.

Silence.

"Hannah? Hello?"

"I'm here."

"I'm really sorry I yelled at you."

No response. I had an idea: I could use a "when you _____, I feel _____ because _____" statement, like we learned to do in our life skills unit.

"When you told me everything I did wrong, it made me feel angry because it's hard to hear the truth about yourself."

A pause. "OK."

"I never should have messed around with Mac. I convinced myself that it wasn't a big deal, but now I realize it was, and I feel terrible. And I shouldn't have stopped confiding in you. You're right: I ditched you for Tristan."

Silence.

"The only thing you shouldn't judge me for is changing. I changed, and that's normal. I'm not sorry about that."

A long pause. Then she said, "I'm sorry I called you an only child."

"It's OK."

I asked her to sleep over on Thursday, and she agreed.

She'll probably never stop annoying me, and I'll probably never stop offending her, but that's OK. You can't throw away friends you've loved since kindergarten. Besides, even if it's uncomfortable, I need to hear the truth about my horrible behavior from *someone*.

Wednesday, June 29

Dear Sienna,

I'm so sorry about what I did. I'm guessing
you hate me, and you're right to. I tried to steal
Mac from you for months. How could I do
that to another girl? I lied to myself about you.
I decided you were too paranoid and clingy to

deserve Mac. Sometimes I convinced myself
you were so beautiful and popular you don't
have feelings like other people and you wouldn't
even care if Mac cheated on you; you'd shrug
and move on to the next guy. Mostly I pushed
you out of my mind. I didn't think of you as a
real person.

Recently I've been imagining, what if someone
did this to my mom? Stole away my dad? It
would be so unfair to my poor mother. She
would be devastated. She'd cry and lose weight.
Dark circles would form under her eyes. Anyway,
that's a hypothetical that doesn't matter. What
I'm saying is, I understand now how horrible I
was, and I'm sorry, I'm sorry.

Chloe

When I sent the draft out for feedback, Tristan said,
"Are you insane? She'll put it online and every college admissions officer will find it in three years," and
Hannah replied, "I agree with Tristan. And of course
you want her to forgive you so you'll feel better, but it's
kind of selfish to make her read your apology and feel all
her feelings again. Plus, you can't say that thing about

paranoid and clingy." I was furious for a second, but Hannah's right again, dammit.

In the end I emailed, "I'm sorry for everything," and left it at that.

Thursday, June 30

I got the scoop at our sleepover. It turns out all of Hannah's worrying about parents was for nothing. She introduced hers to Josh, and he introduced his to her, and everyone loved each other. The Egans thought Josh was a gentleman and a genius, and the Menakers thought Hannah was respectful and sweet. The two sets of parents met before the prom and drank a ton of wine and made fun of Hannah and Josh and it was great. But then he went away for an accepted students weekend at his college, and when he came back, he told her he doesn't want to be tied down at school. All men are garbage.

I had to interrogate her for hours to get a few measly scraps of sex information out of her. Did it hurt? No. Not even the first time? Not really, no. Did she bleed? Chloe! No, for your information. How many times did they do it? Chloe, come on. Less than 12? Yes. More than five? Yes. Was it fun? Yes, very. Did she feel guilty afterward? Yes, horribly, especially when she was in church. Did they use condoms? Of course. What does it feel like, exactly? Like . . . like . . . It's impossible to describe. Like being stabbed? No! Like what, then? She doesn't know, just good. Did it make it sadder to break up? Yes. Was she sorry she did it? . . . No.

Friday, July 1

Dad said it's totally unacceptable that I'm lying around the pool all day every day by myself. I said I'm not by myself, I'm with our friendly neighbors, and I'm not lying around, I'm reading great works of literature. Which is true! I only look at my phone for roughly two hours a day, which is practically nothing by modern standards. Dad said he sometimes thinks I'm a reader like Uncle Julian is a drinker. One time Uncle Julian drank so much at a dinner party that he had to sleep on the couch, and in the morning Mom discovered he'd peed in the downstairs coat closet in the middle of the night and called him an out-of-control alcoholic to his face. "But it's good to be addicted to books," I said.

"Not if you're using them to escape from your own life," he said.

"My life sucks," I said. Then we got in a big fight about gratitude and being spoiled and how many summer jobs Dad had when he was my age, and in the end he told me I have to come up with an employment plan.

Saturday, July 2

At dinner tonight Dad asked me if I've given any thought to what kind of job I want to get, and I said yes, tons, but I wasn't ready to talk about it yet.

Ummmm job. Job, job, job. I could babysit. It's pretty easy if you do it at night, and you get to snoop around looking for vibrators and bank statements. But I only know two families with little kids, and Dad wants me to find something steady. Also, kids are so incredibly boring when you have to be with them for long stretches of time. The movie theater? No windows, too depressing, plus your hair would always smell like popcorn. McDonald's? Even more depressing, plus French-fry hair. One of those nice restaurants in the town center? That would be OK, and useful experience for when I move to New York and need to make rent money. But I don't think they let 15-year-olds serve cocktails.

Sunday, July 3

Got an email from Mom!

> Hi, darling—
>
> A quick note to say I'm off on a spontaneous adventure with no internet—but WiFi has miraculously appeared just for the

moment—I haven't forgotten about your email
and am giving it so much careful thought and
really letting it marinate. Talk to you soon, rabbit
of my dreams.

Mommy

While Dad and I were working on the cake, I said,
"Dad, if Mom wanted me to move to Mexico, would you
let me?"

He put down a pint of blueberries and looked at me.
"What did she say?"

"Nothing yet. I asked her if I could, and she's thinking about it."

His face looked like—I can't describe it. Like nothing I've ever seen before. I think I need to read more
books before I can understand his expression. Maybe
"stricken" is the right word.

"There would be a lot to consider. School, mostly."

"But you're not saying no?"

He looked into the blueberries. "It could get pretty
weird without you around. Who would tell me how ugly
my jeans are?"

"I hate it here, Dad. I hate the people I go to school
with and I hate this town."

He pulled his head back. "Got it."

I feel guilty, but I shouldn't! He's the one who ruined everything!

Monday, July 4

The party's over.

Tris and Roy came.

So did Hannah and her parents. And Josh.

And Mom.

Everything's awful, unless everything's OK.

I can't write. I feel like a robot forced by a mad scientist to feel every human emotion simultaneously. My circuit board is broken.

Tuesday, July 5

The king in *Alice's Adventures in Wonderland* says, "Begin at the beginning, and go on till you come to the end: then stop." OK. I'll take his advice.

It was a perfect hot summer day. I woke up early (9 a.m.) to help Dad string up lights, put ice and beer in the cooler, sweep yard junk off the back patio, etc. We listened to the Pixies, Dad's favorite old-timey band, on *compact disc*! We were both starving by lunchtime, and Dad made us huge sandwiches with salami, ham, cheese, pickles, mayo, mustard, and tomatoes. We debated which Doritos flavor is better, Cool Ranch or Nacho Cheese. Dad accused me of arguing for Cool Ranch just to be *cool*, which is his idea of a joke. Then he blew my mind by telling me that in Canada there's a flavor called Roulette, and one out of every seven chips is hot. When I said I didn't believe him, he showed me on his phone. It was our best conversation in ages. I only remembered Miss Murphy at the end of it, and even then, the pain felt more like a headache than like my arm was being sawed off.

A few people arrived right at 4:00, more came at 4:30, and by 5:00 the backyard was full. Tris and Roy and I sat on the swing set, swaying back and forth.

"Remember how fun it was to swing when you were little?" Tris said. "Now it makes me queasy."

"Sad," I said.

"I know. So sad."

Roy laughed. "I didn't realize it was even possible to be nostalgic about your childhood before you're old enough to drive."

I wanted to glare at him, but instead I dug my toe into the dirt. He's too cheerful; that's his whole problem.

It was a green and blue and gold afternoon. The smell of hot dogs and hamburgers floated in the air. The sun shone down through the leaves. Someone brought out a football to toss around, and people played croquet on the flat stretch of our backyard. The neighborhood kids worked up the courage to ask us if they could use the swing set, so we got off and went to talk to Hannah, who was standing next to her parents, looking nervous. The four of us loaded up plates with food and sat on a blanket on the grass. I'd just crammed a huge forkful of potato salad into my mouth when Roy said, "Who's *that*?"

I looked up and saw a hot guy, a stranger. Older than us, but not old. Maybe in his late twenties. He had long hair pulled back in a ponytail, deep-set eyes, and a right angle for a jaw. His clothes didn't match his handsomeness; he was wearing a cheap white T-shirt and baggy pastel blue jeans, '90s style, and not in a cool way. He had a curious, confident look despite his embarrassing outfit.

And then he took a few steps to the side, and I saw— my mom.

Hannah gasped. "What?" said Roy and Tristan simultaneously, and for the first time in months I felt closer to Hannah than to Tris. She's known me for so long.

"It's my mother," I said.

She was wearing a white dress, red lipstick, and a big silver necklace with chunks of turquoise in it, a lot like the one she gave me for Christmas. She was looking around the crowd, scanning, and then we locked eyes and she was moving toward me fast, smiling and dodging people in her way. Out of the corner of my eye, I saw Dad standing by the grill with his mouth hanging open, a spatula dangling from his hand.

"BUNNY!" She hugged me hard, lifting me off my feet.

"Mom!" Oh, her smell, her smell!

She set me down, pulled back, and cupped my face in her hands, looking at me and smiling and smiling.

"I'm so happy to see you, honey," she said.

I looked down. All my friends were clustered around our feet, staring up at us.

"Let's stand—um . . ." I walked to the edge of the lawn, where it meets the trees. When I turned around, Mom was there, and so was the hot stranger.

"This is Chloe, no?" he said.

"*Si, mi cielo*," she said.

He grabbed my hand and shook it. "Chloe, *mucho gusto*. Is so nice to meet you finally."

"Nice to meet you too," I said.

"Sweetie," she said, "this is Javi." She picked up his hand and held it. "My friend."

I stared at their hands. They both smiled at me.

"Javi, like Javier," I said. Stupid. What was this, Spanish class?

"I actually mentioned him to you before, rabbit. He's the matador?"

Oh my God. My mother was boning the bullfighter. I was right all those months ago. I looked over at my friends. They quickly looked away and pretended to talk to each other. I didn't blame them. It's hard not to stare at an awkward teenager talking to her runaway mother and her runaway mother's much younger matador boyfriend.

Then my dad was at my side. He was wearing a novelty apron (LICENSED TO GRILL), which made my heart hurt for him. But at least Javier looked like he'd escaped from 1991. And maybe didn't understand old movie references well enough to understand that my dad should be embarrassed.

"Veronica," said Dad. "This is a surprise."

"Charlie, hello," my mother said. "This is Javi."

My dad and Javi shook hands politely. *Why are you pretending everything's normal?* I wanted to scream at them. *Nothing about this is normal! You're shaking hands with Mom's boyfriend! And you have a girlfriend she doesn't know about, probably! Everyone at this party is staring at us while pretending not to stare at us!* But I'm a hypocrite, because what was I doing that was so great? Standing there trying to pretend everything was normal, just like they were.

"Are you staying for long?" Dad said.

Mom shrugged. "*Vamos a ver.*"

I could feel Dad grimacing without looking at him. "Did you find a hotel?"

"We're at the Marriott," Mom said. Oh. Right. She couldn't stay in our house with her boyfriend.

I found myself turning away and walking through the crowd at a reasonable pace. Tris started to get up, and I waved at him cheerfully and then gave him the A-OK sign, which I don't think I've formed with my fingers since I was about five years old. As I passed Hannah's mom, she gave me a worried look, and I said, "Hi, Mrs. Egan!"

My chest started hurting when I got inside and my throat got tight on the stairs. I had to run down the hall to my room to get there before the serious crying started. Snickers looked up from the bed, startled, and I threw myself down next to him and sobbed into his neck. The scent of a campfire drifted into my room. Dad was going ahead with the traditional marshmallow toasting even though the world had exploded. How dadly of him.

Someone knocked at my door.

"WHAT," I sobbed.

Mom poked her head in. She was alone.

"Oh, sweetheart."

It wasn't fair. I wanted her to leave forever, but I couldn't stop her when she sat down on my bed and started stroking my hair, because I also wanted her to stay forever.

"What's wrong? Tell me. I promise to listen without judgment."

I shook my head.

"Was it a shock, seeing me with Javi? I guess I wasn't thinking. He's such a part of my life now; I feel as if you must know him already because *I* know him so well. Anyway, this wasn't how I envisioned today going at all. I thought you'd be so happy to see me."

She looked at me expectantly, like I might get up and start tossing confetti in the air, or at least say, "I am, Mom." But I didn't say anything.

She sighed. "I'm sorry this year has been so confusing for you."

Confusing for *me*? This was not my problem. This was two adults acting like human garbage. Four adults, if you counted Javi and Miss Murphy.

"Has Dad told you about his girlfriend?" I asked.

Her face turned white.

"Miss Murphy," I said. "She used to be a Broadway actress, but she moved back here to take care of her mother."

I could see her struggling for a second, and then she managed to smile. Who did she think she was fooling? I've known her for 15 years. I can tell when she's furious and shocked no matter how much she tries to look like the Mona Lisa.

"Chloe," she said, and took my hand. "Your father feels strongly that it's inappropriate to discuss our marriage with you, and for the most part, I agree with him.

But I can see how abandoned you feel, how deeply hurt and angry you are, and I think a dose of honesty is in order. Your father and I have been growing apart for some years. It's no one's fault. In the end, we're not a good match. He's earth and roots and paying your taxes; I'm air and light and staying up until 3 a.m. to look at the stars. Opposites attract, but opposites repel. Now, with Javi, I've finally found someone who complements me, who makes me my best self."

"When did Dad find out about Javi?"

"I don't know that that's—"

"Just tell me, Mom. Tell me, tell me, *tell me, TELL ME*."

"Chloe! What's gotten into you? I told him at Christmas, all right?"

He knew for months before he started dating Miss Murphy. And he never blamed Mom. He never said, "She cheated first."

"We're covering a lot of ground here, but I know you can handle it, my strong, smart little rabbit. Do you know why Javi and I came here today?"

I looked at her.

"To invite you to move to Mexico with us. I've found a new rental in San Miguel, a beautiful place on the mountainside. You can study online, like you wanted to. You'll meet all these fantastic kids your age and bomb around on ATVs with them—you should see how they fly. We'll go on excursions to the beach on the weekends, see the ruins, see the caves, see Javi in the Plaza de Toros, see everything. I know how hard it will be to leave your father, but you won't be leaving him, really. You'll come back on holidays. Think of it as a surprising, sunny interlude between the hell that is high school and the glory that will be college. I miss you terribly, my darling. It's true that I needed some time apart from you and your father to clarify my own thoughts and get my novel truly off the ground. I thank you for granting me that time. But now I need my girl by my side. My reader, my writer, my ruminator. Will you come with me?"

She looked at me. Snickers looked at me. I stood up, pulled my box of treasures off the shelf, and walked downstairs. Mom trailed after me as I went outside, walked through the crowd, and stopped in front of the fire. There were my friends, huddled together, probably discussing me. There were Mr. and Mrs. Egan, staring at Javi, who was looking around the yard in fascination, like an anthropologist. There was Dad, holding an opened bag of marshmallows, still wearing his apron.

I knew what I wanted to say.

You left me. I don't feel abandoned. I am abandoned. I was the lead in the high school musical, I lost my best friend, I made a new best friend, I fell in love with a guy and acted like a monster, and YOU MISSED ALL OF IT. *You'll never know me completely because you don't know what happened to me this year. Move to Mexico? I would NEVER go ANYWHERE with you. I wouldn't go to Chipotle with you, let alone to another country. Who picked me up after every rehearsal? Who made me breakfast and dinner every day? Who did my laundry when I was too lazy to do it and never told me my period underpants were gross? Who shoveled the driveway on snow days so I could sleep in? Who made me an Easter basket? Who put up with your crap for year after year, probably for my sake, so I could have a mother, even a mother as useless and narcissistic as you? Dad.*

I didn't say any of that, but I did scream "I'm not your rabbit!" at her. I opened the box, picked up the bunny, and threw it into the fire as hard as I could. Then I ran back up to my room and slammed the door, and opened it again, and slammed it, and slammed it, and slammed it, and slammed it.

I guess I killed the party. From my window, I watched people scurrying away, probably impatient to get home and start gossiping. When I saw the little kids leaving, I felt bad. I hoped I didn't scare them. I could see Mom sobbing and hiding her face in Javi's neck. Is that where I get my crying from, her? I hope it's my hormones and not hereditary.

Finally she and Javi left without talking to anyone. The marshmallow fire was still going. When everyone was gone, Dad put his hands on his hips and looked around. Then he went inside and emerged a minute later carrying some trash bags. I went down to help him.

"You OK?" he called.

"Yeah," I said. When I got to the fire, I opened my treasure box, pulled out all my Mac memorabilia, and dropped it in. The papers went up first. The ChapStick took a while to melt. The bracelet I threw in last. After everything was burned up, I tossed the box on the fire, picked up a trash bag, and started collecting plastic cups. By the time we'd finished, it was dark. We went inside without talking. I walked upstairs, brushed my teeth, got in bed with Snickers, and slept for 12 hours.

Wednesday, July 6

I didn't see my mother yesterday, but Dad did. He drove over to her hotel and they went to a Starbucks. When he got back, he asked if I wanted to talk, and I said no.

She came over for dinner tonight. By herself. No Javi. I knew she was coming, so I hid in my room, texting with Tris and feeling sick. I considered refusing to emerge, but a few minutes after I heard the delivery guy ring the doorbell, I went downstairs. Dad was getting glasses out of the cabinet and Mom was leaning against the island. When she saw me, she moved toward me with her arms out, but I gave her a wave and started setting the table.

"It's impossible to get good pizza in Mexico," she said when we were sitting down. "Not that this pizza remotely resembles the real thing, but it's like Arturo's compared to the nonsense we get down there."

Dad smiled politely. I didn't look up from my plate. They'd ordered my favorite: Hawaiian. A full pie, not even half Hawaiian and half pepper and onion, like they normally do. Did.

I picked up my slice. Dad cleared his throat. "Chloe, we want to talk to you. You probably know what about." His eyes had tears in the corners.

"You're getting a divorce, right?"

I thought I knew the answer already, but it turned out I didn't. I only knew it once they looked at each other and then back at me, and Dad said, "Yes."

Mom said, "We adore you, bunn—Chloe. We're splitting up because we grew apart, not because of anything you did. We both love you so much. Nothing will ever change that."

It was like she'd Googled "how to tell your kid you're getting a divorce," except she probably wouldn't bother to do research beforehand.

"It will take at least a few months," Dad said. "I'll stay here, in this house." He must have seen something in my expression, because he said, "I mean, you and I will stay here together."

"Or you'll move to Mexico with me," Mom said.

"Veronica."

"*Charlie*. We agreed it's up to her. Chloe, wherever you make your primary residence, of course you'll see the other parent quite often, at least once a month."

I had vowed to myself not to say a single word during this conversation, but I panicked. "I don't want to go to Mexico."

Mom said, "You mean you want to live with your father?"

"I mean, I never want to go to Mexico."

Mom's eyes filled with tears. I felt nothing.

Dad said, "Well, it's possible your mother will move back at some point."

"But not likely," Mom said. Dad gave her a look. "It's *not* likely," she said. "Chloe, you might as well know that my relationship with Javi is serious. I envision a future with him in Mexico. How this will affect my writing, I don't know. There's an unfortunate perception that you must live in Brooklyn to be a 'real' writer." She made air quotes with her hands.

"Veronica, let's talk about that later, OK?" It was weird how nice Dad was being. Normally he'd snap at her if she interrupted an important conversation to talk about her dumb dream of being a famous author, which will never, *never* come true.

"Don't feel you have to rush into a decision, Chloe," said Mom. "Take all the time you need to mull it over. Moving to Mexico is a big step. I can understand how scary the idea must be, but remember, you've wanted to live with me for months now."

"I know," I said. "But I don't anymore. I'm sorry. I don't need any time to think about it."

We all looked at our pizza. I'd taken one bite of mine. I could see my teeth marks on the cheese.

"Do you have any questions for us?" said Dad.

I had a million questions, but I couldn't ask any of them, and it made me so mad that they didn't know that.

How long were you married before you realized you had nothing in common?

How can I stop that from happening to me?

Mom, did you know when you left that you were going to stay in Mexico forever? Was all that stuff about coming back in four months a lie, or did you change your mind?

How old is Javi?

Don't you think it's possible he has some disgusting mother fetish?

Are you aware of all the porn on the internet? A lot has changed since you were a teenager.

Did you guys agree you were allowed to date other people before Mom vanished?

Are you mad at each other about Javi and Miss Murphy?

Did you decide it was OK to see other people but then hate each other for actually doing it?

You didn't agree to an open marriage at all, right? You didn't talk about much of anything, did you? Mom just announced she was leaving and then did it and Dad was furious? And then he found out about Javi and decided if Mom had a boyfriend, it was OK for him to date Miss Murphy?

Dad, are you going to marry Miss Murphy now that you and Mom are getting a divorce?

Why did you let Mom complain about you to me for all those years? Why didn't you complain about her to me? She brainwashed me into thinking you were a boring loser.

Will you fight over custody?

What will happen to Mom's clothes, which are all stuffed into my dresser drawers, and her boxes of old journals, and all the other junk she left behind? Can we make another marshmallow fire and burn them to ashes?

How can you love your mother more than anyone else one day and hate her the next? Do you know how scary it is to realize that I don't understand my own feelings at all?

Do you think there's any chance I'm bipolar?

Would it be expensive to see a shrink? Can you find one on the internet?

Why couldn't you stay together and secretly have affairs I'd never find out about and be polite friends until I left for college? Why are you so selfish?

Is Javi even old enough to drink?

Do either of you care about me at all? OK, that was a question for Mom, and I already know the answer.

But all I said was, "I guess not. Not right now." Mom said she had a flight in the morning and wouldn't see me again before she left. I let her give me a hug. I was standing there like an overcooked noodle, but at the last minute I decided I would probably be crushed by guilt later if I didn't hug her now, so I put my arms around her and squeezed. She was crying into my hair. "I love you so much," she said, and I said, "Love you too." Everyone knows it doesn't count if you leave off the "I."

Thursday, July 7

I guess Mom's back in Mexico now. My heart is a burned-up bracelet.

Friday, July 8

Things I hate about Mom:

1. Her embarrassingly long hair
2. The sound she makes when she's eating spaghetti

3. The way she and her friend Mimi got drunk in the middle of the day. Once they thought I was upstairs doing my homework, but I was sitting at the top of the stairs, and I heard Mom doing an impression of me. She said "like" and "totally" every other word, which I don't do at all
4. The ancient disintegrating rabbit slippers she wears
5. Her disgusting pathetic dreams
6. The way she ran away to Mexico like she's 18 and has no responsibilities
7. That she turned me against Dad like some kind of cult leader

Saturday, July 9
Before I fall asleep every night, I think, *Well, I've used up all my tears. That's the last time I'll cry.* But it never turns out to be true.

Sunday, July 10
Tris is being really sympathetic, but at some point I'll have to stop making him analyze recent events with me for hours every day.

Monday, July 11
Why did I hug her? I hate her! I should have said, *Great, get a divorce. It's the best idea you've ever had. I hope you*

hire an incompetent lawyer and Dad doesn't have to pay
you a single penny, and I hope that Javi gives you HPV
and your vagina falls off and I hope Dad marries Miss
Murphy. You're not my mother anymore.

Tuesday, July 12

I used to be traffic-light green. Then this year happened.
Now I'm a very pale mint.

Wednesday, July 13

Hannah and I went to the pool for eight hours today, from
10 to 6. We spent the entire time eating ICEE Freeze
Squeeze Ups, drinking Diet Cokes, and analyzing our
breakups. It was so fun, I almost forgot about Mom for a
few hours. Around lunchtime (hot dogs from the concession stand), we agreed that although Mac is a beautiful
cheating jock and Josh is a brilliant pint-size geek, what
they did to us isn't that different. By 4 p.m., we realized
that it's actually a blessing (Hannah's word, obviously)
that we're going through this now, because imagine the
humiliation of pining away all fall only to get dumped
during Thanksgiving break. On the walk home, Hannah
told me when I feel sad, I should think about Mac's chin
zits. I told her when she feels sad, she should think about
Josh's tiny feet.

"Well, well, well, if it isn't Splish and Splash," said

Dad when we got home. That's what he's called us since second grade, when we got in a fight because I accidentally bumped Hannah into a puddle and she ruined her red sequined Dorothy shoes.

From now on, I'm going to be a better friend to Hannah.

Thursday, July 14

You know what? Mac's a DICK. He cheated on his girlfriend with a freshman, and he would have done it forever. He only stopped because everyone found out about it and he had to. He didn't stick up for me or even say, *I'm so sorry people booed you and squirted pee on you.* He's homophobic. He was rude to Hannah. He was rude to my dad!

And you know what else? He's DUMB. He's not strong and silent. He's stupid and silent. He never asked me questions about myself. He didn't have opinions about anything. He'd never heard of *To Kill a Mockingbird*! What kind of moron gets through high school without *hearing* of that book? I should call his college and tell them most of his papers are slightly reworded SparkNotes. Why did I waste my brainpower worrying about him? I should have been studying great literature or books about acting technique instead of expending all my mental energy on a half-wit.

The worst part, the part that really confuses me, is that I knew all that stuff when we were messing around and I ignored it. Why? Because I liked his body and the way he smelled so much. And I kind of liked that he was a dumb dick. I still like it. That part I really don't understand. Maybe I will when I'm much older.

Friday, July 15

Dad came home at lunch and caught me and Snickers still sleeping. He asked me if I think I'm excused from finding a summer job just because Mom is gone. I said no, of course not, even though I actually did think that. He said I was about a week overdue with my employment plan. I said I had a plan, and when he asked what it was, the answer came to me: "I'm going to be a lifeguard." Dad raised his eyebrows and said it wasn't a terrible idea, but it was probably way too late to get trained and hired for this summer, and had I made any inquiries? I said almost.

Saturday, July 16

Dad was right. They hire lifeguards in April. But Mrs. Franco said they need someone to work in the concession stand. I start on Tuesday. The pay is peanuts and I don't get free rocket pops (I asked). But I don't think I'll mind the work, and Mrs. Franco said I can take a training course in August and apply to be a lifeguard next spring.

Sunday, July 17

Tris and I went to my future workplace and lay on lounge chairs, talking. He said Roy's parents have invited him on vacation with them four times, and they keep saying *of course* he and Roy will share a bedroom; that's not even a question. We agreed if he goes, he will be signing on to star in a massive Facebook album called "Double-Dating in Maine!" Meanwhile, Tris's mom printed out and framed an 8 x 10 picture of Tris and Roy at the prom.

"Has your dad said anything?" I asked.

"Nope."

"Do you think he knows?"

"He must. I guess he's never going to say anything, and neither will I."

Tris gave a big shrug like, *Oh whatever,* and even though I'm sure he doesn't really feel like that, I didn't want to force him to be emotional about it.

"Has Roy been to accepted students weekend at his college?" I asked.

"Yeah. How come?"

"No reason," I said. "Does he want to move to New York when he graduates?"

"Chloe, I promise we're going to be best friends and live in New York. Even if Roy and I get married."

"Do you think you'll marry him?"

"No! I'm 15 years old!"

Then we read our magazines and phones for a while. Kids jumped into the pool. The sun poured vitamin D into my skin. The air smelled like chlorine and sunscreen. I had new fluorescent-yellow polish on my nails and the complete Chronicles of Barsetshire, by Anthony Trollope, on my phone. Tris and I were the only high school kids in the vicinity.

"Doesn't it feel like this year lasted for about a century?" I said.

Tris put down *Us Weekly*. "Sort of. But it feels like the Love Notes auditions happened yesterday."

"Remember how upset we were when Bernadette didn't choose us?"

We laughed. It was cute and sad to remember our younger selves, so clueless about everything that would happen to us.

Monday, July 18

Some days I'm a firework shot into the sky by the power of hating my mother. Some days I'm a piece of party streamer that got left in the rain overnight.

I wish I could decide "I hate my mother" or "I love my

father." If I had one clear feeling about them, I wouldn't have to think about them so much. But I feel two contradictory things at once, which is uncomfortable. I pick at my own thoughts like I'm trying to untie a knot. I loathe my mother, but I want her to come home and give me head rubs, read me Shouts & Murmurs from the *New Yorker*, and make fun of our town with me. I love my dorky father, but I still can't forgive him for dating Miss Murphy. And it's not that I hate Miss Murphy. I even feel bad that Dad broke up with her. She's nice, and smart, and she only did exactly the same thing I did, falling for someone who was taken. It's just that she's not Mom.

Tuesday, July 19

I forgot I wouldn't be able to work on my tan from inside the concession stand. It's OK, though, because there are about two customers per hour, so I have plenty of time to read. At the beginning of my shift, Mrs. Franco trained me, which took 15 minutes. She showed me how to work the old-timey cash register, fill out the stock sheet, and balance the drawer. It feels pretty good, having a job and a little to-do list.

Tonight Dad said he has to throw away the charcoal grill before we both get cancer, and I said I'd rather die young than eat burgers from a gas grill. As you can see, we're both acting more normal now.

Wednesday, July 20

Sometimes I remember sophomore year is coming in a month and a half and my entire body turns bright red from the panic. Then I remember: Bernadette won't be there, and neither will Sienna, and neither will Mac. Other horrible things will happen, but not those three things.

Thursday, July 21

This guy named Grady works with me during the "busier" days, a.k.a. the days when we have ten customers per hour instead of one. Maybe Mrs. Franco sent him to spy on me and make sure I'm not stealing. He's about my height and even skinnier than me, so already I don't like him. Another problem: his face is prettier than mine. He looks like someone Mac would accidentally step on while jogging to football practice. Today, as I was counting the singles, he said, "Your nail polish is cool." Now I like him a little better.

Friday, July 22

Roy is away on a Habitat for Humanity summer program, so I get Tris to myself for an entire week. Tonight we went to the movies, which I hate, because everyone looks at their phones the entire time and I can't concentrate because I'm so angry. When I'm an old lady, I hope I remember that the problem isn't teenagers. The problem is *everyone*. Some mom next to me tonight was typing *with her keypad sounds on*. *Click-click-click-click* until I almost punched her in the hands. Maybe the high school has anger-management classes for sophomores.

Saturday, July 23

I slept in until 1 p.m., so late that I had a horrible eye socket ache when I woke up. But eating chocolate chip ice cream and iced coffee for "breakfast" cured it. As I was licking the last of the ice cream off my spoon, I thought, *Some pretty bad stuff happened. Mom abandoned me. I fell in love with a huge jerk who broke my heart without ever even being my boyfriend. Seniors tormented me. And I'm still OK, and sometimes I even feel happy.* Then I went back upstairs, opened all my curtains and the windows, put on some Motown, and danced in front of the mirror in my underpants. Snickers looked at me from the bed like, *Wut is she doing now smh.* It was 80 degrees, dry, blue. I put on my bikini and went to the pool to enjoy being young and alive.

Sunday, July 24

Here are my goals for sophomore year:

  * Go to bed earlier so I don't fall asleep in class
  * Get the lead in the musical

* If I do get the lead, be humble about it
* If I don't get the lead, be equanimous about it
* Be a polite professional to Miss Murphy
* Do generous things for Hannah and Tristan; ask them about their lives instead of always talking about mine
* Stop obsessing about guys so much
* Buy some clothes that reflect my true personality
* Find out what my true personality is
* Complete lifeguard training
* Do some extracurriculars
* Get my learner's permit
* Be nice to Dad
* Think nice things about Mom — or at least stop imagining how I would feel if she leaned too far into a bullring while cheering for her boyfriend and got gored

Here are some things I'll probably keep doing without trying, so they don't count as goals, but I want to write them down because I'm proud of them:

* Read at least one book a week; keep a list
* Get good grades
* Write in my diary every single day

Monday, July 25

Tris and I wasted the entire afternoon watching musicals on YouTube and trying to guess which one Miss Murphy will pick next year. He's rooting for *West Side Story*; I want *Annie Get Your Gun*. When Dad got home and found us staring at the laptop screen in the dark, watching clips from *Into the Woods*, he whipped up the shades and shouted "Aha! See how zhee vampires scurry away from zhee light!" in a Dracula accent, which doesn't even make sense, but then, what Dad Joke actually makes sense?

Tuesday, July 26

Grady is wearing the same thing every time I see him: Chuck Taylors, Dickies cut off at the knees, a black T-shirt, and two old beige rubber bands around his left wrist. He wants to talk about music all the time. He tells me about bands with names like the Bloody Wolves or the Rickets or something, and I'm like, "I only listen to Top 40 music," and he's like, "Oh, yeah, pop music can be cool too." But then half an hour later, after we've sold bottled water to some moms and ice cream sandwiches to some kids and I've completely forgotten our conversation, he'll say, "But the thing is, Top 40 is like gummy watermelons compared to real ones." So I say, "Gummy watermelons are delicious." It's very relaxing, talking to a guy who's so much younger than me. I couldn't care less what he thinks of me. I wonder how old he is? Probably 12. I should have asked him on our first day. Now it would be awkward.

Wednesday, July 27

Reading helps me drown out my thoughts. Whenever I can't read because it's physically impossible, because I'm emptying the dishwasher or sweeping the concession stand floor or whatever, my mind wanders, and before I know it, I've spent 15 minutes wondering what Javi and my mom even talk about, and whether my mom now does the stuff she considered demeaning when she lived here, like cleaning up and going grocery shopping, and whether they click on their laptops after dinner like a normal couple or whether Javi irons his matador cape while my mother makes offerings to the writing muses.

The other thing I think about all the time now is Dad dying. Whenever he goes on a run, I imagine a car hitting him. Like, in really vivid detail. I see him flying through the air and landing hard by the side of the road, breaking his neck. Tonight he got home from work 10 minutes late and I was convinced someone had run a red light and smashed into his car. So you see why I have to read all the time.

Thursday, July 28

Today Grady gave me a mixtape. Literally *a tape*, a cassette tape, from the '90s. I was like, "Thank you, but I don't have a way to listen to this," and he was like, "Oh, here you go," and shoved a yellow Walkman at me with the headphones all tangled. When I write it down, it sounds like he has a crush on me, but he definitely doesn't. If I had to describe him in three adjectives, I would choose "weird," "short," and "opinionated."

I looked it up, and yellow Walkmans cost a ton of money on eBay! What a world. When I told Hannah, she said, "He likes you, dumb-dumb!"

I knew from the "dumb-dumb" that she was in a great mood.

"I'm sure he found the Walkman in his dad's junk drawer, or something."

"Hmm. Or something."

"You sound happy," I said.

It turns out she's been flirting with someone in her summer Bible study class! The Lord moves in mysterious ways.

Friday, July 29

We're going on vacation tomorrow. Perfect timing— it's the same week Tris is going to Maine with Roy's family.

The night before the Cape, Mom always made a big salad to use up all the vegetables in the fridge. She listened to the Indigo Girls and Joni Mitchell while she chopped, and when "River" came on, she cried, especially when Joni sang, "Now I've gone and lost the best baby that I ever had."

Mom lost me.

Saturday, July 30
We're here.

Maybe my favorite part of the entire year is when we're done with the highway, and through all the quaint village centers that I'm sure all the teenagers who live there hate with a passion but that look adorable to me, and over the bridge, and past the cheapie beach chair and souvenir stores, and finally we turn onto the road our rental's on, and I roll down my window and smell the ocean. And hear it, and feel the salt air on my face. For a whole week, I won't be in my routine. No TV, and almost no reception here, so no phone, no clicking, no high school stuff. The world the way it was when I was a baby.

Sunday, July 31
Here's what I do at the Cape. Wake up early. Eat breakfast while reading my book. Slather on the sunscreen

and *then* put on my bikini, so I don't get burned around the edges. (Pro tip.) Take my towel, book, chair, lunch, and water down to the beach. Read and read and read. Sit in my chair until my butt falls asleep, then lie on my stomach on my towel until I get too hot. Wave to Dad when he comes down. Maybe go for a walk. Throw a tennis ball for Snickers to catch. Go for swims. Float on my rubber ring. Walk up to the cottage. Clean off in the outdoor shower. Look at the sunset and the ocean while rinsing off all the sunscreen and salt. Wonder if anything in life will make me as happy as showering outside at the beach does. Play cards and eat Goldfish with Dad while he has a gin and tonic and I have a Coke. Play solitaire while Dad grills something for dinner. Talk while we eat. Read some more. Go to bed early. I'm always hungry for meals here, and my mind is always as sharp as a knife, and I always sleep like the dead.

Monday, August 1

I read an entire book today. *Jane Eyre*. It's only the best novel ever written. When I finished, the sun was setting, and I put my hands in the sand and tried to communicate with the spirit of Charlotte Brontë and say, "Thank you for writing this book, and thank you for making the protagonist a smart girl with a lot of grit." Then I thought of all the girls and women who've read *Jane Eyre* over the years and the hard things some of them were going through when they read it. Maybe they'd just gotten dumped, or found out everyone hates them, or lost a mother. Or maybe they were orphans, or couldn't get pregnant, or had cancer. I sent a message into the air to every girl who's loved *Jane Eyre*: *I hope you stuck up for yourself, and I hope you liked yourself, and I hope that you were as happy as you could possibly be.*

Tuesday, August 2
Cried this morning because the week is almost half over. Hashtag hormones.

Wednesday, August 3
What is it about being on vacation that makes you think about how you want to change your life when you get home? I'm going to go through all my clothes and trinkets and makeup and throw away everything I don't use. And I'm going to stop looking at my phone. Or, no, I'm only going to look at it for 10 minutes in the afternoon, as a reward after I do my homework. Speaking of homework, I'm going to do it slowly and methodically instead of in a panic at the last second. Most of all I'm going to transform my mind from a dirty ball pit of anxiety into, like, a calm lake of serenity. I'll start meditating! I read an article about how teenagers who meditate for five minutes a day have higher GPAs. But that's not even

the point. The point is, I'm not going to drift away from the real world to think about Mom, only to snap back to reality and find that I'm frowning so hard I gave myself a headache.

Thursday, August 4

Dad and I drove to town to do some errands. There's reception there, so while he went to pick up groceries, I sat on a bench outside the store and looked at my phone. I was flipping through a slide show of unlikely animal friendships when Hannah called.

"I miss you!" I said, instead of "Hi."

She laughed. "I miss you, too!"

"How's Bible study guy?"

"He's OK. He's not Josh."

"You don't know him as well yet, though. He'll probably seem way better than Josh in a few months."

"Maybe you're right." She paused. "Josh and I have been texting."

"Really??"

"And sometimes we say X-rated stuff."

"Whoa!"

"I know. And sometimes I send him pictures."

"Not with your face showing!"

"No! I'm not a total idiot."

I watched a little girl walking by wearing nothing

but Crocs and a yellow one-piece. I tried not to think about her growing up and sexting some cheating elf.

"It's bad, right?" said Hannah.

"Not necessarily. I don't know. Only if it's making you upset."

"It's exciting at the time, but I feel terrible afterward."

"Well, I'm not judging you," I said. "I'm not that big of a hypocrite."

We were quiet. "What are you doing right now?" I said.

"I'm in the kitchen looking into the backyard. My dad's picking up sticks. OK, now my mom is bringing him a glass of water and he's, oh, well, yep, he's squeezing her butt."

"I'm so jealous," I said.

"Of my gross parents?"

"Yes. I wish my parents were together and in love."

"I know," she said. Her voice was kind. "I'm lucky. It's not fair."

"It's OK," I said. "I'm glad you're lucky."

I meant it.

Friday, August 5

Dad and I went for a long walk on the beach today. How romantic! Speaking of being a big perv, we talked about whether it's OK to keep liking Woody Allen movies even though his stepdaughter says he molested her. Then about whether *Manhattan* is completely disgusting. At first I was on the fence, but then Dad said, "So you'd enjoy dating a 42-year-old in two years?" and I saw his point. We walked for a while without talking. The tide was out, and we were close to the water on the firm sand, picking our way between the rocks. The sun and the wind were on our backs.

"How's Miss Murphy?" I asked.

"Fine, as far as I know."

"You haven't talked to her?"

"Nope."

I bent down to look at an oyster shell. Not pretty enough for my collection.

"You should call her, if you want," I said.

He looked at me. We kept walking.

I said, "I mean, whatever. It's your decision. But she's nice. And Mom . . ." I waved my hands at him like, *is living in Mexico with her underage matador.* I think he knew what I meant.

Saturday, August 6

It was so sad to leave, but Dad let me listen to my music on the drive, and when we got home, Snickers tore around the house like a madman. I think he'd assumed we'd moved to the Cape forever. If only, Snickers.

Tris drove over the second I texted him. He was so

excited to see me that he jumped into my arms, and we both fell on the driveway and I got a huge scrape on my knee. He felt terrible and ground *his* knee against the driveway until it bled, and then we spontaneously pressed our knees together to be blood siblings. Then we freaked out and looked up "STDs blood virgins?" for half an hour before deciding we were OK.

He gave Maine a B+/A-. "I was worried Roy and I would run out of stuff to talk about, but it was actually great. We couldn't possibly talk the whole time, so it didn't feel awkward when we were quiet. Sometimes we took long walks and discussed all this stuff we never have before. He told me he tries every day to believe in God, even though it doesn't work, because he misses his grandmother so much and he wants to think she's in heaven."

"So everything was perfect!"

"Kind of. I'm never going in a lake again. The bottom is all squishy and full of fronds, and you feel like you're stepping on the hair of a huge corpse. The last day we were there, we were swimming, and I looked to my left, and there was a snake swimming along next to me. A snake!"

"You were probably swimming with that snake every single day!"

"That snake, singular? There were probably hundreds of them."

"Come to the Cape next year. No snakes."

"Roy's parents would die. They're even more in love with me now. We sat around for hours after dinner every night, playing board games and talking. I beat everyone at Trivial Pursuit one night and I thought they were going to adopt me on the spot."

"They sound so nice."

"They are."

We were crammed into the downstairs bathroom, putting Neosporin on our knees. Tris went rummaging for the Band-Aid box. "They're much nicer than my parents. Or than my dad, at least. But I was still so happy to come home. Why is that?"

I shrugged. "Your parents are your parents, I guess. They're like comfy pants. It doesn't matter how stained and full of holes they get. You still love them."

He nodded and handed me a Band-Aid. "Other people's parents are like jeans. They'll never be that comfy."

Hannah came over for dinner. Afterward, we went to the backyard, spread out an old sheet, and lay down on it, talking and looking at the sky until it got dark.

"Have you talked to your mom?" she said.

"No."

"Do you miss her?"

A year ago, I would have bitten her head off for asking a question like that. "Yeah, I do," I said. "I'll never forgive her, but I miss her a ton."

Hannah didn't say anything, but I knew she was listening. A plane flew overhead, leaving a white mark on the pink sky.

"I can't believe we're done with freshman year," she said. "I was so scared of it for so long, and now it's over."

"Sophomore year is like the Tuesday of high school. Neither here nor there."

"Maybe it'll be relaxing. Maybe nothing exciting will happen at all."

"Yeah, right," I said. "It'll probably be nonstop drama again. But that's OK. That's high school, I guess."

No matter how bad the school years are, they end eventually. And unless Dad dies in a car accident, we'll always go to the beach during the summer. At least one week of the year will be perfect. And most of the other ones will be pretty OK too.

Sunday, August 7

Mom Skyped me today, and I picked up. She walked around with the laptop facing out to show me her new apartment. It looked nice. Billowing curtains, tile floors, chairs with black curlicues for backs. When she flipped her laptop back around, she said, "What do you think? Isn't it fantastic?"

"It's pretty."

"You know, Chloe, the offer still stands. If you ever change your mind—"

"Yeah, Mom, thanks, OK. I have to go."

"Well, at the very least, promise me you'll be here for Thanksgiving. I can't—"

"I really have to go. Bye, Mom."

Monday, August 8

I worked with Grady today. First time I'd seen him since vacation. His face looked like it had gotten prettier while I was away. What did he do, buy some eyeliner?

"Where were you?" he said. No "Hi."

"At the Cape."

"You got tanner."

I pulled my shirt to one side so he could see the tan line from my halter top. He looked scandalized. Ha! It's fun to terrify children.

Around the middle of our shift, he said, "Is high school as bad as junior high?"

I thought. "In some ways, yeah. But I had a really bad freshman year. Why do you ask?"

"I'm starting ninth grade in the fall."

"Oh. Well, I'll say hi to you in the halls."

"Cool."

We both looked out at the pool.

"Why was your freshman year so bad?" he said.

"You really want to hear about it?"

"Yeah," he said. "Of course."

"OK. I'll tell you," I said, and I did, even the worst parts, and he listened.

Tuesday, August 9

Tris and Hannah met me at the pool after my shift. We sat on the steps in the shallow end with our hats and sunglasses on, like old ladies, and chatted about our childhoods and crushed Santa dreams.

Tris said, "My sister found out at school, and my dad didn't want to bother keeping up the illusion just for me, so he sat me down and told me. I cried so hard I threw up."

Hannah said, "My fourth-grade teacher asked us to write an essay about the day we found out Santa's not real, and I was like, *Santa's not real?!?*"

I said, "I never believed in Santa. My mother didn't want to lie to me."

"That's sad," Tris said. "Or maybe it's kind of nice."

"It made me feel like a grown-up," I said. "But it was terrible, knowing this secret and not being able to tell anyone."

"Thank you for not telling me," Hannah said.

"You're welcome."

We floated our hands on the top of the water, where it's warmest. The sun was on my shoulders. Hannah was smiling, and so was Tristan, and so was I. My heart was full of love for them.

I can't believe that one day we'll be 16, and then 17, 18, 21. Driving, going to college, being grown-ups. It'll be horrible, and amazing, and I can't wait.

Acknowledgments

My most affectionate thanks to . . .

Jesseca Salky, for finding me in the slush pile, representing me so brilliantly, holding my hand at every step, and doing all the hard, scary parts. I would be lost without you. Carrie Hannigan, for helping make my dream come true. Liesa Abrams, who is not only right about everything, but is unfailingly kind and understanding.

The wizards at Simon Pulse: Mara Anastas and Mary Marotta, Katherine Devendorf, Sara Berko, Jodie Hockensmith, Lucille Rettino, Carolyn Swerdloff and team, Christina Pecorale and team, Jessica Handelman, Mike Rosamilia, Penina Lopez, and Erica Stahler.

My writing and English professors at Barnard College: Mary Gordon, Jhumpa Lahiri, Peter Platt, and Timea Szell, all of whom paid such generous attention to their students.

My professors at Boston University's creative writing program: Leslie Epstein, who taught us fundamentals of the craft. Ha Jin, for forcing us to outline. Jennifer Haigh, who told us that talent is meaningless if you're not willing to do the work. Andrew J. Wilson, my friend and grad school soul mate.

Melissa Albert and Susanne Grabowski, who read this manuscript in draft form, and who are two of the best writers

I know. Suzi Pacaut, whose friendship was like water in the desert. Laura Davies, who is a kindred spirit. Lauren Passell, the warmest friend and reader. Emily Winter, whose funny, honest writing made me want to stop showing off and try to write something real. Milan Popelka, my friend since fifth grade, for his essential help and advice.

My parents, Patricia Anne Chastain and David Chastain, who gave me everything, and who are the smartest, most interesting people I know. Special thanks to my mother for raising her children so thoughtfully and lovingly, for reading to us every day, and for being absolutely nothing like Veronica. My late grandmother, Frances Chastain Shanor, who showed me by example that it is possible to make a living writing and editing. My grandmother Anita Lannom, whose love is boundless and who sees the world like a novelist. My brother, Carl Chastain, who is so capable, bright, and brave. My sister, Laura Chastain Emmons, who lights up a room and my life.

Jared Hunter, for marrying me. There has never been, and there never will be, a better husband. And my sons, Wesley Hunter and Malcolm Hunter. I love you more than words can say.

Emma Chastain is a graduate of Barnard College and the creative writing MFA program at Boston University. She lives in Brooklyn, New York, with her husband and children.